TIME WAS

A romantic comedy ....

....with a kink

PAUL ADAMS

H
Halcyon Publishing

TEXT COPYRIGHT

©2013

PAUL ADAMS

ALL RIGHTS RESERVED

Without limiting the rights under copyright above, no part of this publication shall be produced, stored in or introduced into a retrieval system, or transmitted in any form or by any means (electronic, mechanical, photocopying, recording or otherwise), without prior permission of both the copyright owner and the publisher of this book.

ISBN

Paperback – 978-0-9923-407-0-4

Published by Halcyon Publishing, Perth, WA, Australia - © 2013

Printed and bound by Lightning Source, USA, UK & Australia

Cover photograph – Paul Adams

Cover design by Paul Adams

Cover and text formatting by Ares Jun

About the author

Paul Adams was born and educated in Hampton, England.

After graduating from Lancaster University, he was part of the alternative comedy scene in London in the 1980's, but failed to make a living where so many others succeeded.

He then worked in the Civil Service for far too many years, before deciding that he needed to get a life.....so he resigned in order to dedicate his time to writing fiction and designing gardens.

This is his first novel, published in 2013.

The sequel, 'Blythe's Spirit', was published later the same year.

At least two further novels are planned in the Henry Blythe series.

'Bad Man Rising' is due for publication in early 2014, with at least one more instalment, (as yet untitled) to be published later that year.

He is also planning to write crime novels from 2014 onwards, as this is his professional background.

Paul Adams now lives in Western Australia, where the beer is not as good but at least it doesn't rain as often.

**What is this life if, full of care,
We have no time to stand and stare?.....**

**No time to wait till her mouth can
Enrich that smile her eyes began?**

**A poor life this if, full of care,
We have no time to stand and stare**

Extract from the poem – 'Leisure' by W H Davies. p. 1910.

PART ONE

OUT OF TIME......

I

Oh, bum!

Oh bugger, oh bugger, oh bum!

A quarter past sodding eight. I'm s'posed to be at the office at nine. 'Nine sharp' the old trout at staffing said. I can't cock this up. I can't *afford* to cock this up. I mean, I really, *really* need this job. I know, I know, it isn't much, but hey, you've gotta start somewhere, as my mate Emms always tells me, usually when she's pulled some bloke that looks like he's just walked into a lamp post, all squashed nose and bulging eyes. The bloke, that is, not Emms. 'You gotta start somewhere', she says, and in her case she's right. From there on in her blokes always seem to get worse.

So there I am sorting through heaps of clothes all of which shoulda been washed like *weeks* ago, sniffing at panties and bras and blouses, errr..... what *is* that smell? trying not to retch, just hoping upon hope that somewhere in this festering pile there is something that is reasonably clean and doesn't stink like the local gym or something.

And I'm pulling on about three things at once, looking for bits of make-up, it'll have to wait... stick it in my bag, I can do it on my way in, clothing can't wait though, not unless I wanna get arrested, so I have skirt, blouse, underwear. Oh bum again, where's my underwear? I toy briefly with going without. A whole day at a new job *sans* panties. Hmmm. Why hello Mr Blythe, nice to see you and yes you're absolutely right it *is* a lovely, warm day, isn't it?... *so* lovely and warm, in fact, that I decided not to......

No. Don't go there, girl. You *know* what not wearing pants does to you.

So I finally find a pair that I probably wore like weeks ago, that isn't contaminated by one stain or another (yugh!) and, after giving them a quick wave around the room, they seem to have lost most of their aroma and I give them a quick squirt of my favourite 'light and breezy' perfume, the combination creating a kind of 'Eau de Pussey'.

It'll have to do. I really don't have time.

And then I'm out of the door, hoping I look vaguely presentable but inside feeling like my head is about to explode and my stomach empty most of its very acidic contents onto the floor in front of me. Shouldn't have had that last tequila slammer. But I manage to keep most of this down...I'll need some mints to get rid of that acrid taste and smell. Coo, didn't even get a chance to clean my teeth. They seem to have developed a stucco coating.

But, on the train in, I get time to lightly apply and check my make-up. Not looking too bad, girl, even if I say so myself, and I'm just putting a brush through my hair, applying the finishing touches, so to speak, when I notice a man sitting opposite me staring as bold as anything at my legs, like my *upper* legs, the bloody perve and I wriggle in my seat coz now I'm conscious of my skirt and how short it is coz it's ridden up my thighs and, oh shit, maybe it is a bit *too* short and what will the people at my new job think? She's a bloody tart, that's what they'll think...why oh why didn't I put something more sensible on?... well I know why, coz nothing whatsoever is clean, that's why...and as I feel more and more uncomfortable in my seat, suddenly the perve opposite's eyebrows shoot up like someone switched on a light bulb and his eyes are fairly popping out of his sockets as his eyes bore into the area between my tightly crossed legs and thank heavens I *did* put some panties on after all, coz by now he'd have had a right eyeful.

So, anyway, now I'm glaring back at the old bugger but he just keeps staring back at me, or rather my at my 'bits' and I want desperately to pull down at my skirt but don't want to give the perve the satisfaction, so I just glare even harder and he just keeps on staring totally oblivious to my 'retaliation from Hell' until it's his stop and he gets up and people move out of his way to let him off and it's then that I see his dog......well his *guide* dog!

Oh bum!

Well my jaw must have been hovering around floor level by then and then I catch the eye of another person opposite and I guess he must have seen the whole thing coz he's grinning like it's just *the* funniest thing, so I stick my tongue out at him like a little schoolgirl and he just starts laughing to himself so I get up and move, pretending that I'm getting off, although I'm not, but I just don't need this right now, OK?

And then I'm running for the next I don't know how far and burst through the door at precisely ten past all huffing and puffing and sweaty and horrible and feeling like death and there's this woman at reception, where I'm supposed to be, and then she's giving *me* the evil eye coz I suppose she's guessed who I am and that, yes, I'm late and even as I'm approaching the desk she's looking at her watch as if every second counted, the little......

Hi, I gasp, I'm.... but she cuts me off, Yes I *know* who you are, she says all stuck up, you're *supposed* to be the new receptionist. No supposed about it, I interrupt, coz I'm not gonna let this little madam get the better of me. Is this where I sit? I say sliding into a seat next to her and I suppose you're here to show me the ropes

I say, deliberately not looking her in the eye. She sighs as if to say we've got a right one here, but I choose to rise above this, so she introduces herself, all hoity toity, as Hollie, with an 'I E', so I say '...and I'm Sophie Macdonald, that's MacDonald with an 'E I E I O'', and try not to smirk.

She doesn't see the funny side.

Glad that we get off on the right foot, I then proceed to quiz her on all aspects of the exciting career that I have chosen for myself. The 'Face of Blythe Enterprises' as 'Hollie with an I E' likes to call it. *Just* a bloody receptionist is my take on things. I look at her as if to say '*you* were the Face of Blythe Enterprises before I came along? Dear god, how *have* they managed to stay in business?' She has a chin you could plough snow with.

So I learn to operate the switchboard, 'Blythe Enterprises, Good morning. Blythe Enterprises, good morning. Blythe Enterprises, howdya sodding well do-oo!!? And by midday I'm bored stupid and the 'Eau de Poisson', as I'm now calling it, is beginning to wear off and 'Hollie with an I E's nose is starting to twitch. And by the time Madam asks if I can manage on my own from then on in, I am ready to hit the nearest bar and drink it dry.

'I won't be here tomorrow, as I'll be starting my new job 'upstairs',' she informed me for possibly the fifth time that day as if 'upstairs' was something to be in awe of. I almost ask if she can manage the stairs at her age, but resist the temptation...I mean she must be nearly *forty*!

And as I sit with my wee glass of blanc de blanc, all I can think is, 'is this it? Is this all life has in store for me? Hour after hour, day after day, week in week out of 'Blythe Enterprises, good *fucking* morning'', ('scuse my French) smiling politely even though my stomach feels like the bottom of a bucket of rancid meat, my mouth tastes of sick and what's left of my brain is determined to leave my skull by whatever exit is nearest.....probably my forehead.

What else is there? None of the blokes that work there are vaguely fanciable, even if they could stop letching at me for just one second. The odd courier that pops in *could* be shaggable...all that black leather.....hmm hmmm! ... but let's face it, what are the chances, eh, even if they did take off their crash helmets? 'Hollie with a IE' kept going on and on about the Big Boss.....Mr Blythe this, Mr Blythe that, blah blah blah....I got the distinct impression that this little Madam just wasn't getting any. No, I'll revise that.... had never *had* any! I was beginning to feel some empathy there, but it didn't last.

With work again tomorrow, I can't afford to stay for more than one drink.....not that I'm being conscientious or anything....I literally can't *afford* another drink, my purse being filled with not so fresh air yet again. Besides, I had somehow attracted the attention of some old perve at the bar, who kept grinning at me as if he was one fairy light short of a Christmas tree. Someone really should wipe that dribble off his chin. I waited for him to turn his back to order another drink, and then I slunk off home. Maybe I'll get in early tomorrow, just to show willing.

    Maybe.......

II

So. The Williamson account.

Nope. Nothing.

I can't do this. I don't even feel vaguely inclined.

So many files, so many reports. All meaningless.

Can't concentrate on a damned thing these days. Lack of sleep is half of the problem. The other half being a complete lack of interest.

What do I do, eh? If I don't get this contract signed by the end of the month, then I might as well give up. Three months I've been working on this and if only everyone else knew how damned important it was they wouldn't act so.......well, *blithely*.

I haven't had a decent night's sleep in weeks. I keep waking up after only three hours remembering things that I haven't done, that I *should* have done, things that I need to do, things that can wait. And I lie there fretting, staring off into the blackness, listening to the slow, rhythmic breathing beside me. Oblivious to my plight.

Time was that I could have coped with the stress. When I started out, I would have *thrived* on the stress. But not now. Oh no. Now it just seems to be dragging me down. Each new problem just feels like another nail in the coffin. I know that that's morbid, but sometimes....sometimes I feel that's all I have to look forward to.

Where did it all go, eh? My youth, all that time, all those years, all that ambition. And for what? To end up here struggling to keep things together. Did it die overnight? No. It just drifted away.

What I would give to be twenty five again. What I *wouldn't* give would be a shorter list. Hmmm...twenty five....oh man, what a *great* age that was to be. Things seemed so possible then. Every day brought new ventures, new opportunities, new challenges. And I'm not just talking about business, oh man, no. The women.....the booze, the parties.....wine, women and song. Make the most of it, some wag once told me and did I? In spades, my friend, in spades.

But now?

Hmmm.....each and every day seems to bring grief. And as soon as one problem is sort of dealt with, there are two more lining up to take its place. A conveyor belt of misery. Don't let the bastards drag you down, Nick tells me, ever one to quote a threadbare cliché at me. 'They are not, bastards or otherwise', I tell him staring blankly into the bottom of my now empty glass, wondering where that pint that I'd just bought had disappeared to, 'they are not dragging me down' I repeat, *'they* are wearing me out. If I was being dragged down' I continue with the analogy, *'If* I was being dragged down.....I'd take a few last gulps of air and it would be all over in a matter of seconds. Thank you and goodnight.' I wave my glass at the barman and point to Nick's, barely touched drink. He shakes his head, but he gets one anyway. 'It's like a constant war of *attrition.*' 'Ah' he interjects, 'don't let the bastards *grind* you down?' 'Zactly!' Oh dear, fourth pint and I'm already slurring my speech.

'But you know the worst thing? Hmmmm? I'm tired. Not just *tired* tired,' I sigh, 'I'm tired of doing the same thing day in day out, tired of wondering where the next buck is coming from, tired of having to fight for every last scrap of income, tired of always having to please other people, tired of painting on a plastic smile coz, if this little shit across the table doesn't sign on the dotted line, I can't put food on the table....' the mention of food making my stomach cringe '....tired of the responsibility for the people I employ, tired of dealing with staff 'issues', tired of the incessant bills that snatch the cash away before it's even hit my bank account.' I pause for breath.

'Rant over?' asks Nick.

'I'm tired of.....'

Nick mutters - 'I'll take that as a 'No' then....'

'........not getting just one decent night's sleep a week, bugger that, once a *month* would be good, tired of never seeing my wife, tired of never *fuc*......no, best not go there, tired of having no time to myself, tired of all the worry, the hassle, the grief, just to shut it all out and have time to draw breath, tired of the *mundanity* of it all.... and do you know what?

Nick, under his breath, 'no, but I've a feeling you're about to tell me......'

'....I'm simply tired of *being* tired.'

'Boy, you've got it bad. Just as long as you're not tired of life, eh....?' Nick says, trying vainly to bring some cheer.

'Nope, not yet. But I'm getting there.' I stare into the dregs of beer. 'Fuck, I'm even tired of finding daily solace in the bottom of a pint glass.'

'Wo, things *is* bad. Never thought I'd hear old H say such a thing. That's almost blasphemy. Your last pint then?' I answer with a nod. 'Suits me, it was my round,' he giggles and smiles his toothy grin.

Food, must get something inside me. 'Fancy some grub?'

'Not as much as I fancy that,' he retorts, nodding to some space over my shoulder. I give him the courtesy quick glance.

'She's young enough to be your wotsit'.

'Cheers, mate...maybe just what *you* need though?'

'Me? Sure, if Sarah got one whiff of me sniffing round some young floosie....'

'Floosie? What the fuck is a floosie?' he giggles as he exchanges his empty glass for the full one on the bar. The one that he hadn't wanted.

'Just one more thing that I can't have. Just one more thing that makes life's burden seem almost unbearable......just one more thing that....'

'*That's* the one thing you do need, mate' nodding and grinning like some inane letch. 'Young, pretty, dark, lithe. I bet she goes off like a rocket.' I take a cursory glance again. He's right of course. Not that this young woman is what I want, but she is all of those things that Nick said...and in an instant I'm back in the days of my youth. Her name was Sam. A country pub, the warm haze of a late summer's day drifting into a long sultry evening, long, long blonde hair, dazzling blue eyes, that cheeky grin, that light summer dress barely concealing those awesome....oh fuck! And yes, the fuck. The fuck in the field of barely ripened wheat, pressed hard to the ground, the removal of that dress with, oh man, nothing underneath and hands just about everywhere and.....

'Who the fuck is Sam?'

'What?'

'You just said 'Sam'.

'Did I? ...hmmmm, just someone I used to...you know?'

'Someone you used to shag? What, you gone gay on me?'

'Sam, as in *Samantha*.'

'Oooooh' He says with mock realisation. That same lecherous grin. I gaze longingly into my half empty glass, wishing for something more inspiring to look back at me than that insipid brown liquid. 'Someone I used to.....know'. I take a deep breath. 'Look, if you don't want to eat, that's fine, but I need to and there's bound to be nothing at home so......'

'I'm fine where I am mate' still avoiding eye contact. So I leave him to it. Leave him to drool over some young woman that would never give him a second glance. Leave him to fantasise that, at the tender age of forty six, and nursing a gut the approximate shape and size of a small cathedral dome, he had anything other than a snowball in hell's chance of getting anywhere near bedding someone close to the age of his own daughter. Even if he did wipe the dribble off of his chin.

But I've had enough. I am exhausted. The alcohol, once a palliative to stress, just seems to exacerbate the condition now. Sure, it takes the edge off, until about the end of the second pint, but after that......I'm just drowning. Many moons ago, booze was just the starter. The kick start to an evening of over and self indulgence and I could just keep on going, confident in the belief that life would just keep on keeping on. But not now. Somewhere in the last twenty years it had imperceptibly all gone into reverse. Year after year of living like there was no tomorrow just to wake up one morning and realise that tomorrow is only a few hours away. From behaving like you are immortal, to being painfully aware of your own mortality. Long gone is the perpetual buzz that life presented me with. Long gone is all the drive that that buzz generated.

Give me one day....just *one* day of that vim, that vitality that I had when I was twenty five. Yeah.....if only.....

Well there's no point in dwelling on it is there. Never could roll your life back to the past. No point in even thinking about it.

No point.

So, concentrate Henry, the Williamson account.....

Nope.

Still nothing.

III

Oh bugger, oh bum.

Here we go again! Five past blood eight! I'm really gonna have to get that clock fixed....or at least remember to set the sodding alarm. I can't even blame the booze this time. One glass of vin de plonk and then it was home for some microwaved mush and an early night.

Have to find summink different to wear....oh, bugger! Can't wear the *same* panties as yesterday. Not *again*. I sat there the whole afternoon bathing in the aroma rising from my seat, secretly blowing at my nethers everytime I thought that no-one was watching. So I rummage round my room and finally find a vintage pair under my bed. A bit dusty but any lingering odour has long gone...well I *tell* myself it has. I know, I know. How can I live like this? Well I do, is all I can say. Organisation is not my middle name, OK?

So, a quick squirt of Eau de Pussey and I'm off.........

And in through the main door by 9 a.m. sharp!

Damn, I'm good. If there was an Olympic sport in getting out of bed and in to work in less time than most people take to have their breakfast, I'd get the gold medal every time. So OK, I did manage to put my panties on inside out but only *I* know that. Not much chance of anyone *else* finding out around here, is there? Which reminds me ..... I simply *must* sort a clean pair for tomorrow. I reckon I've used up my nine lives when it comes to clean-ish undies. Tomorrow it's all or nothing......and I know how I get when it's nothing, so that's *not* an option.

So I sit with a sigh and wonder why on earth I hurried. I mean, here I am for the next eight hours, nothing to do except answer the phone and smile sweetly at the people coming and going and 'Good morning, Blythe Enterprises.....' and pretty soon I'm bored silly and it's not even nine thirty yet.

Ho hum. Tuesday, half nine. How many hours is it til me and Emms head out on the town? ..... 'on the pull', more accurately. Do you know how many days it is since I last got off with anyone? No. Let me rephrase that. Do you know how many *weeks* it is? And, if I was to be totally honest, it's probably into the months by now. Kevin, I think his name was. I should have known better. I mean, *Kevin*! Honestly, just the name should have been enough to put me off, but then I only learned that after the event, so to speak. And I'm using the word 'event' in its loosest possible sense. Two hours of spittle-sprayed shouting at each other over the noise in the club, followed by a short ride home and an even shorter ride in bed. After, I insisted that he wrote his number on the back of my hand, safe in the knowledge that the first thing I'd do when I got home was to have a shower and watch that oh so valuable information drain off down the plughole. Hopefully he'd have better luck with the number I gave him.... Alcoholics Anonymous.

Works for me.

And before that? Well there was Dave (hmmm...), Geoff (yewww....), Darren (oh my *god*!), Colin (oh puke! No really, I *did*....absolutely everywhere!), Nigel (a bit posh, face like a horse), and the one who shouted 'Goal' when he came ..... which was more than I ever did. And so many others, names and faces now lost in the mists of time, if I ever knew them in the first place. And that's it for the last ..... how long? Two years? Three? And nothing to show for it but a zero bank balance and a course of antibiotics.

Things really have to change.

Wednesday – hey, I met the big boss today. Mr Blythe himself. Seems pleasant enough, but I can't help feeling that he carries the weight of the world on his shoulders, as my mum says. He wandered in mid-morning, introduced himself, smiled briefly and wandered off towards the lift, which I guess was courteous, if nothing else. Some bosses are so far up their own bum .... Honestly, though, he owns a big company, must be rolling in it, what the hell has *he* got to worry about? Cheer up mate, it might never happen.

Emms wants to hit some new club on Thursday night. I tell her I'm skint and will be for two weeks til my first wages come in. She reckons she'll sub me, but I'm not so keen. I mean, she's *always* subbing me. I must owe her loads by now and she never asks for it back. Maybe it's a mark of how desperate she is. I mean, she's lovely, is Emms, but if I wasn't there to go out with, I doubt she'd ever get laid. Not that I'm great looking, or anything, but we are a bit of a cliché when we're together. The slim one and the *not* slim one. But that's OK coz she's such fun, especially once she gets her second wind and she's past her sixth tequila, and somehow she just seems to attract the guys, coz she gets so LOUD, which you might think is a good thing, guys flocking round, but if you saw the *kind* of guys you wouldn't be so sure.

So rather than her getting *my* seconds, it's usually the other way round, except that I don't even rate her firsts, so I'm not even slightly interested in her leftovers. Such an unassuming girl when sober. Butter wouldn't melt.... You'd never guess what a little devil she turns into when she's had a few. I mean, once she just couldn't decide which of two guys she preferred, so she ended up leaving with *both* of them! Honestly! I don't know what it is they put in that tequila, but they should bottle it.

So once little Emms has hit the road with whatever lowlife has got his hand up her skirt and his eyes down her cleavage, I retire to the bar to survey the scenery in the increasingly vain hope that some halfway decent guy will be worth talking to and, even better, worth shagging. Sometimes it works, sometimes it doesn't. Hence Dave and Geoff and Darren and Colin and.......

Roll on Thursday.

IV

Sarah had gone by the time I had got up. Can't remember the last time we were together long enough to do more than exchange a few perfunctory remarks or, in my case, utter a few perfunctory grunts.

Never at my best first thing in the morning. Not much better the rest of the day for that matter. I'm standing, staring blankly out of the window, cup of coffee in hand and I really should eat something because my stomach is turning somersaults and burning at the same time, like some ancient boiler replete with the requisite gurgles. Coffee on an empty stomach. Probably not a good idea. Never did get any supper. Fridge empty as usual. And I can't get the Williamson account out of my head. Spent half the night lying awake worrying about whether or not there'll be enough money coming in at the end of the month. Hell! *Any* money would be good!

Got to work late. New receptionist. Pleasant enough. Can we afford her? Probably not. Hollie harassing me as soon as I stepped through the door. So-and-so called and wants this-and-that, so-and-so needs.....so-and-so reminding you that.....and don't forget the meeting with.....and I've rescheduled for tomorrow as so-and-so can't make it and .... OK, OK, just *back off* will you? Whatever persuaded me to employ Ms. Twigg as my assistant? Well, I know that she's good at what she does, the very model of efficiency and I should be pleased with that. And she was clearly wasted in reception, even though it was always understood that that was a temporary post, just until we could get someone else in. So why does she annoy me so? Probably that sycophantic way of hers. It's just plain cringeworthy. I'm sure that she doesn't even realise she's doing it. She's about the only one who doesn't.

I suppose that the bottom line is that there was simply no-one else. I really couldn't be bothered to go through that whole rigmarole of advertising, sifting, interviewing and then selecting the most promising candidate. Better the devil.......? Maybe.

So. The Williamson account. It really has come to this. When I first started in this lark, I'd be out there rustling up new accounts, new *prestigious* accounts. The young buck with all to strive for....showing all and sundry how it was done, and yet here I am..... hmmmm, yes here I am now trying to *save* one of those same prestigious accounts. Not drumming up new trade, as I should be doing, but tentatively clinging on to the only halfway decent client I have left. A sign of the times? Maybe? Or just a sign of *my* time? Come in, Henry Blythe, your time is up! Well, not if I can help it. This old tanker is not going down without a fight.

So, client meeting end of the month. Three weeks to sort out a presentation, show what we're *still* made of, show them that we still matter, show them that *they* still matter and Bob's yer wotsit. 'Hollie, team meeting, one hour, my office' 'Yes Mr Blythe' and the treacle positively drips from the intercom.

Should take about an hour. Could murder a pint right now....and I really should eat, sometime.

The meeting goes reasonably well, but it's still the same old faces and I can't help thinking that maybe we need some new blood here and that maybe, just maybe, that's part of the problem, why Williamson is causing the ructions that he is. And I can understand that. No-one wants something that has become jaded. They require innovation, novelty and, bugger me, that's what they're going to get .... even if it kills me.

So I'm feeling upbeat as I bound through the bar door. Nick's already lined them up and I insist that I'm only staying for the one because I can be sensible like that, especially when I know I have things to do. And now I really do have things to do. A sense of challenge abounds.

True to my word, I'm out of there three pints later, and everything and everyone has taken on a rosy glow as I head back to the office with something approaching a new lease of life. There's a pile of papers waiting for me on my desk, courtesy of Ms Twigg, which gives me something to peruse during the rest of the afternoon, as the ale wears off, but the more I read on, the more depressed I get because it's the same-old, same-old and my gut reaction is that it's simply *not* good enough. I mean, come on boys and girls, let's at least *try* here! A general rallying cry goes out – Pull your finger out, team! Three out of ten. Must try harder! But there's a sense that I'm just going through the motions. I'm hoping that no-one else picks up on this and that I've succeeded in instilling some kind of enthusiasm into my staff. But I'm not so sure.

If your heart's not in it, well.....

V

Thursday night doesn't come round quick enough. Eight o'clock sharp-ish and Emms is already sat at a table by the time I pile through the door, and by the way she slurs a 'hello' I'm guessing that she's well on her way already.....the seven empty shot glasses are also a bit of a clue.

'I've come to the concloooshon zat I should zave time by getting pizzed an *awful* lot earlier than I normally do. That way I can pull a bloke, get him 'ome and shagged *before* he falls azleep. A girl can only take *so* much, ya know. Last bloke nearly squashed the life ouda me. Two hours of his snoring in my left ear before he *finally* decides to roll off. Did wonders for me figure though!' she says looking down at her ample curves, and she cackles that raucous laugh of hers that some men seem to find attractive. Men with their brains in their scrotums.

She waves cash at me and I order a double coz I've evidently got *alot* of catching up to do and we settle down for a chinwag and I fill her in on my four days of dazzlingly intellectual stimulation at the glamorous surroundings of Blythe Enterprises....which takes about three minutes.

Emms then launches into a long spiel about the guy she ended up with the previous Saturday night, explaining in graphic detail how she'd produced this vibrator from her handbag in the taxi to his place and how she'd insisted that he use it on her during the ride home and how the taxi driver thought that the noise was a problem with his radio and kept hitting it. The radio, that is, not the vibrator.

'But zat was just the start of it' she goes on, knocking back another tequila shot, 'by ze time we get out of the taxi, I'm abzlutely dripping, but when we get indoors all thiz guy wants to do is 'ave me use the bloody thing on *him*!' She feigns shock, all wide-eyed and gobsmacked, but by this time I'm only half paying attention coz I've just caught sight of the old fellah at the next table who is earwigging every word that Emms is saying and looks on the verge of a heart attack. Despite me trying to get Emms to quieten down a bit, she continues at full tilt 'Well you know me....anything for a laff' and she cackles, her ample cleavage joining in with the mirth, the old fellah's eyes on stalks and his chin now at table level, 'so I'm giving it the old one-two and he's telling me 'deeper, deeper' and I guess I must 'ave got carried away by it all, coz the lube gets abzlutely *everywhere* and I lose my grip and suddenly I'm looking down at my hand.... my *empty* hand, wondering how the hell I managed *that* dizappearing trick, then I realise that the bloke's going 'ooo...ooo...ooo....' and I think, oh my gaaaard! It isn't? it hasn't?....but it *must* 'ave, coz *I* can't see it!'

And by now we are both in fits of giggles, Emms from her reminiscences and me from watching the old fellah miss his gaping mouth by a good three inches and tipping his beer down his shirt front. Oblivious, she goes on... 'so the bloke lookzat me over his shoulder, seez me looking aghast at my empty 'ands and says, all seriouz, "you have *got* to be kidding me" and I just goes 'nope!' and he goes 'Fuck!' and I sez 'Not any more, you're not!'

And for the next twenty minutes she goes into grossest detail about how, passion spent, they came up with a way of getting the damned thing out without having to go to hospital and explain exactly *what* it was, and exactly *where* it was, to some student nurse on night shift in A & E.

Oh, dear Emms. I'm not sure what shocked the old bugger next door more, the graphic images of her exploits or the fact that it was delivered in an accent that could cut crystal glass, courtesy of the most expensive education that money could buy.

I can't help loving her for it!

By about eleven we're in some noise den and Emms is giving it some, strangely ignoring the inbreds that have dragged their knuckles to the edge of the dance floor. Maybe last weekend's experiences have taught her to get a grip?... so to speak. And I am joining in coz right now the dance floor seems to be the safest place – it's certainly a neanderthal-free zone for the first half hour, but then I have to go to the loo and I find that I'm no longer alone coz some no-brain excuse for the male of the species seems to have latched on to me and is making every effort to catch my eye with his leery smile. He even follows me into the ladies, before he spots the tampon machine on the wall and realises where he is. Excuse my French, but for *fuck's* sake! Is this what it's come to? I'm feeling ever so, *ever* so slightly pissed off by now and struggle to resist the urge just to walk straight out of there.

I can't coz I'm with Emms and she's paid for the whole evening and there's no way I can just up and abandon her. But when I get back to the dance floor there's some spider-like, gangly youth draped over her shoulders bawling into her ear. I catch her eye and indicate I'm going and blow her a kiss safe in the knowledge if anyone can look after herself, she can. I take one last look at the grinning spiderman and start to feel just a teeny bit queasy, trying to imagine him with a dildo stuck up his bum.

VI

New day, new regime. I actually manage to get to the gym on the way to work. First time in over a week, but at least my lack of exercise is more than compensated for by my lack of food. Low calorie intake negating the need for calorie burning. Really should get something sorted with Sarah about buying more than the occasional pint of milk. Fridge seems to be a food-free zone. She might as well keep her legal files in there....along with her libido.

Man cannot live on coffee alone.

New receptionist didn't look her best this morning. Not her usual cheerful self. 'Late night?' I asked, all innocent. She smiled meekly and nodded, as if uttering a single word would bring forth something she might regret. I had to sympathise. Many a morning I've felt like that. Can't let her give a bad impression though. 'Face of Blythe Enterprises' I quipped, mimicking Ms Twigg, and raising a brief smile from Ms Whateverhernameis. 'Strong coffee and two ibuprofen. Can't beat it' She points to same on the reception desk. 'Great minds' I add, heading for the lift.

VII

I don't know what *he's* got to look so pleased about! 'Strong coffee and two ibuprofen.' Like I didn't *know* that! God's sakes, I've had *years* of practice. I guess the old bugger got laid last night. Which is more than I did. Surprised he can still manage it at his age. I mean, he must be nearly fifty. He's *ancient*!!

He does a good piss take of Hollie-with-an-I E, though. Now that *was* funny.

VIII

Two weeks in and I'm not convinced that this is going to work. I keep pushing the team to come up with something fresh, something inspiring, but it's as if they've run out of steam. I'm worn out with the stress and the worry, but I can't relax for one moment. Only I know how important this is. The imperative of success. The impossibility of failure.

Nick is concerned by my absence from our usual watering hole and seems unimpressed by my excuses that work has come on top recently and requires all hands on deck. He's just lonely though. Happy to cruise through life with a pint glass in his hand and several kilos of flab overhanging his belt, he doesn't understand the responsibilities that I carry.

Good grief, the man even turned up at my office once. Thought that presenting himself in person might sway the balance in favour of a session. Found him letching over the receptionist, Ms Thingummy, as I exited the lift on my way to a meeting...

'Could swear I've seen you somewhere before,' as he edges closer, palms flat on her desk, beery fumes emanating from his open mouth 'Never forget a face......' and then his eyes are on her tits '.....or a nice pair of........' and I had to practically drag him off the poor girl. 'Steady on, H. Just being friendly.' 'Sorry' I say over my shoulder to the young lady, guiding him towards the exit. 'He's probably in need of a drink.'

So I promise to join him for a pint, 'just give me five minutes to sort something out.' Placated, he heads off. So do I. In the opposite direction.... and I won't be back today.

IX

What's a girl to do? I haven't even been here a month yet and I am *so* bored! 'Ennui', my mum would call it.

I mean, it's not as if it's exactly busy at reception. Not what you'd call a hive of industry. People come and people go. The busy times seem to be when they arrive for work – all over in half an hour of 'good mornings' – or leave in the evenings, drifting off in dribs and drabs... 'good night...good night...thank you and good *bloody* night.' I know, I know, I shouldn't be nasty like that. It's a job and I should be grateful, but it is *just* a job and it's not exactly scintillating, is it?

And that's the problem? No-one to actually *talk* to all day. Other than 'good morning', 'Blythe Enterprises, how can I help you?' and 'Good night.' It's not what you'd call conversation is it? No wonder I look forward so much to seeing Emms at the weekend.

So I tried playing a few games, which helped to pass the time.

I have the most fun when answering the phone.

'Hello, Blythe Enterprise, how can I hurt you?' Most don't even cotton on to what I've said and just ask for the extension or a particular person but some say 'I beg your pardon?' 'Blythe Enterprises, how can I help you?' I repeat, all innocent. One sharp chap caught on straight away and, after a brief pause, asked if I could give him a good spanking. Cheeky!

Then there's the accents. Emms says I'm really good at them, so I thought I'd get some practice in while I had the chance.

'Oooo dat dere?'

'Erm, can I speak to Jeffrey Cummings please?'

'What?!'

'Erm, Jeffrey Cummings?'

'Ooo cummin? Jeffrey's cumming? Dat's *dizgosting*, ya dutty mon. Wash your mout' wit soap. Raaass clart!' and I suck my teeth for good effect, then hang up.

Thirty seconds later there's this tentative call back from the same person....they wait to hear me say 'Blythe Enterprises, how can I help you?' but I say nothing until I hear '....err, hello? Is that Blythe Enterprises? Hello?'

'Blythe Enterprises, how can I help you?' I almost bawl down the phone and I swear I can hear them kack their pants......just before I piss mine!

My favourite, of course, is my French accent. Not a difficult one to pull off, under the circumstances, but the one I can have most fun with....especially if the caller is a man.

'Aaaaallo?' I drawl.

'Hello, can I speak with Janet Blake please?'

In the deepest voice I can manage. 'Wah do you warnt to spik wiz 'errrr?....when you can tock to *me*...?'

'Erm, and who might you be?'

'*Marr* name is........Izzza-belllllar.' I sigh. 'And wart is yerz?' Coy.

'Err........well, errrr.....Isabella?'

'No, no no, NO,' I interject playfully, '....not Isabella....' I growl even deeper, 'Izzza-bellllar. Can you say?'

'Errr....' his voice shaking, 'Well, Izzza-bellllar' .... and I can almost feel him sweating.

'Oooh, I sink you are verrry sexy man.'

'Really?' he says, but it comes out as a sort of squeak.....like a strangled mouse....... and I can't believe this guy's still on the line. He must be *desperate* for someone to talk to.

'Yes verrrry sexy man wiz verrrrry sexy voice.... I lark yerr voice verrrrrry *verrry* maaarch....will you say mar name again..... for me, pliz? Oh, and mar second name is Marcoque'

And I hear him take a deep breath at which point I make a click on the line just before he growls 'Izzzar-belllar ma cock.'

'Oh my god,' I shriek in my poshest English accent, 'I've got a dirty phone call!!! Hollie, Hollie, call the police. There's a perve on the line....and don't think I don't know who you are, either you slimeball, coz your number's come up on the switchboard'...and then I hang up.

That one didn't call back for, like, *hours* after....and even then made every effort to disguise his voice. Funny that.

But, otherwise, it's just snoresville. I'm counting down the days and hours til the next piss up with Emms.

X

Just two days to go now and I can't sleep for the worry. Only I know that this is literally make or break for both me and probably the company. The work's completed. It's not great. It's not bad, either, for that matter but it's too late to start tweaking it now. I have two others joining me for the trip, although one of those is my 'assistant' Hollie, so she's not really a team member, as such. Just there to make sure that things go according to plan.

But I spend the day flicking through what we've prepared only to have this nagging thought, scratching at the back of my mind, that this really isn't *that* good. And, to be honest, if I was in their shoes, well....let's just say I'd be tempted to try elsewhere. This is not good. Trust your instincts, I always say. If my gut feeling is this negative, then there's a bloody good reason for it.

And then, at five past five, Jeff pops his head round the door.

'On my way, H. Just to let you know, I'm not feeling too good. Rough throat. Should be good for tomorrow, though. I know how important it is.'

I just smile....grimly. No you don't, mate, I'm thinking. You really haven't a clue. But I say nothing, just – Mind how you go. Early night. Keep warm. See you bright and early...... and anything else appropriately trite that comes to mind...all the while thinking, let me down, mate, and you are *seriously* fucked!

*

DISASTER!!! Total fucking *disaster!!*

7 a.m. I get a call from Jeff. All hoarse and wheezy. Says he hasn't slept all night. Temperature. Losing his voice. Headache. Headache? I'll give him a fucking headache. And I'm afraid I lose it. I'm standing there shouting down the phone as Sarah walks in, looks at me askance and flounces out again without so much as a word. After a deep, deep breath I just tell Jeff to see how it goes, maybe he'll feel better later, can catch us up, knowing full well he won't. I mean, I *know* he's ill, that he's absolutely not one to pull a sickie just for the sake of it. And I know *he* knows that this is important, he's just not aware quite *how* important......but all I see and feel, as I stand there, is my whole life slipping away from me.

So I'm in no mood to be friendly by the time I bound through the office door and Ms Whatsit says a cheerful 'Good morning...' which I answer with one of my grunts and head for the lift. Hollie finds me slumped in my chair head in hands on the desk. 'Strong coffee and two ibuprofen...?'

'I do *not* have a hangover...' I snarl, eyeing her through splayed fingers, then fill her in on the absence of our number one presentation man.

'Ah' she says breezily, 'well I'm sure we'll manage.'

'How....?' I pause for effect. '...exactly?' She stares at me blankly for a moment. 'Leaving in one hour then Mr Blythe.' and off she goes. Thanks.

So that's yet another thing that gets me about Hollie. Completely useless in a crisis. Just carries on regardless as if the crisis didn't exist at all, thereby solving it. And humourless? Dear god! I swear if she ever cracked more than that thin smile her head would fall in two. If only she'd inherited her parents' sense of humour ..... calling her Hollie. I guess it could've been Hazel. Useful when looking for water.

Speaking of which, it's five past nine and I need a drink already. In fact, I need a whole day slowly immersing myself in a velvet cocoon of warm beer, brass fittings, the aroma of salt and vinegar crisps and decades of stale cigarette smoke.

But I can't. No matter how much I just want to give up, right here, right now, I know that I have to make this one last effort.

With Hollie as my back up.

Shit.

*

So at 10 o'clock sharp I'm in reception, pacing the floor impatiently, checking my watch every ten seconds after the last time I checked it.

'Problem, Mr Blythe?'

I wheel round to face the origin of the question, but only manage to stare blankly at Ms Whojammerflip, as if she's some kind of weird alien creature beamed down in place of my receptionist. Sent to taunt the fuck out of me. 'What?!' I almost scream at her. She's shocked. I back-peddle rapidly. 'Nothing' – is all I can manage, just as Ms Twigg exits the lift.

They say these things are supposed to happen in slow motion. Well they don't. Whoever said that clearly had never had anything dramatic happen to them. Ever.

What happened, happened in the blink of an eye. In a heartbeat.

Heel. Spiked. Slid. Over. Ankle. Twisted.

Crack.

Fall.

And all I can do is stand and gape. And only *then* does time slow right down, as I realise the full repercussion of what I've just witnessed, the full devastating effect of that simple fall and it seems like a full minute before I register Hollie's screams.

And I'm over to her in a flash and try dragging her to her feet with – can't be that bad, probably just a sprain, try walking on it, no?, there, there, it'll soon pass, there not so bad now, is it? Better hurry, mustn't miss our appointment....come on Hollie, you're not trying, walk damn you, *walk* woman.....as I man-handle her around and around in ever decreasing circles.

For fuck's sake, what is *wrong* with you?!

But all I can hear is that awful, soul destroying CRACK and I know it my heart of hearts that it will *not* be alright, that it is *not* a sprain and that the only thing that will soon pass is my own life before my very eyes as the vessel is lost and the captain goes down for that third and final time.

So, as I lower Hollie into the nearest chair, I follow suit but end up on the floor at her feet and it's not until I hear Ms Whatzername say 'Mr Blythe?' for possibly the fifth time that I realise that I am shaking violently and I'm blubbing like a child.

XI

Oh my good god! There's even green stuff coming out of his nose! Oooo, now *that's* gross.

So, that's Hollie-with-an-IE slumped on a chair, *probably* with a broken ankle, screaming blue murder and bawling like a baby. That's Mr Blythe lying on the floor, probably having some kind of breakdown, blowing bubbles out of his nose and bawling like a baby........

So I'm doing what I do best in these kind of situations.

Dither.

Errrr.....ambulance . Must get an ambulance. Mr Blythe may be a bit of a mess, albeit an increasingly gooey mess, but Hollie is in serious pain here and, much as I'd like to maintain that particular status quo for a few minutes longer, I dash for the phone.

When I get back a small crowd has gathered...well there are two other people anyway, but both seem to be concentrating on Hollie and Hollie's ankle. Men! Honestly. Any excuse. Neither seems bothered that My Blythe is now flat out on his back, snorting back snot and coughing almost simultaneously. I don't really know how to comfort someone in this situation. I mean do you pat them, hug them, try to get them to sit up? stand up? drink some water? Well what? So I kind of do all of them, one after the other in quick succession. The pat just feels silly, the hug is a struggle as I try to prevent my pristine blouse from making contact with Mr Blythe's increasingly messy nose, sitting him up was a real effort until I accidentally stood on his foot (ooops) and, from there, getting him to stand was frankly a doddle.

Minutes later, I have him back in his office and am handing him liberal amounts of tissues from a box on his desk. He's calming down pretty quickly now and I guess he's embarrassed by the fact that he let himself go in front of me.

'So what the hell was all that about?' trying to make conversation and divert his attention.

'It's all finished' is all he says shaking his head.....and then it all comes out, last chance for the company, Jeff goes sick, Hollie breaks a leg, no-one left but himself, can't do it on his own and it's all just falling apart. And I try to tell him that it can't be that bad, but even I have to admit that, yes, actually it is pretty bloody crap......

So then I have a brainwave. Why don't I go with him? He looks at me as if I'm some kind of idiot, and even I have to admit it does seem like a stupid suggestion, but I press it and say even if it's just for moral support it has to be better than going on his own. So he asks me why would I want to go, not sure that I can be much help and I'm thinking, bugger this, *anything* has to be better than sitting behind that bloody reception desk for another day, but I don't say that, I say, go on, it'll be fun... then think - Oh shut up Sophie, have you any idea how dumb that sounds?

But he seems to warm to the idea and almost jumps up from behind his desk, gives me a big hug and then strides out of the room, bag in hand. Come on then, no time to lose.

Well, here's a turn up for the books. Within an hour we've stopped at my place just long enough for me to pack an overnight bag, including brand new knickers, and for Mr Blythe to advise a change of blouse given the gunge that seems to have attached itself to my right shoulder (that last bloody hug!) and we're on our way. I feel like I'm going on holiday. I could almost sing.

XII

We sit side by side, in total silence, for what seems like an absolute age. What do you say in such circumstances? Sorry, my dear, (too patronising? I really *must* remember her name) .... but I've really been under *alot* of strain recently and, I don't know about you, but I find the best way to deal with things is to lie on the floor and throw a fit. Works everytime. Embarrassed? Who me? Good heavens no, comes quite naturally after the first time.

Doesn't really cover it when you've just made a complete fool of yourself in front of your most junior member of staff. And here we are now, on my last fateful journey, nothing to say to her, except maybe – Please stop that humming, I'm finding it *really* aggravating. But I make light of it – Someone's happy – Sorry was I annoying you? – No, I lie, fine by me.

I try a change of tack. 'If you want to make yourself useful, there are some papers you can read. Bring you up to speed with what we will be doing tomorrow.' But I can see her eyes glaze over and I guess that's no surprise. She's a bloody receptionist, for godsakes, not my number one presentation skills expert type person. What possible interest can she have in what we are on this trip for, other than what looks nice out of the window? I sigh - 'or maybe not eh?'

'No, no' - she says brightening a little. 'That would be most interesting, ('...most interesting'?). 'I should at least know what's going on.'

'If you're sure?'

'What? You think I can't handle it?'

'No, no, really it's just it's a bit dry and probably not your area of expertise and.....'

'You think I'm thick. That's it, isn't it?'

I try to act shocked but, when that fails, I say 'I'm shocked'.

'Well you could at least look it!'

Bugger. Rumbled.

But minutes later she's got her head stuck into a bundle of files, reports, proposals, so I can't complain about her apparent dedication. Just her sodding humming. After a further ten minutes of this tuneless droning, a kind of aural Chinese water torture, I have to interject.

'So?' A pause while she keeps reading. 'What do you think?'

'Well, it's a bit dry and not *really* my area of expertise......'

I can't help myself, but a smile breaks out across my face. It almost hurts. 'Are you taking the piss?'

'Yup.' Slapping the last file shut '...I think it's the only way, don't you?'

'That bad, huh?'

'Well, it's not exactly the latest blockbuster, is it? I don't see it winning any prizes for literary merit or witty insight'

Literary merit and witty insight? What the......? 'You think it's boring?'

'Hmmmm....who am I to say. Like I said, not my area of expertise.'

'Yes, you said,' I can't win here can I? .....and we lapse into silence and stay that way until we arrive.

XIII

Oh my gaaaaaard, as Emms would say, I feel like a princess. Well, old Blythey's company may be going down the pan but he certainly knows how to live the lifestyle. I have never, and I mean NEVER, stayed in anywhere as plush as this before. The carpets that you just seem to sink into, the bathroom...all that marble, all those little bottles of toiletry stuff to play with, the furniture, like something out of a French bodice-ripper... and the bed, ohmygaaaaard, the bed! I mean you could have an *orgy* on the damn thing, it's so big!

So here I am waiting in the bar, all bathed and perfumed and refreshed and feeling like the cat got the proverbial, but I've not got a drink coz, bugger me, have you seen the prices? And I'm starting to feel uncomfortable and wishing that Emms was here, coz I know that she could handle this better than I can, when in strolls Mr Blythe dressed all cajj, but still looking more than a little uptight.

He's at the bar briefly then heads my way with an ice bucket with a bottle of bubbly sticking out of the top....... 'Saw you hadn't got a drink. Hope champers is OK?'

'It'll have to do, I s'pose' I say, all nonchalant, but ohmagaaaaard, I'm thinking how much did THAT cost?!

'You didn't have to wait for me though' he says, expertly pouring a glass whilst perched on the edge of his chair.

'Wait for *you*? Are you kidding me? I'd need to work for you for a week to afford one glass of vin de plonk in here!'

He kind of smiles and goes 'I don't think they sell plonk here ...... but you could've put it on your room, you know?'

Oh bum, why didn't *I* think of that. Twenty minutes dry. Twenty minutes wasted. 'I didn't like to presume, Mr Blythe.'

Passing me a glass.... 'Henry, please.' And I raise the glass to my lips, trying to disguise a grin as I finally discover Mr Blythe's first name. Henry. Ewww.....

'And here's to you, errrrr.......ummm, and a successful trip' and I'm forced to clink 'cheers' with him still smirking til he looks at me over the rim of his glass and says 'you can call me 'H' if you prefer.......'

'OK, errr H.........are we going to eat and will I need a bank loan?'

'Probably, it's your shout.'

'Whaaaat.........?!' and I'm devastated... 'you *are* kidding me?....' (til he grins) '..... you bastard!' as the relief floods over me.

And you know what? It's OK. It really is. The more we eat and drink and chat and laugh the lower and lower his shoulders get and the stress just seems to seep out of him. He kinda turns from this uptight wreck into, well, OK, a kinda *drunken* wreck.

Coz of course the wine starts to flow and he seems to be getting louder and louder and getting funny looks from the people at nearby tables....until we're halfway through some glorious fish dish and I say '...and you know what the really, *really* funny thing is...' and he's giggling and shaking his head '....you've absolutely *no idea* what my name is, have you?'

'Yezzihave.....' all defiant, but I just sit there with my eyebrows raised, challenging. And the poor bugger is struggling but then a light seems to come on and his face brightens and he goes...

'Yerr name izz .... IZZZABELLLLA!' and he throws his hands in the air in mock awe.

And if the waiter had come up to me and set fire to my knickers, I swear I wouldn't have moved a muscle. I'm mortified. All the thoughts that were rushing through my alcohol soused mind, where? when? HOW!? Oh fuck, oh fuck, I am in *serious* trouble here and Old Blythey is milking it for everything he can get, just sitting there, stone faced, waiting for a reaction..... the wee shite.

'Bu...bu.... bu.... bu .....I....I...' and that is the sum total of all that I can get out, until he leans forward and hoarse whispers ..... 'Izzzabella Marcoque' and winks slowly at me.

There is a clatter as my cutlery hits my plate and a sudden hush descends on the room. I wait, frozen, for the hubbub to return, gather my thoughts before venturing 'What makes you say that?' all innocent.

'Hmmmmm.' Milking it again, 'maybe you should look over your shoulder the next time you want to play games on reception.'

'You mean you......?'

And he nods.

'And you....?'

He keeps nodding

'...everything I.....'

Still nodding.

'Oh BUM!'

And he starts laughing out loud and slaps the table. The waiter looks nervous.

Bowing my head, examining the pattern on the tablecloth ... 'I am so, *so* sorry, I.........'

'Don't be' he interrupts, holding both hands up, palms towards me, 'Bezz laugh I've had in weeks!' Oh the relief! 'And furzermore....' (furzermore?!), '....you're abslootely right. I have absloootely no idea (and he takes a deep breath) who you are.' And he just keeps giggling and shaking his head 'None whazzoever!' He leans forward, 'Who the fuck *are* you?' and he slaps one hand over his mouth in mock horror at his profanity.....this last line let out just a teeny bit too loud, raising disapproving looks from all others present. I have to calm things down a wee bit.

'Sophie MacDonald, pleased to meet you', offering a hand.

'Sophie MacDonald, eh? Of course I could tell by your accent that you were a 'wee bit Scots' (lousy accent, H. I'll have to give you lessons), but there's more than a hint of something else in there, isn't there?'

Well, my *father* was Scottish, my mother is French.'

'Ahhhh, so does that make you a gaelic gallic? Or maybe a garlic?' and he chuckles to himself, '....and no prizes for guessing who did the cooking, eh?' And he thinks that's hilarious, like I haven't heard it before, but I give him the benefit of the doubt and laugh politely anyway.

'Culleen skink, blerrrrrgg, haggis, yuggggh!' OK, OK, he's getting just a *little* bit out of hand here and I know I'm pissed but I'm not *that* pissed. We're on our third bottle but this is just warming up for me. He's already heading for the exit.

So I hurry past pudding coz even though I'd just love to try something off this menu for kings I reckon my colleague (colleague? Boss!) needs to ease off a bit. He has other ideas. Like me he skips pudd, but only so that he can get stuck into the liqueurs. Large ones of course. But he's calmer now as we 'retire to the drawing room' and there's lovely big sofas and armchairs and a roaring fire (do fires roar?)

and it's a bit more private, because all the other guests are either still eating or have headed off to their enormous beds for an orgy.......or maybe even to sleep.

If only Emms could see me now, 'lap of lux' she'd call it. Though, of course, she'd be more used to this than me. Just think, I could be in my cold and cramped bedsit right now, instead I'm....I'm...I'm HERE!

Waiter - 'Brandy, madam?'

'Actually the name's Sophie....' He ignores me. No sense of humour.

Henry - 'Or Izzzabell.......'

'Don't! Just don't.' I say staring goggle-eyed at the Boss. 'Pleeease.'

'OK, cheeeers.' Raising his glass. I take a sip and it burns its way down. Fair takes my breath away but I try not to show it. 'Not really a brandy drinker, eh?'

'Tequila's more my line. Shots. Short and salty...like an orgas....' but I stop myself before I finish the line, bury my nose in the globe-like glass and mumble 'S nice.'

'Some things you need to take your time over,' he says swirling the amber liquid around and around before taking a long draft, savouring the fire and swallowing in one go.

And before I know it, there's another on the little table in front of me and he's swirling his second.

Now I know what you're thinking. He's trying to get me pissed in order to try it on, so to speak. But I just don't get a hint of that and I've had plenty of experience of that sort of thing, believe me! More to the point, if he's trying to drink me under the table, he's losing *big* time coz he's pretty much comatose by now, eyelids drooping, slid so far down in his armchair his bum's nearly on the floor. I reckon one more of those Napoleon wotsits and it's lights out, thank you and goodnight.

So I take my leave and head off to my giant's sleigh-ride in the sky.

XIV

'Mmmm nn nmm mn nnnnnmm nmmnm'

Why mouth not working?

'Mmmm nnnmnmmmn mmmmnnn nnnnmmmm....'

Why head hurt?

'aaaa....oooooo...oh'

Why sick taste, mouth?

'Eeeeeewwwww.....'

And used cat litter?

'Accchhhh......cchhhhh'

Thirsty?

'Nnnnggggg....'

Hungry? No, just thirsty. Water!

'Warrr...aaaaarrrrr'

Owwwww! Shhh, headache!

Wha...what...what time? Time? Open eyes. Clock? Noooo...watch. Have watch. Hmmm...can't seem to move arm...lying on it...oooh....can't seem to focus eyes...... erm....five past...hmmmm...thaz OK then. Five past. Hmmmm....five past. Five past what?...hmmmm fiiiive....paaaast.......eight. Thaz OK then, five past eight. Zzzzzzzz.......five past eight...hmmmmm......eight .... five past.....OH FUCK!

FIVE PAST FUCKING EIGHT!

And suddenly I'm upright. Five past eight. Oh fuck! Giddy. Seriously giddy. Gonna be sick.....no mustn't be sick. Gotta get up, crawl to edge of bed....gotta get dressed. Fuck, *already* dressed! Trousers, shirt, tie, jacket, how the f......? Oh god, slept in them all! Look down. Oh gooord, everything's a mess. Look like a sack of potatoes. Gotta get to bathroom. Need water. Water. Leave light off. Headache. Water, hmmmmm water. Oooo smells sick. I didn't, did I? Must've done. Ewwwww......

Back into the bedroom, errr...breakfast......no, no time......gotta get smartened up though. Everything crumpled. Err....trouser press, yes trouser press. Quick. Must get trousers off. Shoes first. Who thought of shoelaces? Twat! Just get trousers off *over* shoes. Much easier.

Oh bugger, such a bloody headache!

Trousers cooking nicely. Fresh shirt. Can do that. Underwear? Yes. Tie? yes. Socks? Yes. Can do, can do......

Shower.....yes must wake up. Cold shower....nooo.....cool shower...noooo.... warmish shower....OK, that'll do.

And coffee....pleeeease coffee! Strong and hot and two.......

And suddenly the banging in my head is getting louder as if my brain is trying to escape my skull.

Stop. Please stop.

'Mr Blythe.....Mr Blythe?' bang, bang, bang.........

Whaaa.....what?

'Are you up Mr Blythe? Time we were going, Mr Blythe?'

And before I know it Ms Thingummyjig is in the room looking me up and down like a school ma'am with a particularly grubby schoolboy.

'Aren't you supposed to put your shoes on *after* your trousers?'

'Probably......only I haven't actually taken them off yet. Nor anything else for that matter'

'Except your trousers...? I see. Well aren't *I* the lucky one?' and she smiles rather cheekily, but I'm in no mood to oblige her humour, then spot the coffee cup she is balancing on the palm of one hand and the two white tablets on the other.

'You lifesaver!' and I guzzle gratefully.

'Now we really do have to get you sorted, don't we? Why don't you go and take a shower and I'll sort your clothes for you.'

And I stand there like a twit wondering why this young woman is treating me like a kid, but then realise that, let's face, I *am* a kid right now and who the hell am I to complain? So I shuffle off to the shower leaving Ms Madam to sort the rest of me out.

When I reappear, I'm horrified to see her holding up my freshly cooked trousers. My freshly cooked trousers with a big, brown, squidgy, sticky mess stuck to the bottom area.

Oh bugger. I've shat myself!

Not only have I shat myself, I've let my receptionist in on the event.

Oh bugger.

'I think you have a problem, Mr Blythe.'

Is incontinence a problem? Yes, I suppose it is. Especially in one so young. She registers the look of horror on my face.

'Oh no, don't worry. It's not poo. Not unless your poo has a peppermint flavour?' Does it? I haven't checked recently. She pauses as if awaiting a response, then registers my little boy lost look.... 'it's a chocolate *mint*...must've been on your pillow last night. Only instead of *eating* it....' and she waves the offending article at me.

Oh, the relief!

Then 'but what am I going to do? I only have the one pair.....' and she offers to clean it up as best possible and suggests I make sure I keep my jacket on and keep my back away from all and sundry and I say yes, great idea, that I can do.

So we set about rescuing the good ship Blythe and we are in reception in half an hour, even though I know I'm running on empty and would rather just curl up somewhere quiet and die.

XV

Well here's a turn up for the books. I come along just for the ride, so to speak, and end up acting as nursemaid. Dear me, he did look a state first thing this morning. Jacket, shirt, tie, shoes ...... and no trousers. If only I'd had a camera.

Nice legs though.

Well apparently he'd stayed up til nearly three and reckons he must've had five large nightcaps. He says he was in such a good mood, had had such a great evening that he just didn't want it to end.....even after I'd left. Unable to remember much after that, like getting back to his room, like sticking a chocolate in his back pocket for later, like sicking up in the sink, until the morning brought it all back to him in grim reality......Poor sod, he just sits there behind his dark glasses, glum, silent, rancid alcohol seeping from every pore.

Not the best of company, then.

Much to our mutual surprise we actually arrive on time as Willamson's office and are shown into a large room with all mod cons ready to go. Mr Blythe, (I still can't bring myself to call him H, let alone Henry!) sets about his preparations which seem to take twice as long as need be, hindered by the fact that he is evidently suffering the DTs and, less evidently, still drunk.

Some kind of secretary pops her head round the door and asks us if we'd like coffee. Mr Blythe almost melts with gratitude. Then in marches a procession of rather humourless looking individuals, most of whom seem to know the boss and I'm introduced to them one by one, then Mr Blythe says '....and this is Miss... ermmmm'

First he notices how much his outstretched hand is shaking and quickly hides it behind his back. Then we *both* realise that he has forgotten my name...again!

'Sophie MacDonald' I say and raise a hand and wave round the room. I'm met with a mixture of slight nods and blank stares. These people know how to make a person feel welcome.

Then their big boss arrives and I'm surprised to discover that there actually is a *Mr* Williamson. He sits at the head of the table, furthest from Mr Blythe.

To say that Mr Blythe's performance is lacklustre would be an understatement. If he's actually read what's in the files he seems to have forgotten most of it and is forever rifling through his papers in search of something he never seems to find. But he stumbles on regardless with the aid of all the audio visuals that his team has thrown together, until he virtually collapses into his chair, completely spent.

There is silence.

Then someone shifts in their seat.

Then there is more silence.

A cough, then someone fiddles with their pen.

At last Mr Williamson...... 'well thank you, Henry, a most ...*interesting* talk. I'm just not sure that it's what we're looking for. I'm thinking it's a little....bland, a little ordinary' He lets this sink in. Mr Blythe is barely holding it together. I swear I could see a tear begin to form in his eye. Poor bugger. I can't stand to see him suffer like this.

The silence returns.

'With due respect......' all eyes turn to me. Most don't look particularly supportive, '.....Mr Williamson, you may have missed the point here.' His eyebrows raise in query. A slight nod tells me to continue. 'The point is........' and I'm thinking back to ploughing through the files yesterday, wondering where the hell I'm going with this and then '...the point is (I repeat) ...... we're taking the piss!'

Ooooo, sharp intakes of breath all round.

Williamson - 'I beg your pardon, Miss ermmmm......'

'Marcoque!' blurts out Mr Blythe. 'It's Marcoque!'

Just when you think things couldn't get any worse...........

Now it's raised eyebrows and open mouths all round. All eyes are on Henry.

'MacDonald! Miss ...ermm ...MacDonald....I meant to say...' he trails off and slumps even further into his seat.

Back to me, 'Perhaps you'd like to elucidate, Ms MacDonald?'

I certainly would, you pompous twat, I think, but instead say 'What you've seen here today is not what you think you've seen' and I can't help but picture Mr

Blythe with no trousers on. 'What you *think* you've seen is something really rather ...... bland,' acknowledging Mr Williamson's remark. Reluctant nods all round. '... somewhat predictable , a little mundane maybe, lacklustre even' I find myself waving in Mr Blythe's direction here, for whom bland, mundane, lacklustre would actually seem like a promotion .... 'but what you've actually seen is us, as I said, taking the piss.' And I swear I hear a slight whimper from Henry's direction.

'So what we have seen so far is what, exactly?' asks Williamson, feigning intrigue.

'What you expected to see, what everyone expected to see. The same old stuff in the same old way.' And I find myself waving in H's direction again. Oooops. 'But what if we turn it on its head and present it in such a fashion that people realise that, actually, ...'

'You are taking the......hmmmmm, I think I prefer the word *satire*.'

'...or parody' I say, trying to demonstrate that I'm not a complete halfwit.

XVI

'Call it what you will, Cedric,' and I'm on my feet now, '.....but, correct me if I'm wrong, my opening gambit bored the pants off of you?' (I, briefly, see myself with no trousers on again) but people aren't exactly tripping over each other in the rush to contradict me '...and you'd be right.'

Williamson's eyebrow twitches. The rest of him is motionless.

But I'm getting into the swing of things now, '.....because that's *exactly* what we wanted you to feel. We wanted to you feel exactly what Joe Public feels when the same old product is rolled out in the same old way by the same old people.' A pause for effect. In for the kill H. 'But what we give them is what I call our Scorpion Strategy... (pause again for effect) something with a sting in the tail (oh, *that* Scorpion Strategy) ...just as they start to think that they've seen this all before, we hit them with a punchline. Pow!' (Pow?) and I slap the table, hard, for good effect. Two people wake up. 'Hey guys, only joking! See?' No-one moves. Not a word.

'What is it we've never had here?' Blank faces. 'Humour. It's time to show them that we don't have to be taken *that* seriously. That we have a softer side.' and I turn towards the board and scrawl, in big letters, 'HUMOUR'.

XVII

All eyes are on Henry and what he is writing. My eyes are on the large brown patch on the seat of Mr Blythe's trouser, but he swings back round before anyone else clocks *his* softer side.

'The human side of Williamson's.' And he turns again and scrawls 'HUMAN'. And one person spots what I've been looking at and her eyes widen before glancing round the room to see if anyone else has seen it .... or were her eyes deceiving her? But Mr Blythe is on a roll now and he's firing on all cylinders coz he's facing the audience. 'What we don't want to see is our audience, our *customers*, thinking 'Bah humbug'' and he turns again and adds 'HUMBUG' to the lengthening list, underlining it for effect.

Humour, human, humbug..... What next, I wonder, Hummus? Hump? 'Humilate' might be appropriate under the circumstances, as H's brown patch is now clearly in view again and more people follow my lead and drift off subject and end up in the region of their presenter's bottom. 'But now is *not* the time to be po-faced,' he continues. Ouch! There are a few titters.

H swings back round and catches his entire audience 'off subject'. Some are gaping like goldfish, others have the smirks. Both of Williamson's eyebrows are twitching violently.

'Gotchya!!' looking at each in turn. He grins at their embarrassment, revelling in it. 'And that's *exactly* what I mean' H ploughs on. 'Just as you think that I'm being serious, you find something to laugh at. I've got your attention *now*, haven't I?'

Cooo, you couldn'ta cut the atmosphere with a scalpel. At long last one brave soul says 'he's gotta point'. A few nods. Eventually, the big man relents.

'Yes, OK. Let's go with it. A bit risky, but it's about time we took a risk.' To H. 'Like your style, Blythe. Had me worried there for a moment. Great presentation. Made your point. Better than most. Glad to see you still have it, blah blah blah.....' and there's was a shaking of hands, a few slapping of backs and smiles all round.

Mr Blythe fairly flew down the steps as we left. By the time we were somewhere private all he could do was rub his hands together and repeat 'yes, yes, yes, yes....' until eventually even I was beginning to tire of it. But I can't help but admire his glee. He's a different man. Flying by the seat of his pants?

Then just as suddenly he stops, turns to me, locks eyes intensely and says, 'Thank you, Sophie MacDonald, thank you *so* much.' And then just keeps shaking his head and staring at me, lost for words for the first time in half an hour.

Well at least he got my name right.

Marcoque, indeed.

*

I can't help admitting I feel great as we leave. I mean I know I was winging it and it hadn't *quite* worked out the way I had intended...alright, I hadn't actually intended it to work out *any* way at all, but it seems to have. Funny that.

By the time we get back to the hotel, we are chatting ten to the dozen and head straight for the bar and a 'celebratory', as H calls it, and I'm still aghast as to the change in the man. You'd never have guessed the skinful he'd had last night. First thing, he had clearly been in need of a very minor top up to be running on full again, but somehow, somewhere, he's sprung a leak on the ride back to the hotel and is now in need of a total refill ... of the finest champagne, of course.

He keeps saying 'We did it Sophie, we did it!' and I like him giving me a nickname (he pronounces it So-ff). And I like the 'we' too.

I like that very much.

XVIII

I like this girl, I like her very much.

Shit, she coulda just saved my company!

And, OK, she didn't clinch it, but she had the nerve and the savvy to open her mouth and give me some direction, some kind of cue as to which way to play it. And it just went so well.

Synchronicity.

Beautiful.

'So Sophe, your call tonight. My treat. Whatever you want.' And she's smiling at me like a kid given free rein in a sweetshop.

'Whatever?'

' Your call. Whatever.'

And you can see the possibilities running through her mind, til 'Right, first a meal, nothing too heavy coz...........' she smiles, '....weee ....are going clubbing!'

My face falls. Well, falls even further than it usually is.

'Go on. It'll be great!' but she can sense my reticence. Clubbing? I haven't been clubbing in *decades*. Do I really wanna be an old fart amongst young bucks. I'll feel a complete twit.

'You said 'whatever'!' she reminds me. I have to admit defeat. OK, clubbing it is then.

Bugger!

*

Six hours later, I'm feeling one hundred percent. A quiet siesta, a leisurely bath, change out of my chocolate flavoured suit into something more casual (although admittedly not casual enough for a nightclub full of kids) and I'm back down the bar toasting myself for a very successful day.

When Sophie turns up she's looking fresh and bubbly and we adjourn to the restaurant. Conversation and wine flow but I'm limiting my intake tonight. Just enough to lubricate the palate and absolutely no nightcaps. Gonna need all my faculties tonight, coz *I* am going clubbing!

Good grief.

*

But I find that nothing much has changed. The same lights, the same thumping, incessant bass that seems ubiquitous no matter what is being played, the same writhing mass of humanity on the dance floor. It could be any generation over the last several decades. Sure there are minor differences, but the only thing that is really different is me. So I stand there feeling like a fish out of the proverbial and even the calculated intake of alcohol (calculated so that I *don't* feel like a fish out of water) doesn't seem to lessen my load.

Sophie senses my unease. 'Come on H, it'll be fun.' Hmmmm...it just isn't fun *yet*. I mean, it was bad enough outside in the queue. I felt like I was Sophie's father accompanying her to the local 'disco', just to make sure she wasn't molested by some young ruffian and, shit, did I get funny looks from the bouncers!? But inside it's not so bad coz the lights are low way down the back by the bar and people can't see exactly *how* old I am and exactly *how* naff my clothes look, just as long as I keep to the shadows.

So I line up the shots (two each) and they've even given me a little bowl of salt and a lime wedge and it's kinda fun to be knocking them back like this and I see Sophie's head is nodding back and forth and her eyes are scanning the dance floor and I know she won't be around for long, but that's OK coz it's her night and she bloody well deserves it!

Well the first shot burned like hell – this is not sophisticated liquor here - so I throw the second down hoping that it'll hit my stomach before it recovers from the first one. It just about makes it ..... and the lime wedge helps.

So I'm standing there feeling the fire, when I'm grabbed by the hand and dragged bodily towards the mêlée and find myself squashed in amongst all and sundry. Dance? You serious? There's no *room* for fuck's sake! Besides, I really, *really* do not want to be the one person on the dance floor that dances like everyone else's dad, i.e. like a complete tit.

Which is what I already feel.

XIX

Oh god, what have I done? Dragged the poor bugger up to dance....He's gonna dance like someone's dad. I can see it already. A spasticated spider.

And sure as eggs is eggs, he starts to twitch.

Oh well. Here goes.

So I'm picking up the music's rhythm and I'm getting into the swing of things and turning away coz I really can't bear to look and there's this guy behind me who's actually quite cute so I shuffle over and we smile at each other and we're kinda moving in synch and I guess I lose track of time coz it seems like an age before I turn round to find H, but when I do he's not there and everyone's looking kinda strange coz, well, they're *not* looking. They're looking the other way. So, being a nosey sod, I squeeze through and there's this space in the dancing which is really odd coz it's like packed in here and then my chin hits the floor.

There's H doing his thing on the dance floor and a crowd has gathered to watch and they're not laughing at him, they're going with the flow, so to speak, and clapping and whooping and I look at H but he doesn't see me coz he's really getting into things and my god...but he's *good*!

He's bloody good!

You coulda blown me over with a sneeze!

I can't help but join in with the crowd...and then join in with the dancing and me and H are giving it some stick and he's swinging me round like I'm as light as and I'm gobsmacked that he's got that kinda strength but boy can this man go...and keep going by the looks of it.

But then, just as suddenly, he's stopped, thumbs towards the bar and we're back on the shots and gabbing and laughing and this is all just so funny and I just have to tell him that I thought that he was brilliant this morning the way he picked up my lead and just went with it.... 'just brilliant, H, brilliant!'

'No shit?' he asks... and there's a pause and we both burst out laughing. Sure it's a crap joke, so to speak, but neither of us cares coz we both know it's a crap joke and that's what makes it so funny!

And then he says 'couldn't have done it without you, Sophe! Great team, eh?' and we chink glasses and throw them back and we go on at each other, massaging each other's egos, but it's cool coz we're both having a great time, shot then a dance then a shot and this is way better than most nights with Emms coz at least I'm with a guy that I like being with, who's funny and smart and not like one of the drongos that normally hang around me and Emms.

Before you know it, we're heading back to the hotel both hideously pissed hanging on to each other for dear life but we're very sensible tonight coz we don't head for nightcaps 'time for bed says Henry!' and we wend our way upstairs and H escorts me to my room and gives me a big hug on my doorstep, says thanks, once again, and then there's one of those 'moments' (as Emms says) where we hold the look for just a moment too long, lips just so close to each other's that says - hmmm...this could get interesting....if only we moved a little closer and... But H breaks away and so I give him a big, quick smacker on the lips anyway and tell him thanks for a great night and head for my bed where my dreams feature large, spastic spiders ...... for some reason.

XX

Oooooh, when will I ever learn? How many tequilas exactly? Lost count after about five. And then there was the wine .... and that champagne!

I'm talking to myself in the mirror. At least I think I am. I seem to be having a conversation anyway. Not sure if I'm actually speaking though. Probably not. Headache tells me that wouldn't be a great idea.

What was I thinking of? Dancing and drinking like a twenty five year old! Good grief, at the end of the evening I could even have ......with ......no, do *not* even go there!

So you deserve to look like a rats scrotum this morning. Back to reality mate. Red eyes, sagging, creased skin with a slightly grey tinge to it, breath like a dog's fart. Well, it couldn't last could it? This morning is payback time. One night of hellraising and another month off your life.

Bloody good night though. The best in....*how* many years?

Worth it, then!

*

'Of course, with Hollie off for god knows how long, I'm going to need a new secretary.'

'I don't know anyone who could.....' I give an almost imperceptible twitch to the corner of my mouth... '...you don't mean....me?' I purse my lips and raise my eyebrows. I'm playing with her and it's fun. I find that I like to tease. 'Oh, wow, does that mean, like, tens of thousands extra a year?'

'Well maybe one....' her mouth forms a perfect O, '.....possibly two...tens of, that is.' Now her mouth is agape. 'How's your typing speed?' I continue.

'Probably about as good as yours.'

'That bad, huh?'

'Lousy, actually'.

'Maybe 'PA' might be more appropriate, then?'

'Me? Your PA? You *are* kidding me?'

'And why would I do that? I owe you alot.' Actually, I owe you *everything*! 'Are you game?'

So there you have it. I have a new PA and, you're right, I have absolutely no idea what I've let myself in for because I know absolutely nothing about the woman..... except that she can drink like a fish and ermmmmm ......oh, and that she can drink like a fish.

Gets my vote!

XXI

Needless to say it's put a few noses out of joint. There was a definite atmosphere in the office when the news got out and I moved into my new station outside Mr Blythe's office. I could guess what they were saying coz I'd heard it said of others. She's only got where she is coz she's shagged her way there. Simple, eh? Not coz of my ability, brains, savvy, nous, no...no...no...it's coz I opened my legs for Sir.

Well fuck that! (Steady on, Sophie.)

So I got H to put everyone right at the earliest opportunity.

'Sophie is here today because of her efforts with the Williamson account. Thanks largely to her, we still have that account. Believe me when I say, we almost lost it.' Eyes are on Jeff, sniffling into his hanky. 'Whilst I won't go into detail (*I bet you won't!*), it's safe to say that, through some very quick thinking, Sophie has put the good ship Blythe Enterprises back on a steady course and as far as I'm concerned, every good turn deserves. She will be standing in for Hollie, until she is better, and will then take on an advisory role, nominally as my PA.'

Great talk H, I'm just not sure it helped any. Whichever way I look at it, every line can be twisted. As far as everyone else is concerned, I shagged myself into this position.

So to speak.

*

Well the weeks and weeks go by and it's fun and really I'm not complaining coz it's waaay better than sitting on that bloody reception desk all day and I'm certainly not complaining about the pay increase. So OK, it was only ten grand more, but it coulda taken me years to get that kinda pay rise. Do you know how many new pairs of knickers I can buy with the extra money? No, me neither. Though it hasn't helped with actually doing any laundry. Probably a disincentive if anything. Easier to buy new than to wash old. The piles of festering stuff just keep growing.

And there's a definite buzz around the office now and not all of it is people talking about me behind my back. H has geed everyone up, seems to have found some new verve now that his account hasn't gone down the toilet. It's really put some life back into the old bugger, he looks fitter, smarter, livelier. It's good to see him with a smile on his face....pretty much most of the time.

XXII

Leaner, fitter, hungrier, happier. Who thinks up these mantras? Do they really have nothing else better to do? Funny how I took this as gospel all those years ago.

But for some reason I'm harking back to the good old, bad old days and at last have something to work for again. Who'd'a believed it?! Gym, tailor, hairdresser, no alcohol (well, *less* alcohol anyway. Can't be perfect.) Of course it's set Old Nick awhinging . Never go out. Used to booze all night. Not the same anymore, is it?... which I guess is the bottom line. It's him that's missing the company. He doesn't have anyone else. I do. I have *my* company.

Even Sarah has noticed that I'm more chipper than usual. She jokingly accused me of having another woman. At least I *think* she was joking...you never can tell with a lawyer. But, in a way, I do. Have another woman, that is. Because it's down to one woman that things are the way they are. In fact, it's down to one woman that there is now such a vibe in the office. She's just what the doctor ordered. Young blood.

And with that increasing vibe comes additional contracts. First off we hit our existing customers. New broom boys and girls. Complete rethink. Treat this as a new company. Forget what went before. That's the past. Another country. New campaigns all round. Are you in? .... because if you're not well, you're going to miss out big time. And I'm doing what I used to do. Instilling enthusiasm. Passion. And there are those that are happy to sit on their laurels. Keep things as they've always been, but that's not me anymore. Sure we'll keep them on as clients. Hell why not? It's easy money after all, but do you really want to live in the past? Times are changing ladies and gents. Are you all aboard the good ship Blythe? Great. Well full steam ahead.

And it's amazing how one good thing leads on to another. New contracts come in from those that want to see progress, to modernise. To give their companies a damn good kick up the proverbial. Like I've just done to mine. And, as they say, success breeds success and I have no doubt that this will lead to greater things, once word gets out that Blythe Enterprises is on the up.

And I just needed that one thing to turn it all around. Well that one person.

Which has got the rest of the staff all afluster. Some have caught the buzz. Some don't or can't quite get it. Jeff just sits in his room perpetually filling his hanky. He'll have to go. Gotta be ruthless to survive. No place for sentimentality.

Another work trip next week. Two nights away. Will have to take Jeff and Carla along for the ride.

And Sophie, of course.

XXIII

A night out on the piss with Emms.

Woo hoo!

I haven't done this for weeks and I'm really into it. It's been work, work, work... oh and shop, shop, shop, what with all the extra money I'm now getting. So I'm spoilt for choice when it comes to the glad rags. So much to chose from, so few nights out!

So when I get to my meet with my mate, I look bloody *gorgeous*, even though I say so myself! Emms, as usual, is already halfway to alcohol heaven by the time I get there, which annoys me a little bit coz I've insisted that I pay for everything tonight. As far as I'm concerned, it's payback time. Years (literally) of sponging off Emms (and her trust fund) have to end.....at least for tonight, so this is *supposed* to be my treat. Well it is from now on.

'So, shots all round then?' but Emms shakes her head and points to some clear, fizzy stuff in a whisky glass. I give my quizzical look.

'G and T. Better make it a large one.' Ah. Something's wrong here. Not just the change in drink (gin – bad sign) but she's not her usual bubbly self. Exuberant, H would call it. And I'm standing at the bar, chewing my lip, wondering what it can be....bloke? job? health? No, bloke. Has to be.

Sure enough, she's got the bloke blues. It transpires that the one with the dildo stuck up his bum managed to get it out in the end, so to speak, only to come back for more! He'd had the time of his life apparently, and Emms was more than happy to oblige with an encore. This had been going on for weeks then suddenly all contact stopped. Nothing. Try as she might, her efforts were met with a blank wall. So here she is. 'Bereft' she says, whatever *that* means and I'm expecting her to swoon any minute. So I try to gee her up and say best thing is a night on the piss with her bestest mate and see what we can find, but I'm kinda guessing that the bloke blues might just be too much for Emms to bear and I'll be dragging round one miserable mate all night. Well we'll see.

*

So the music is thumping and me and Emms are jumping around and I'm having the best time since me and H were out way back whenever it was and even Emms seems brighter now she's had her usual skinful and I've kept the subject off blokes all evening, boring her to death with my new job and how amazing things have turned out.

But, as we are heading for the bar who should we both spot standing there, but Mr Dildo himself. Some blond tart, all tits and teeth, hanging on his arm. There's gonna be trouble.

Big trouble.

Coz Emms is over there in a flash and ohmygaaaard, you should hear the language. I mean, I know I swear a *bit* but she's effing this and effing that, she's like a woman possessed, pointing, pushing, shoving, shouting. You can even hear that diamond accent over the noise of the music. I don't know where to look, really I don't. And then the big guns come out.

'Has he told you he likes a dildo up his arse?' Heads turn. This to the blond tartlet. 'No?' Then to Mr D – ' Already progressed to a strap-on, have you?' Then back to the tartlet (for the audience it's like watching a tennis match) 'I have a whole *tub* of lube you can borrow. Don't worry, it's only *just* been dipped into. (At Mr D) Nearly new, one careful owner.' And with this she storms off towards the exit.

Luckily there are no large drinks in the vicinity coz I could have seen Mr D taking an early shower.

Then Emms storms back in, empties the pint she is carrying over *both* the new arrivals and exits stage left.

Spoke too soon.

*

I spend the next half an hour trying to calm her down to a level that enables her to get into a taxi and head home. Honestly, what an evening.

Men are complete shits, aren't they!?

XXIV

Sarah's been a complete shit this morning. Used to our customary mutual grunts at the opening of the day's business, today I was surprised with 'why are you going away, where are you going, who are you going with?' I just sit there in silence, staring blankly at her. 'What's brought all this on?' I ask in all innocence....

'We never spend any time together.' Yes, I'm thinking, so what's new? I say nothing, waiting for more of the same. 'Why can't we go away, have a holiday?'

I don't know, why can't we go away, have a holiday? But still I say nothing. I'm waiting for her to blow herself out......or get to the crux of the matter.

She collapses onto a stool, exasperated. 'I work too much', she admits. '*We* work too much', she accuses.

And....?

'There has to be more, hasn't there?' She looks me in the eye for the first time in what must be months, maybe years. She's looking tired, old even.

'Yes...' I venture, not wanting to rock the boat. Tentatively, 'so where would you like to go?' Not tentative enough.

'I don't know! Why does it always have to be *me* that decides?! It was my idea! *You* think of something for once!!' And with that she storms off, slamming the door for good measure. Case adjourned.

The remnants of my coffee end up in the sink.

*

So we are all lined up like a bunch of excited kids heading off on a school trip and I take the lead with the others chatting behind me. We have a good trip. The vibe that has infected the office is carried with us and even Jeff seems to have lost his handkerchief. It was probably due a wash, anyway. Carla and Sophie are getting on well, although I have no doubt that, knowing Carla, she is trying to get the measure of her younger colleague. Threat or no threat? We shall see.

The evening is all very civilised, a few drinks, leisurely meal, single nightcap and then bed. Another big day tomorrow....

.....which, as it happens, goes like a dream. We really are in the zone, aren't we? There are big grins all round as we leave and a small celebration is called for, so I suggest a night out at the best restaurant in town and make sure that it's appreciated that there will be no early night tonight. 'So are we going clubbing?' enthuses Sophie...I laugh and try not to sound too patronising when I decline her suggestion...at my age? I imply..... Really?

She picks up on my intonation and lets the subject drop. Smart girl.

So I spend the evening mulling over various points with Jeff, while the two ladies are locked in conversation that escapes me because I'm concentrating on what Jeff has to say, all the while looking for that chink of weakness, a flaw that might give me an excuse to get rid of him or, at least, find him better employed. There is no doubt in my mind that his best days are passed. If there's one thing that Sophie has reminded me of, it is that young blood can breathe new life into a business and that, *with the right guidance*, that new life can flourish and all can benefit.

I hardly speak to Sophie all evening, until she corners me on a trip to the toilets. 'You ignoring me?' she challenges. I shake my head. 'So why the cold shoulder?'

'Trying to do you a favour.'

'How does that work, then?' Head tilted to one side, she's not angry, just curious.

'To scotch the rumours that are doing the rounds in the office.' Raised eyebrows from the lady in front of me. 'Don't tell me you're not aware.....' She rocks her head from side to side, and pouts noncommittally. '....that people think, people *assume,* that there's something going on between us and that *that's* why you're no longer just a receptionist.'

'And Jeff and Carla are....?'

'....witnesses to the facts. Which is why you have a room next to Carla.....' and then she gets it....

'...and you have a room next to Jeff?' She looks at the floor between us and makes a small round O with her lips. 'You did all of this for me?'

'Yes' but I'm thinking – *and* for me too.

Then I'm looking down into two large, dark brown eyes which seem just a little too watery, with a pupils just a little too dilated, eyes that I could just dive head first into, and she simply says 'that's *really* kind,' and is about to say something else, but the words escape her.

She just whispers 'thank you' and leaves.

XXV

I can't sleep tonight. I'm lying here staring off into the dark at where I think the ceiling must be (thanks to three *large* brandies the room keeps turning topsy turvy) and my mind is racing.

That someone could do that, could plan that, so calculating, so clever, so simply brilliant.

And all for me.

OK, I'm not kidding myself too much. I know that he probably did it as much for himself as for me but, let's face it, I'm the one with everything to lose here. I'm the one that people think only got where she is by opening her legs to the relevant person. I'm the one with the tainted reputation, not H. People would only think the better of him for bedding the young tart in reception. Especially the men. Bloody typical.

Nope. I'm the one who has the most to gain from H's little ruse. All of this. All of these people. Here. Just for me.

'Thank you' seems inadequate, under the circumstances. But it wasn't what I'd said, it was what I'd wanted to do. What I'd *wanted* to do was throw my arms around his neck and give him a big hug.

Too risky. If someone had seen, all that preparation and planning would have gone out of the window. So I left.

But now I roll myself into a tight little ball and as I drift off I think, maybe 'thank you' was enough.....after all.

XXVI

I haven't been disconcerted like that in a long time. It's not as if I don't look. Of course I do. Every...well, *most* blokes do, don't they? Look, I mean. It just doesn't occur to me that anything more will happen. I'm married, for fucksake. I'm married to a *lawyer* for fucksake! Nearly twenty years of wedded bliss. Well, of being wedded, anyway. But to be suddenly affected like that was, like I said, disconcerting.

'Thank you,' she said. Then left. But what I wanted her to *do* was plant another of those smackeroonies on my lips, like she did once before. Only this time to really *mean* it.

Maybe I do need a holiday? Rekindle my life with Sarah?

I'll get some brochures tomorrow.

XXVII

Holiday brochures!

You have got to be kidding me? You want me to go and get you holiday brochures?! You honestly think that I have nothing better to do? You honestly think that's all I'm good for? Your skivvy! Your runaround!

But I say none of this, just 'Yes Mr Blythe' and scoot off.

So I'm standing in the first travel agency that I find scanning the shelves for something suitable for a company director and his lawyer wife and soon I'm winging off to the all these exotic destinations around the globe ....

The Caribbean - Barbados, Martinique, Antigua, Trinidad – hmmmm, all that loverly rum!

The south of France...ooooo, scrummy wine ...and brandy too! Yum, yum!

Mexico – TEQUILA!!!! Yay!

The Greek Islands – ouzo...bleeuurrrgh!!

The Maldives – erm...what do they drink in the Maldives? – ANYTHING YOU WANT, BABY!

YEAH!!!

And, I can't help myself, but I picture me and H knocking back the cocktails and gabbing away ten to the dozen and laughing and swimming and sunbathing and .... and, hey, it would be *such* a laugh.

Then I remember that this is not for me and him, it's for him and his wife and suddenly I find myself envious of someone I've never met before, never even spoken to.

This is not good.

XXVIII

Sophie's not in a good mood when she gets back with the brochures. I knew that something was up when she called me 'Mr Blythe'. She hasn't called me that for months. Only ever does that when she wants to put some distance between us. But why? Just because I asked her to get something for me? I mean, what's the big deal? Holiday brochures.

Maybe she's in need of a holiday herself? Yes, maybe that's it. Maybe I should drop the hint that she's due some time off and leave her a few of my brochures. OK, so not quite the far flung destinations that she seems to have deemed appropriate for me, but there's plenty to see, plenty do closer to home.

So the hint is dropped …. and meets with a mixed reception, but she noticeably brightens when I suggest maybe she has a friend, or boyfriend, who she could ……?

XXIX

A holiday with Emms.

Woo hoo! YES!

Thanks for that H, great idea! Not that I let him see that. I can't have him thinking he's a *complete* smartarse.

But where to?

Well Spain is the obvious one. Hmmm, some nice wines there....not sure about the brandy, though, probably rot the fillings in your teeth, and as for Spanish men? Yeah, well....not *really* my cup of tea. All lithe and wriggly ... like a snake. Plenty of other nationalities there though. On holiday.

France? ...hmmm, yeah, better food *and* better wine. Better looking men? Errrrr, well, maybe.

Greece....yeah, well, a bit basic on all counts...

Hey, what about Italy? Yeah, now we're talking. Great food, great wine and great fuc...... great guys. Italy. Yeah.

So that evening......'Emms what about Italy for a week or two?'

'Oooo, yes please! Italian cock! Yummeee!' Typical Emms.

'They're probably all gay, Emms.'

'Not when I get hold of them, they won't be.' And she wiggles her tits to emphasise the point, 'Hey, I've just thought, I have an uncle who has a villa on Capri. He's absolutely *loaded*.'

'Where's Capri?'

'ITALY!!'

'YAY!'

And we both drink to that!

XXX

Every year we have a reception for all of our clients.....a reception that, as the years have ticked by, has been getting smaller and smaller. Last time out, I had seriously considered cancelling the whole affair. I mean, it doesn't create a great impression when you only have a handful of clients left, does it? All I could think of doing was making the venue smaller to compensate. But that would have just added to the sense of a company in decline.

This year is going to be different. This year we are a company on the rise. Same venue, same faces, only this time out, a whole load more faces too. Which is going to create exactly the impression I want.

I'm thinking of a need for something different. Something that says 'dynamic'. Something that says 'imaginative'....only trouble is, I'm drawing a blank. No dynamism, no imagination. Maybe I *do* need a holiday. Oh well, not long now.

Sophie breezes in with papers to sign and reports to read and I run this quandary past her.

'You mean a mega piss-up? Yeah, count me in H, never miss out on a decent bevvy.'

'No, I didn't think you would, but I don't have to count you in. I'm *counting* on you being there. Only trouble is, I'm not sure what we should do to liven it up a little. Give it some vim. Some pizzazz. Just do something different for once.'

'How 'bout pole dancers and male strippers?'

That girl is taking the piss again. I don't move a muscle. Just glare.

'OK, OK, eeerrrrmmm...how 'bout...fancy dress?!' I *know* it's a bit naff, but we can have a theme, say French revolution, errr Hollywood .... Super Heroes! Yeah, Super Heroes! I can see you as Superman, H, yeah?'

I don't know, she thinks she can butter me up with flattery. As if.

But Superman I like. Yeeees.

Superman it is then.

XXXI

It's awfully quiet without H. Quiet and a little boring. Two weeks he's gone for. Two weeks with his wife. Two weeks not here.

But there's plenty to do, as ever, so at least I'm busy and I just kinda immerse myself in me work. 'Knuckle doon', as my dad used to say.

Carla has been extra friendly. I don't trust her. I mean she *seems* nice, but we all know what 'seems' did, don't we? I think she's watching her back. Making sure I'm not trying to muscle in on her territory. As if.

H has left his number two in charge. John Smith (seriously!). A non-descript, go-getter type who wears shiny grey suits and has an attitude to match. Slippery ....like phlegm, H let slip once. The comment, that is, not the phlegm. But he's competent at what he does, otherwise he wouldn't be doing it. I actually have a little less to do, as John has his own PA, so I fill the gap by minding H's back, in his absence. Making a mental note of what is going on, who is saying what, who is doing what (or who). I can't have others backstabbing my boss now, can I?

Only another twelve days to go. Ho hum.

*

I'm a little disconcerted with Emms' absence too. 'Disconcerted' is one of H's words. I know what he means. Once upon a time, I would have said 'put out', but it doesn't really cover it does it?

Several times this last week I've tried to make contact with her only to be met with no reply. Nothing. It's not like her. I'm sure that she's over Mr Dildo, sure she was over him the moment that beer hit his scalp, so I can't believe it's down to him. But there's bound to be a man at the bottom of it all....err, so to speak.

*

You'll never guess who calls in today?

Hollie! Yes, Hollie-with-an-IE. Remember her? Well I hadn't. I'd completely forgotten about her. I mean, it's been months and months since she had her wee accident when, out of the wide blue yonder, she comes limping in, leaning heavily on a walking stick. Apparently there had been 'complications', whatever that means, which has kept her off work for so long, but she's now looking forward to returning to the fold..... if only I'd get the hell out of her desk and back to bloody reception!

She doesn't say that last bit, of course.

She doesn't have to. I can read it on her face...in her eyes. Mean, calculating, beady little eyes. Like a rat.

So, I say it's *lovely* to see her again and that Mr Blythe will be back in a week's time and that perhaps she can bring the subject up with him thereafter (thereafter?) ...*if* he can spare the time, I add for good measure.

I know. That's a bitchy thing to say, but I really can't help myself.

*

Emms is back! Woo hoo!

It seems she has 'reverted to type' and has been nobbing (or, maybe, 'knobbing'?) with the country set again. She's spent the last week at a series of dos involving polo, weddings and charities : or horses, hitches and Henrietta's, as she put it. She reckons she hasn't been sober once since she got there and just *had* to come home 'for a rest'. All that champers. Poor girl is exhausted.

'There' as she put it, was Uncle Seymour's place, some massive pile way out in the sticks. Somethinghamshire, or thereabouts. She reckoned she had to do a bit of buttering up of the old fellah to see if the villa in Capri was a goer. Well she bided her time (it really was the *only* option, what with all that fizz around), and managed to get him in a nostalgic mood coz. After half a bottle of finest malt, they got chatting about holidays she'd had when she was a wean, then went on to talk about the Med, then he mentioned Capri, then he mentioned the villa and then Emms mentioned she'd had a *great* hols there once like *yonks* ago and then Seymour suggested she goes again, hardly ever used, a waste really and Bob's your wotsit! Anytime we want it, just name the day!

Ohmygaaaard!

We are going to **Italy!**

'When, when, when?' asks Emms. But I have the work's do first. Two weeks away. 'Can I come, can I come, can I come?' she begs.

'Sorry Emms, it's *work*....' and I hate to even think it, but the thought of Emms at my annual work reception, pissed and with her tits on the loose, does not sit easy.

So we settle on the beginning of the week after the reception, so I have a few days to lose my headache and pack and then two weeks of sand, sea, sun and anything else beginning with 's'……that might just happen along the way.

*

I'm in early Monday morning. H is due back today and I want to make sure that I'm there when he arrives, make sure that everything is pristine for him and that I'm in position to brief him on all that he has missed. Bang on eight thirty and he bowls through the door and I'm confronted by someone I barely recognise. Gone is drawn, grey, washed out and slightly haggard looking man that left this office two and a half weeks ago; here is the slim, fit, bronzed, dapper man about town that I'm guessing he probably used to be maybe ten or more years ago. I mean, he seemed to have turned himself around since the business began to pick up, but that was nothing in comparison. The transformation is astonishing and it's not til he says 'good morning Sophe, lovely to see you, as ever' that I recognise his dulcet tones and am convinced that I have the right man.

But there is something else. Something else that has changed. Yes. There is a slight swagger about him, a certain slouching roll of the hips, a casual reclining of the shoulders that indicates a loss of stress, a total relaxation of body, mind and soul ……..and then it hits me.

He's been fucking his wife.

How *dare* he!?

XXXII

It's half past nine and I'm still struggling to shake off the holiday mood. Sophie drifts in and out and so does Carla. Both all smiles and pleased-to-see-mes and how was your holiday and don't I look well and thank you yes I feel great, refreshed and raring to go, but try as I might I can't shift myself back into gear and deal with all the crap that has piled up. In reality, not an awful lot *has* piled up, as Smithy seems to have kept on top of it all. Sophe does her best to bring me up to date, but my mind keeps drifting off to turquoise seas, and white beaches with palm trees swaying in the tropical breeze and stark, white tropic birds soaring and circling in the azure sky .... and poor old Sophe has to keep stopping in order to drag me back to the real world.

So, really, the first day back is a bit of a write-off, as I can't concentrate on much at all and I look forward to the journey home where I can daydream to my heart's content about warm breezes, and clear skies and the luxury villa on stilts over the tranquil lagoon, with its glass floor and underwater lights that come on at dusk so that you can just lie there and watch the tropical fish dart and flit in a myriad of iridescent hues.......

Why is two weeks never enough?

This thought jolts me out of my reverie. I mean, the reality of the situation was that the first week was actually not unlike being at home. Sure we were in a tropical paradise, but really we could have been anywhere. Still the same silences or occasional grunts, the petty bickering, the banning from personal space, the leading of separate lives.....in a wooden hut, on stilts, in the middle of the Indian Ocean fergodsakes! Then, as the stress leeched away and the tropical dream seeped in, communication increased, irritability waned and contact was restored. We actually started to enjoy ourselves, laugh, play and (blow me down with a feather) ... TALK!

By the last night we were playing in the open air Jacuzzi under the stars and a little bit tiddly on a bottle of fizzy plonk, when Sarah actually came on to me, straddled me and started a bit of bump and grind ... or maybe that should be splish and splosh, coz the water went everywhere and pretty soon we were inside the hut and on the glass floor and the lights were on and the fishes were doing their thing and so were Henry and Sarah and she's whispering all sorts of wonderful filth in my ear, just like she always used to and like I haven't heard for *years* and I'm getting hot as hell and she's on her back, bent double, knees up to her chest and I'm inside her and she's yes, yes, yessing and I'm going for what seems ages but it feels good, so that's not a problem, even though I don't think I'm gonna *ever* make it and just then this baby shark appears beneath us, but only I see it over Sarah's shoulder as it circles below her back, as she's pressed hard against the glass and as it spins in a languorous figure of eight, I close my eyes and still see the circles it makes but they change and merge and reappear as two dark, dark eyes looking up at me like two deep, deep pools and I just want to dive head first into them....

...and at that very point, as Sarah sinks her nails into my back, and whispers 'cum baby' I hold perfectly still and feel part of my life drain out of me .... again and again and again.

*

By the time I get home, I'm more than a little surprised to find Sarah already there, in the kitchen, preparing food. She's taken a short day for some reason, visited a *'supermarket'* and has decided to *'cook'*.

There are things on all the worktops. There is *food* in the fridge!

This is not normal behaviour. It's a bit scary.

So I buzz round her, asking what's for supper, sidle up behind her, arm around her waist, whisper 'and for afters?' and then there's this shiver that runs through her and she almost shrugs me off. Can't I see she's busy, you're in the way there, etc etc etc..... It appears that she's having a dinner party at the weekend and has invited over some very important clients. She needs to put in some practice, so if you wouldn't mind staying out of the way until dinner is served then it would be appreciated, thank you very much. I say I'll just check my diary. I *think* I'm free, but my jest is dismissed with a tut.

Didn't take long for things to return to normal, now, did it?

So that's sex done and dusted for another year, then.

Business as usual.

XXXIII

Only two weeks to go to holiday time. *Less* than two weeks to go to party time! Party followed by holiday. Perfect combination.

H has me organising things with the help of two others. But you'll be in charge, he says. Most of this has been done so many times before there's not really an awful lot of new preparation required. Fancy dress is the new thing though and I make it my responsibility to let all guests know where they can hire their costumes from. I also make it clear that no-one is to come as Superman, as that's H's role. And Superwoman is a no-no, as his wife is insisting on coming too, for some reason.

I've already chosen my costume, just to make sure no-one else gets in there first.

It's going to be a ball....errr, so to speak.

*

H is in a funny mood today. I popped in to drop some paperwork on his desk and his eyes just followed me round the room and he didn't say a word. Not even hello. I'm not sure that he was all there. Well, it's the end of his first week back and it looks like the holiday mood has already faded into the distance....just as I'm gearing up for mine.

Funny that.

XXXIV

Some things never change. Two weeks away and there's Sophie to welcome me back, always smiling, always cheerful, always ready with a witty quip and the very model of health and efficiency. I don't know how she does it sometimes. I mean, I've been buzzing for months now and, apart from the occasional come down, still feel pretty good about myself. But Sophe. She just keeps going. Never misses a beat. There's probably a bloke behind her somewhere, keeping her pecker up...or maybe the other way round. There's more than a hint of envy in my thoughts.

*

Finally back in the groove and just in time. Tonight is the night. I'm winging my way round the room in my superhero get up, feeling like a proper little kid, swirling my cape behind me, but it's in the spirit of the occasion, so what the hell. Carla is drifting about the place dressed as Wonder Woman and trying to look important and largely failing; Jeff (who, somehow, is *still* with us) has a full supply of hankies which look somewhat incongruous with his Batman costume (though he *has* found a use for the utility belt); whilst John looks out of character as Spiderman. I've always had him down as slimy rather than sticky. Hollie is limping around as Batgirl with her wings clipped. Sophie is nowhere to be seen. Gone off to get changed apparently.

And there's Sarah, who seems to have adopted a permanent scowl. Scrutinising everyone as if they are defendants in one of her murder trials. She should be at work, of course. She hopes that I appreciate that.

Sarah and myself are the meeters and greeters, the hosts with the mosts and pretty much everyone else is left to their own devices, to enjoy themselves as best they can. Carla seems to be hanging around a little too much though. I get the impression that she wants to be seen with the boss and impress a few of our clients in the process. I'll have to keep an eye on her. She has an agenda. We've even stretched to a disco and lights and I have to say it's all very festive, thanks to Sophie. Who is nowhere to be seen. But then there must be over a hundred people here now, well up on last year, so she'll be lost in the crowd somewhere. Must've slipped in whilst I wasn't looking.

Wrong.

As more guests stroll in and I press the flesh and am all smiles and conviviality, I look back, to meet the next entrant, to be met by this .... statue. For a moment I am at a loss. Then it moves but it still doesn't register. For it being a 'her' there is no doubt. A mask might be hiding her face, but her costume is barely hiding anything at all. Or rather it is, but it's leaving nothing to the imagination. A one piece, black, lamé catsuit that simply melts into lines and curves that really should be made illegal in public. Matched with deadly stilettos and a diamante mask with pointed ears that covers all except her bouffant, black hair and dark eyes. The transformation is remarkable. She purrs at me ...then miaows and makes to scratch my eyes out.

Me? I'm rooted to the spot. Agog. Sarah sidles up and I make a quick recovery. 'Sophie! Lovely to see you. Sophie, Sarah.' Introductions made, Sophe brandishes her claws at Sarah, purrs and dances into the crowd without a word.

Sarah's scowl is back.

But generally the evening goes brilliantly and all are very complimentary as they are poured into taxis all the worse for wear but happy and smiling. Honestly, you've never seen such a motley crew. Superheroes indeed. Most look like they've been standing next to the radiators for too long and have melted along with their costumes. Bits sag and ripple everywhere. Not so much *Super* Heroes, as supine. I can't imagine any of this lot leaping tall buildings. Maybe the odd, uneven paving slab? But I'm guessing that this is exactly the point that the originator of the idea wished to make. I can't help but smile.

Finally I manage to shake off Carla, retrieve Sarah from the liquid charms of Mr Smith and am just heading for the door as Sophie appears sandwiched between two young chaps with a further entourage in tow. 'Going clubbing H! You coming?' I don't even need to look at Sarah to know what my answer will be. If that furrow between her eyebrows gets any deeper she'll be able to plant potatoes. 'Have a great time,' I call, as Sophie and that figure of hers head for the exit. I watch her leave with more than a hint of envy. Again. It's like watching my youth walk out the door.

Time was, Henry.

Time was

XXXV

Party done. Holiday next. Woo hoo. Two weeks of living it up in I-ta-leee!

Hopefully I'll do better than I did at the party. I mean loads of blokes there but nothing special. Most were *way* too old. The only one that was vaguely passable insisted on pinning me to the wall and shouting in my ear for, like, hours. Kept going on about how 'amazing' I looked. Like I didn't know that? That was the whole point, stupid! As if flattery was going to be a quick way into my knickers? Not in your lifetime, mate! Besides, he really fancied himself and that always puts me off. Smug. Cocky. So I just towed him along with a few others and got a full evening's entertainment and loads of free drinks into the bargain. Just had to make sure that he understood that when the club shut up shop, so did I. He took a *lot* of persuading.

Shoulda said a better goodbye to H though. I forgot I'd be away for yonks.

Two weeks without me. What will he do?

XXXVI

Two weeks with *Hollie*. What am I going to do?

I feel depressed even before I arrive.

And when I do, there she is with her funny lopsided smile because she is *so* pleased to see me, Mr Blythe, so *lovely* to be back and *so* looking forward to assisting you over the next two weeks and *anything* you need don't *hesitate* to ask and wasn't the party just *wonderful,* simply *devine,* Mr Blythe.

I'm straight on the phone to Nick.

'Drink?'

*

'God you make me sick!' I tip my head in response, '...will you just fuckin' look at yerself?! Tanned, toned and...and ...'

'Tinned?'

'...and I bet you even got laid recently!'

I don't answer.

'You bastard!' He takes a long draft of his ale ...he has a gut to feed. 'So go on, to what do I owe the pleasure?'

'Just fancied a pint.' He fixes me with his weaselly stare. I'm not believed. 'OK, just needed to get out of the office, bit of a breather, you know.'

'And..?'

'And nothing. Had a seriously good year. Work is hectic as ever. Cash is rolling in once again. Long holiday.'

'Oh, do shut up. You're beginning to depress me.'

'Funny, I was thinking the same thing myself this morning.'

Nick's glare is back. Then he slowly shakes his head. 'What is it with you? Never happy are you? When things are going shit, you're miserable. When things are going great, you're *still*.....'

'Yeah, well, you know me. Always striving for something more. Never one to rest on.....'

'And, whilst we're on the subject, how *is* the lovely Sarah?'

Were we? On the subject? Then I see what he means, '....got laid recently.'

'She's......' I struggle with the next word '.....*fine*.'

'Oh *dear*.'

'What?'

'That pause does *not* bode well. Which means....' I'm being scrutinised again. His face turns into a revelation. '.... you little bugger...it *wasn't* Sarah was it?!' I'm genuinely taken aback by this. '*You*......' waving as accusatorial finger at me '..... have been shagging someone *else*!'

My hackles rise. 'The fuck I have! And don't you ever, *ever* repeat that in public. Understood?'

Nick backs off. He knows he's over stepped the mark but is taken aback by how far. I'm left thinking that maybe Henry doth protest too much...and wonder why. This ale doesn't taste so good any more. I make my excuses and leave, my glass half empty on the bar.

*

By three, I think that I'm going to pull my hair out. No matter what I try I just can't seem to settle, can't seem to concentrate. I'm on edge with everything I do, nervous, uptight, irritable. Only one thing for it, I surmise, go work it off at the gym.

Fifteen minutes later, I'm kitted out and pulling, pushing and pressing weights like it's some kind of race. It's not what I need. What I need is to hit something. Something hard. Then I'm attacking this punchbag until exhaustion sets in, my arms ache and my knuckles bleed, but that's not working either. So I resign myself to a run on the treadmill, but I just end up getting seriously pissed off by all the other inmates in there, pacing up and down as if they are in desperate need of a piss but can't quite comprehend the concept of a gents' toilet, their arms sticking out at odd angles due to imaginary biceps the size of watermelons, making them vaguely resemble constipated apes with a bladder complaint. What is it with some men? Do they honestly think that such behaviour is attractive to females? And if so, which species exactly?

After half an hour, I've had enough of the menagerie and stink of stale sweat and head back to the office.

Ms Twigg is in my room before I've even sat down. Urgent phone call, please call back.

I grab some files and the phone message and head for the door.

'Be at home if anyone needs me, needs me *urgently*, that is. Otherwise I'm not contactable. Reports to read,' waving papers at her. Hollie looks deflated which, given how skinny she is, means she virtually disappears.

And then I'm gone, too.

*

Being at home is a little more relaxing. There's a fine rouge on the go with a little paté and cheese and a baguette that I picked up along the way. Reclining on the sofa, juggling glass and papers, I manage to salvage what's left of the first day of two weeks. Papers cleared by five, hunger long since satiated, an hour of television then an early night. The front door bangs just as I'm drifting off...my last thoughts that day.....?

'Two weeks with Hollie. Two weeks *without* Sophie.'

What *is* a man to do?

*

Easy, came the answer in the middle of the night, get the hell outa there. Next morning, first thing, I'm arranging a PR visit to our biggest client for the following week. This breaks the spell. Now I have something to look forward to for the rest of this week and most of next week I'll be away. Carla can keep me company. Hollie can stay put. Despite her evident disappointment, Hollie engages the task of making the arrangements with relish and obsequiousness in equal measure. I swear you could get diabetes from standing next to that one for too long.

Despite the prospect of a bit of a jolly, the rest of the week still drags and I'm more than relieved when I hit the road for an RV with Nick, Friday night. In need of a change, I suggest a new venue, so we convene at a contemporary affair, albeit it with the requisite fine ales, so that the past is not quite a foreign country. Nick is full of apologies re the last time we met, acknowledging (with envy) that Sarah and myself is *the* relationship that everyone else looks up to, him now being on his third marriage and all.....but I will hear nothing of it. I'm painfully aware that I over reacted and put the evening on my tab...and even stretch to a curry afterwards. Look after your friends, I think as we say our drunken goodbyes, you never know when you might need them.

*

After a routine weekend with Sarah, it's back in the starting blocks Monday and away for Tuesday night. Carla seems as buoyant as me at the prospect of this trip, but I suspect that her motives are different. Our biggest client. Our BIGGEST client. Ambition bleeds from every orifice and I know she'll make the most of every second. What her endgame is, I can only guess, but an endgame there will be, for sure.

It's as if we have brought a little piece of Hollie with us. Ms Ventura is positively drooling over the head honcho. The only difference appears to be the level of subtlety. Carla has this down to a T. The slowly replaced hair behind the ears, the tilt of the head, the well timed smile, the slight touch to her companion's forearm and a little cleavage. And, of course, Steve Singleton is lapping it up. Singleton? Ever a misnomer. Wife, three kids and just the type to play the field. Easy prey for someone like Carla.

Feminine wiles as fine art.

*

Dinner is at eight and Carla has dressed to impress in the clichéd, but still effective, little black number, killer heels and the merest hint of stocking. Mr Singleton is struggling to keep a straight face and his eyeballs in their sockets for the next two hours as we wine and dine and he clearly thinks she's divine and I'm betting that his shorts are stretched to the limit for most of that time. His reluctance to visit the 'facilities' confirms my suspicions.

I can't blame the poor bugger. She does look eminently shaggable. Except that she isn't.

So it's with a full stomach and a light head that I lay me down to sleep, gazing up at the brass bedstead, its rails and bars glowing dully in the semi-dark ..... à la recherche du temps perdu.

Sweet dreams, Henry.

*

And they were.

I dreamt of the first time I spent the night with Sarah .... all those many, many years ago. It was the bedstead that did it. Brass. All those vertical and horizontal bars. Victorian, or maybe mock-Victorian. But there was nothing mock about Sarah's desire.

Everything started as usual, you know, kissing, petting, heavy petting til rock hard and very wet. But as the final clothes came off for the coup de grâce, Sarah reached under the pillow, pulled out what looked like her dressing gown belt and said 'tie me.'

Oh, shit, I was such a novice. I mean, I'd had plenty of girlfriends by then, but none whatsoever had expressed an interest in anything more adventurous than trying the tradesman's entrance. And that had failed. Miserably.

But this was something new and in those days something new, *anything* new, was exciting and, yeah, I thought, let's give it a go.

So we gave it a go. And another... and another.

It became addictive. And I was hooked.

*

I hate, I mean I really *hate* waking up feeling horny. No. Waking up feeling horny ..... *and* being alone.

No pun intended, but it simply buggers up the rest of the day. And the rest of this day consists of driving back to the office with Carla in the passenger seat beside me, crossing and uncrossing her long, nylon stockinged legs. I seriously doubt that she is trying to wind me up, but her timing is appalling. Actually, come to think of it, I wouldn't put it passed her to have picked up on my mental state and be exploiting it to the full. The little shit!

'Shall we stop off somewhere to grab a bite, H?'

'Errrr....no, ... erm, probably best to head straight back.' I mean, I have the car on cruise control already and it doesn't even sodding well have one.

It should wear off ... in another hour or so.

XXXVII

I-ta-lia, I-ta-lia! Woooo!!

You would not believe the things me and Emms got up to in Capri. Well you probably would, but I'm not going to repeat them. Uh-uh. No way. Well, some other time, eh?

I just don't know how I'm gonna come back down after that wee trip. Two weeks in paradise and now it's back to the grindstone. But two things lift my spirits once I'm back in the office. One, Hollie is back in her proper place and looking miserable for it; two, H is pleased to see me, genuinely pleased, and I have to say, the sentiment is working both ways. He would have loved Capri, I found myself thinking on more than one occasion.

But, that aside, within a few days the holiday is but a distant memory, fading as rapidly as my tan.

H is planning another trip away next week. Going back to see a client that he met up with when I was away. He said that his wee jaunt had drummed up some new custom and he needs to seal the deal. Carla had gone with him that time, but won't be joining us. She had 'more than done her bit' and her reward was three nights away on a jolly - all spa, massage, fine food and relaxation. I'm not sure what H meant by 'more than done her bit.' I didn't like the way he said it. I have my suspicions. I trust her as far as.....

XXXVIII

A quiet weekend at home.

Sarah has been hovering, which is a bit worrying. Out of character to say the least, preferring to keep her distance both mentally and physically. I can't help feeling I'm being examined, *cross*-examined even. Probably just my imagination. Been living with a lawyer too long.

XXXIX

The bastard's having an affair!

All those little signs that on their own don't add up to much, but put them all together......

Losing weight, toning up, new clothes, haircut, cologne, and that persistent bloody humming he's started doing. What's he got to be so damned happy about? *He* reckons it's just because he saved some client's account and that now his business has turned around things are looking very positive....and I, like a bloody fool, took him at his word.

How could I have missed it? How could I have been so *stupid*?!

And no prizes for guessing who the other party is, either. The little madam.

I'll have his balls on a plate....along with *her* head.

XL

Quiet weekend, like fuck!

Something's been brewing all day like a distant storm just over the horizon. Sensed but not seen. With the benefit of hindsight it's probably been building all weekend. And then late this afternoon, I idly mention about work next week, as I'm just getting a bottle of wine from the fridge, and she just explodes at me.

Don't think I don't know what's going on, think you can get away with it, you think I'm stupid, well let me tell you buster (buster?) I worked it all out a *long* time ago, and don't think I don't know who with, the little slut, couldn't keep your hands off, could you? I feel sick just thinking about it...

And I'm standing there just aghast!

I mean, what is the woman *thinking*?

But still she persists.

Not denying it then?

Eh?

Fucking your employee you bastard, your bloody office girl! – she screams.

And I'm thinking – who, ferfucksake – WHO?! And must have said it without realising.......

'Carla! Who else?!'

And I feel relief as a tiny glimmer of guilt is snuffed out.

'Carla? Are you serious? Carla *Ventura*?' And I can't help but laugh, but this just makes Sarah see red and she starts throwing things at me like plates, cutlery, knives (knives !) and she's screaming how dare you, how *dare* you laugh at me! I've seen her. Hanging around you like she's another appendage, hanging on your every word. You think I didn't notice?'

And even though I'm hiding behind the dining table as another piece of something metallic bounces off a nearby chair, I hear the catch in her voice and the hurt as her anger subsides and pain swamps her. So as I raise my head above the parapet to see her head down and shaking.

Tentatively, 'Sarah, Sarah? There is nothing going on between me and Carla? Really. Nothing.'

'Yeah? Prove it,' she protests.

How? How do I prove a negative? 'I have absolutely no interest in her. More to the point, she has absolutely no interest in me. Believe me?' I don't plead. I state my case.

'Why should I?'

'Carla is simply not my type. Or, more to the point, I'm not hers.' Sarah says nothing as she struggles to control herself.

'What makes you so bloody sure?'

'Well for one thing, I have an appendage, as you put it, that she has absolutely no interest in.' I let this sink in, but get no reaction at first. 'Whatsoever.' I add. Then it begins to dawn.

'You mean she's a ......?' I just nod.

'I don't believe you.' she challenges. She's convinced of something that simply isn't true. But her last challenge is now tinged with doubt.

'It's an open secret. Not only is she out of the closet, she brought her whole designer wardrobe with her.'

XLI

I've really fucked up, haven't I? First rule of advocacy. Don't ask a question unless you already know the answer. The problem is, I thought I knew the answer only to find that I didn't. But I know, I just *know* that something is going on. All the signs are there, all of them. I *can't* be wrong. But where's my evidence? Conjecture is not enough.

Fight back. Fight.

Well, if not her, who? What about that little......?

'Sophie' I blurt out 'It's that Sophie....errr whateverherbloodynameis ....'

XLII

I resist the temptation to say 'Marcoque. It's Marcoque!'

It probably wouldn't help.

XLIII

........and I suddenly realise that I'm beginning to sound ridiculous. Clutching at straws. Henry just stands there and stares at me for what seems an age. He doesn't move a muscle. Neither do I. Who will break first?

XLIV

Sophie.

That glimmer of guilt is back.

But I can't show it. I simply cannot show it. Remain motionless. *E*motionless. Nothing. Not a twitch, not a shake of the head, not a sigh, not a word. Nothing that can be interpreted or misinterpreted.

Just stand. Just stare.

Then walk out.

XLV

Bugger!

I have *really* messed this up. I was just so sure, so *bloody* sure! How could I have got it so wrong?

And then to change the charge mid-trial. Plain clumsy, Sarah Blythe. Really, *really* dumb. I'd never have done that in court. Never.

You sounded so *desperate*. And *he* seemed so convincing.

Well, I'm not leaving it at that. I have some checking to do. Then and only then will I be convinced.

Probably..........

XLVI

We didn't speak after that, that night. She went straight to bed with a headache. I sat in the lounge with a sandwich, which had the faint flavour of ashes. Work tomorrow will be something of a relief. I can envisage us both, 5.30 a.m., colliding in the front doorway in a desperate attempt to be the first one out of the house.

We won't speak.

*

Work *is* a relief, but I still can't shake off this cloud. The storm may have passed, but it's aftermath still rankles. Sophie is briefed on the plans for the week and seems pleased with the prospective 'wee jaunt'. So am I, to be honest. Anything not to have to face Sarah for a few days. Time as oil on troubled waters.

I meet Nick that evening for 'a quick one', which turns into 'four quick ones', bringing him up to date with the domestic situation and mockingly accuse him of bringing it all on himself, what with his own remarkably similar accusation not so very long ago, thanks very much mate!

He feels guilty, even though we both know that the link is ridiculous.

But I go with it until he finally volunteers that it's his shout all evening.

*

The next day we are northward bound. Sophe is in her usual chatty mood, all smiles and good humour. Which suits me fine because her good mood always seems to swell my own.

The meeting with Singleton goes swimmingly, well for me at least. He is his usual smarmy self and forgets that Sophie is *not* Carla and mistakenly thinks that he can indulge himself in the same way that he did before.

Wrong.

Sophe is having none of it. She treats him for the creep he really is. There will be no flirting here mate. She is cut from a different cloth than Carla. Why do you think I brought the older woman last time? Assign the skills accordingly.

'My sincerest apologies, Sophe, I should have warned you,' and I'm shaking my head at that little bit of stupidity. She deserves better than that, but brushes it off – 'you should see me out on a Saturday night, H. That wee shite has *nothing* on some of the creeps I usually have to deal with,' and I find that hilarious.

Assign the skills accordingly. Duly noted!

So I promise her a great evening out, just as long as it doesn't include a night club. Having to witness Sophe fighting off 'wee shites' is not on my wants list right now and strutting my stuff amongst the wee kiddies doesn't appeal much either. So we indulge ourselves in great food and fine wines and I'm as happy as Larry by close of play.

I escort Sophe back to her room. Memories of that smacker on the lips the last time come flooding back. I can still taste its sweetness. Feel its stickiness. Savoured it for hours afterwards.

At her door I say goodnight and lean forward to give her a peck on the cheek. I get halfway there and see a slight movement of her head .... to face me .... her mouth now inches from mine.

XLVII

'Oh dear. This is what my friend Emms would call another 'moment',' and I explain it all to H in my slightly sozzled way.

'And are you going to let *this* 'moment' pass?' he asks.

'No,' is all I say.

XLVIII

Those dark, dark eyes, those deep, deep pools. I hold my breath........ and dive in.

XLIX

Oh shit, I've shagged a wrinkly!

What *was* I thinking?

I know what I was thinking. I was thinking 'what a great day, what a lovely evening, I don't want this to end,'.... so I didn't let it.

So I'm lying here with a slight 'head' and a dry mouth, not daring to open my eyes and acknowledge a new day and what that new day may bring.

And all I can feel is an all consuming *ache*.

My legs ache like I've been doing the splits for the last eight hours...only it was probably only two. *Only* two?! My god, where does the man get his energy from?! Just as I thought that was it, let me rest, let me sleep pleeease, he was off again. Luckily, taking *me* along for the ride.

Insatiable.

And then I start to register other aches. Oh, Henry, you bad, *bad* boy! You didn't? Yes, you sodding well *did*!

Oh bum!

...... not only will I not be able to *walk* for a week, but sitting down might just ....

There's a noise from the bathroom and I assume that H is making ready for the day. One eye drags itself open, the other buried in the sheets. The door opens and there he is, perfectly groomed and wrapped in a chunky bathrobe.

'OK?' he asks.

I try an answer. My *jaw* aches.....and my throat doesn't seem to want to work. Henry you've wrecked me! I'd be annoyed if I wasn't so...so....? I can't even come up with a word. 'Content' doesn't even begin to cover it. 'Satisfied'? Getting there. 'Exhausted'?... that's for sure.

I groan, which just about sums it up, then shut my eye and long for more sleep.

L

Up early. Don't seem to need sleep like I used to.

Have to get up and sorted before my companion awakes (awakes?!). Even though my head is killing me and my tongue is like sandpaper. Know how dreadful I look first thing. All sags and bags. Can't let her see me like that. Don't want to put her off....if I haven't already. Oh well, if that's as far as it goes, good while it lasted.

Hell, that's an understatement.

It was bloody brilliant!

I felt twenty six again. Twenty six? Yeah, twenty six was a bloody good year. Sam and then Aisha and finally Sarah.

Sarah.

Hmmmm.... best not dwell on that right now.

Last night. What the hell came over you? No idea. Just went for it. Big time. Too much? Maybe. Could've put her off. No. I kept pushing for more and she just went for it. Give and take. Take and give. Equal measures.

Twenty six, eh?

If only.

So I'm up and washed and dressed before there's as much a grunt from the bed. I've got a hunger on me almost matching the hunger I felt last night. Almost? No, not really. Back to my room. Bed still made. Better sort that. Unmake it. Then change of clothes. Already covering my tracks.

Then breakfast. Leisurely. Reliving last night. What a girl. Who am I kidding. What a *woman*! Insatiable. Just kept coming back for more. Fantastic. Awesome. Doesn't even begin to cover it. Trying not to think of anything else. Difficult.

Sunday's glimmer of guilt is now Tuesday's small bonfire.

Shit.

Still no sign of Sophe. Better go see if she's OK. Tap on the door. A groan. 'It's H.'

'Minute.' Door opens a crack. Dark, dark eyes, hair everywhere, looks a mess. Looks gorgeous. A stirring in me. Not now H. Really? Really. She's wrapped in the bed sheet. Naked beneath. Really? Really. I know what you look like naked. I know how you move. I know the things you do, the things you say.

You're a *bad* girl, Sophie MacDonald, and I think that's wonderful.

But not now. No. Get a grip.

*

An hour later we're heading back and there's an ominous silence. Is she angry with me? Pleased? Tired? What? I'm tempted to ask, but know how crass the 'what are you thinking?' line sounds. I'm not seeking compliments, I'm not seeking criticism.

I guess I'm seeking reassurance.

That it's OK. That I haven't fucked things up. That I haven't just been incredibly stupid, even though I know I have. In so many ways. That it's going to be fine between us. Even though things have changed forever, whichever way I look at it. That something good can be salvaged from the wreckage.

And then there's the guilt. Oh Henry. What *have* you done?

LI

H is not talking to me. I can't say I blame him. I've been really stupid and he blames me. It's my fault. Throwing myself at him like that. He's a married man fergodsakes. I have never, *ever*......

What was I thinking? What is *he* thinking? He must hate me. He smiles, but I can see that he's not quite with me. Not quite in the here and now. I want to do something. Hold his hand, hug him even...... but maybe not while he's driving, eh? I have to stop being dumb *sometime*.

And last night. Oh shit! Last night!

A jumble of thoughts and emotions in my head.

For once I'm lost for words.

LII

What do I say? Err, sorry about last night. What was I thinking? Too much booze. As ever. Stupid of me I know. Can you forgive me? Get things back to normal. Normal? Who are you kidding? Whatever happens from now on, it will never be 'normal'. Welcome to the new norm, H. You have had sex with a much younger woman, an employee, someone you are supposed to be responsible for, she must feel used, exploited even, and you will have to work with her as if nothing has happened.........and you are married ...... to someone else.

Nice one.

LIII

'You OK?' he finally asks. 'Hmmm' is all I give back. Pathetic.

'Look....' and I'm all ears. Make this right H, just make it right. '......what I meant was, are you OK with ..... last night?' The question hangs in the air. I don't know H, is what I want to say. I'm not sure what I've done...except create one big bloody mess...for us both. Is that OK? Does that make me feel OK?

Well, no, not really.

'What we.... *did* .....' he continues.

I have absolutely no idea what he is talking about. 'Did'?

And then realise - Oh *that*. Yes, I'm OK with *that*. *That* was, like, errr great. *That's* just fine. I may never walk again, but *that's* a minor detail. I shift a little in my seat. It's all the other stuff that may not be OK.

'Yeah' is all I say, but it seems to break the ice a little. I raise a smile at the memory. H sees me and smiles back. Good – he says. Then he grabs my hand and gives it a squeeze and his warmth just seems to flood through me. This is making it better, H. Thank you.

'Do you want to......'

And I wonder, is this how we're going communicate with each other from now on? Half a sentence at a time. Do I want to.....?

'.......again?'

Again? He's asking me.....if I want to......AGAIN! Yes! Yes, I do!

And again. And again. And.........

'Yes, please,' is all I can manage.

And all the other crap just seems to fade away, my fate sealed.

LIV

There's that well worn saying 'If you find yourself in a hole, stop digging'

So what do I do? I go and get a bloody big digger and multiply the effort. Tenfold. Brilliant. But I can't help myself. I must *like* digging.

And I know what else I like....and she's sitting right next to me. I just wish she'd stop wriggling like that. It's *doing* things to me. Pretty soon I'll be able to drive hands free.

But she said 'yes, please' and my stomach gave a little lurch or my heart missed a beat. I'm not sure which. Maybe it was both.

There's suddenly so much to do. So much to *organise*. Although I start slowly – we have to be careful, mustn't let anyone else find out, not even your best friend, discretion must be paramount. If anyone, and I mean *anyone*, finds out, I'll have to end it. Understood? It almost turns into a tirade, even though I try to restrain myself. Poor woman doesn't know what's hit her. Don't scare her off, you twit. So she gets her orders. No contact except verbal. Absolute professionalism in the office and with colleagues. No public affection. Nothing that can be misinterpreted. And don't *rush* things. We have all the time.......so enjoy it.

Sorry to go on. This is important to me. Her hand on mine, stroking the back of it with her thumb. 'I know' she says. Really? Really. 'I just have so much to.......'

'Lose?'

Nothing more is said.

I hope she understands. Really I do.

LV

Henry takes control. I like that. But I'm beginning to think that maybe this isn't the first time that he........

His 'orders' sounded just a little too rehearsed, tripped off the tongue a little too easily, as if he'd already...... Henry, you old dog. Exactly how many women have you....? And I guess I think a little less of him, realising that I'm just one of several, maybe one of many?

But I try to be OK with it, coz at that very moment I *am* OK.

It's a quiet, pleasant drive home after that, even though I can't *quite* get comfortable in my seat.

But H is evidently 'pleased to see me', nonetheless.

Maybe if I just lean over and..........

LVI

There's fear flooding through my veins as I turn the key in the lock. This isn't going to be easy. The woman is no fool. Not by any stretch. Pulling the wool over her eyes is going to be as easy as pulling teeth. Pulling my *own* teeth. Let's face it, she earns her living by seeing through lies and deceit and she's good. She's very good.

But all that is washed away as I breeze into the kitchen to find Sarah hard at work at the stove. Big smile, kiss, wine darling? And my fears are swept aside by my wife's bonhomie and, is that seafood? Hmmm... nice wine....and are those....? yes, darling and, maybe later, we can ....and she smiles and even winks.

'What? Twice in one month?' I jest. 'You'll be the death of me!'

............but I'm thinking – 'twice in one *day*?

This'll fucking kill me!'

*

So it's a very tired old Henry that stumbles into the office the next day. Sophe is there already, just as I expected, and she seems to have taken my words to heart. Professional to a T. Not a hint of anything personal......except, errr, *except*, she's taken to calling me HB rather than H. Yes, I'm still pondering whether that's a wise move. Pet names and all that. But I let it pass for the first few times, before I query here choice of soubriquet on the one occasion she comes into my office and actually closes the door behind her. It makes me sound like a *pencil* – I complain.

She looks me straight in the eye, lowers her voice and says slowly – 'believe me, HB, you are *nothing* like a pencil,' and her eyes widen, then she sticks her tongue in her cheek and flounces out.

I don't bat an eyelid, but stifle a smirk.

The little madam.

LVII

Weekend!!!! Wooooo!

And I'm out with Emms for the first time in what seems yonks, but is actually only a couple of weeks. After living together for two weeks on Capri, the break seems like months. She's as hyper as ever, desperate to get a guy for the night, as it's a whole fortnight since her exploits in Italy. Withdrawal symptoms are setting in, she says, squeezing her thighs together and jiggling her tits.

She fills me in on her life since then and I do too, missing out the obvious. We have fun and I'm glad of the change of scene but even Emms notices I'm a little subdued. She guesses a bloke which I'm at pains to deny. In fact I'm horrified given what H has instructed, but try not to show it. I just hope I haven't overdone it. It's just a bit of a come down after the hols – I lie. Maybe a bit under the weather too, but I'm OK and suggest shots and that seems to satisfy her.

The club is a bit more traumatic. The owners have laid on a steady supply of completes bozos who hassle me from the moment I get in there. Emms doesn't seem to mind. A bozo is probably what she is after. It's just for the night – as she says, then squeals – I'm not going to make a *habit* of it – before collapsing in fits.

So I bop around for a while but there's something lacking. It all feels....superficial. Emms tries to cheer me up but realises, after a while, that I'm a lost cause. She can see I'm not depressed or anything like that but – I can't quite put my finger on it – she says, and I add 'so to speak' and we both laugh.

*

I *so* look forward to getting into work these days, but only as long HB is around. Otherwise I'm battling Hollie and rivalling Carla and avoiding Slimeball and every other bugger who works there that has something I don't need. HB makes it all bearable. My raison d'être.

But today things go wrong.

Carla waltzes in with a request for some more info on a client that her and HB are seeing next week. Her and HB? HER and HB?! I miss a beat and then set to it. Professional, remember Sophie? Can't let it show. Mustn't let it show. But all the while I'm turning into a nice wee cassoulet. Stewing. By the time I get to speak to HB, like an hour later, I'm fit to burst.

'Off on a wee trip next week, I hear.' 'Yup. Just a couple of nights.' A couple of nights? Have you any idea what I would give for just *one* night? But say – 'With Carla.' HB is reading where this is going. His eyes, alone, check behind me that the door is shut. Of course it is, HB, *I* shut it. He lowers his voice a shade, 'I'm saying this once only, then you drop it, OK?' I nod. 'I thought it best that we wait a while, so Carla seemed like the best.....' and he's back to unfinished sentences.... '... and safest ... OK?' I bite my bottom lip. And give the slightest of nods.

Then leave, grab my make-up and head for the loos. I'm sitting in a cubicle, lid down and the tears are streaming down my face as I struggle to stay silent.

I can't do this, I just can't.

LVIII

Sophie seems OK with our little talk. Back to her old self as if nothing had happened. That's good. I made myself understood. This is no place for histrionics.

But it's not just her that's getting a bit emotional. Every time she comes into the room, all I find myself wanting to do is bend her over my desk, lift up her skirt, pull down her panties and ....

That old devil called lust.

I just can't show it. Can't afford that. So I carry on regardless counting down the days and hours until the next time.

This *is* killing me.

LIX

Composure regained. Make up reapplied. A few deep breaths and back to work.

Shit, I almost blew it there. HB is right, of course, we can't afford any cock ups, so to speak. I have alot to learn. I'm the novice here. First lesson – keep calm. It *will* happen, just give it time.

Which is not easy, believe me.

It doesn't help that, every time I go into HB's office, all I want him to do is bend me over his desk, lift up my skirt, pull down my panties and.........

Oh bum!

LX

There's been a definite seachange in Sarah. Just once, maybe twice, a week she is making time for me. Getting home at a reasonable hour. Eating meals together. Watching TV....and then bed. Early bed. 'Early enough not to sleep' bed. 'Early enough to play around' bed. 'Early enough to get deep down and dirty' bed.

And I can't help it, but I find myself winging back to the days of our youth when our lust was incessant, when such exploits were not weekly but daily, hell, several *times* daily, and how, now, we try to grasp at that youth, but it slips through our fingers and leaves us empty inside.

She is still beautiful. My wife. My beautiful wife. And my wife still wants me. But I am not all there for her. Not anymore.

Sarah is fighting back, and I'm really flattered that she thinks that I'm worth the effort.

Only I know that I'm not ...... and I feel sad for her.

LXI

Wooo hooo, party time, and my spirits are through the roof.

We are going away again and we are going to party and we are going to...... hopefully!

It seems that we are not the only company that has an annual par-tee. H sprung this on me this morning and I could barely contain my delight. Until he told me that there would be a crowd of us going. Not just the two of us. Invites for four.

Oh bum!

HB and me and Slimeball and Mr Sneezy.

Hoo-bloody-ray.

The wind well and truly taken out of my sails, I settle down to another day of the same old.

It's been three weeks now. Three weeks since HB and I...... since we....since he pretty much *wrecked* me. Physically. Mentally. Each day has been an endurance test. Because I want it again. I want to be wrecked. I want to be *devastated*. By him. And he won't. He just won't.

How can he do that?

*

Well the day has finally arrived and I guess I'm feeling OK about it all. Despite the company, I know that I can still chat to HB and we can party and have a good time and a few laughs. What I really want seems to be out of the question, though, given the circumstances. Too risky. Too many witnesses.

But hey, I guess you can't always get what you want. Second best isn't that bad in this case. It's just miles short of *the* best.

So I'm getting ready and will be dressed to impress, even if it's going to be wasted on others. Full-length mirror. Full impact. Eat your heart out, Henry Blythe. See what you're missing? Yes, you *will* see. So I hitch up my dress and slip off my very brief briefs. I won't be needing those, will I? How's that for a skin tight fit? Now

I *know* what this is going to do to my sex drive, send it through the bloody roof. A roof that is pretty much destroyed anyway. I really don't care anymore.

So, in for a penny.......

*

I try to locate HB, and see he's engrossed in conversation with two other men. Sidling up, just to say 'Hi', I'm introduced to the others with names that go in one ear and straight out the other. There's only one person that I'm interested in. But he just carries on with the conversation and pretty much gives me the cold shoulder so that I'm left standing there like a spare cock at an orgy, so to speak.

That hurt.

So I wander the room, glass of bubbly in hand, introducing myself to anyone that looks like he or she might be interesting and while away a pleasant hour or two. I only catch brief glimpses of HB on odd occasions, but he always seems to be busy.

Finally, *I'm* cornered by someone clearly the worse for wear. A little bit of alcohol and some people become complete dicks, don't they? I, of course, include myself in that statement. Let's face it, when it comes to behaving like a complete dick, I'm a bloody expert, what with Dave and Darren and Colin and the one that looked like a horse. Dobbin? But these were strangers, well, to begin with anyway. Some stayed strangers. But when someone you have known for nearly a year now turns from Mr Nice to Mr Ever So Slightly Weird, it's a bit of an eye opener.

John 'Slimeball' Smith, I would expect it of. But Jeffrey Cummings? Mr. Bloody Sneezy? I mean, come *on*. In some circumstances, *any* kind of attention would be flattering, but someone whose chat up line is to tell me I look gorgeous while emptying the contents of his sinuses into an off-grey and slime green hanky, does not exactly fit the bill. Within a few minutes, he's backed me against the wall, hemmed me in on one side with one arm, then on the other side with the other arm, so he's leaning against the wall with both hands and me in between. Trapped. Then there's a tap on his shoulder. He swings round, almost angrily. 'Can't have you monopolising this lovely young lady all evening there, my man.' My hoped for knight in shining armour turns out to be John sodding Smith, a knight in a shining suit, who eases Snotrag out with the suggestion that I might like a top up and why doesn't he tootle off and get one, there's a good chap.

I'm thankful....for about three minutes. 'So, why don't you and me grab a bottle of bubbly and go check out the view from your room?' Oh, good grief. Out of the frying pan and into the grease pit...... Have things really sunk this low? Yes, they really have.

I could cry.

*

At the earliest opportunity, I make my excuses and then make my escape. It's only just after ten, but I figure it's late enough and that there's little more to be gleaned from the occasion. A quick scout around the room but HB is nowhere to be seen.

I head for the exit.

The lift door is just closing behind me when there's a thump and the doors open again. I turn and Henry is there, slipping in beside me as the doors re-close. 'Almost missed it!' and he slips a card into a slot at the top of the bank of buttons on the lift wall. As soon as the doors are closed, there is the slightest of movements as he turns a fraction towards me. I reciprocate. I have no idea who makes the first proper move. I hope it wasn't me. I hope he did. But pretty soon I don't care because he has me pinned against the wall, lifted up so that our mouths are on the same level, and passion takes over. My skirt is being pushed up my thighs by two hands. Then the lift lurches as it prepares to stop. 'Fifth floor.' By the time the doors open, we are two separate people again. Composed.

A couple, dressed to the nines, are about to get in when Henry says 'I'm going up,' holding out a hand to stop them entering, 'All the way up...' he adds, and I bite my bottom lip to stifle a smirk. They step back as the doors close. Suddenly, my hands are clasped behind my back as our mouths meet and I struggle as I want desperately to throw my arms around his neck. But they are held in place. Then I feel metal. Metal? Cold metal on my wrists. His mouth biting my neck. I gasp. A ratchet sound.

Oh shit, handcuffs!

His hands, now free, hitching up my skirt again, warm skin on my flesh, above my stockings, my inner thigh, between my... 'Oooo you naughty, naughty girl. Been bareback all night, have we?' and my knees go weak, just as a voice says 'Penthouse suite' and the doors slide open.

And Henry is pretty much frog marching me into this large room, one hand in my armpit, dragging me, as I totter forward on my heels hammering the marble floor. There's one wall of glass, which must give magnificent views of the city below, but I barely notice this as he's hissing in my ear '...and we know what happens to naughty girls, don't we?' and before I can even think of an answer (*an answer? Who am I kidding?*) he has me over by the windows and it's an awfully long way down, which is a bit scary and makes me giddy and weak at the knees, and then he is lowering himself onto a long foot stool kind of thing and pulling me face down over his knees, 'that's right, naughty girls have to be punished, don't they?' (*Do they? Are you sure about that?*) and I feel my dress tugged up hard around my waist, everything above my stocking tops is exposed.

'My oh my, now here's something to *wax* lyrical about.' Which is *real* funny, HB, ha-ha, but I'm not really taking it in now because I'm breathing hard, my head is spinning and my heart is racing and the ache that I've kept subdued for, like, *weeks* is back and it's back big time and threatens to explode. And being pinned here, exposed and helpless like this, is just making it worse. I start to say something, I'm not even sure what, but feel my head pulled back by my hair and I am ordered to speak when I'm spoken to, do I understand? Yes HB. No, not HB, 'Sir' to you. Understand? 'Yes, sir.' (*You bastard*)

'Now, how many? Six is always a good place to start. Six of the best for you, young lady? Hmmmm?... I'll take that as a yes, then.' Oh you will, will you? I think, but say nothing.

And the first hits my bare backside with a crack sending my legs flapping into the air, my arms struggling against their chains and a cry lets loose from my throat that peters to a whimper.

'There's a good girl.' I'll give you 'good girl', *Mister* Henry Blythe!

And the next. And the next. Oh merde!! But all I can manage is 'please', please' which just makes it worse (or better?) coz H thinks I want more...and maybe I do coz even though it hurts, it's kinda fun too *and* different *and* I'm really rather enjoying it!

Hee hee.

I'm slowly dragged to my feet again, my dress still up around my waist. Marched firmly to the great expanse of glass. It's an *awfully* long way down! He is standing behind me. My dress is slowly unzipped from behind and eased forward from my shoulders. His mouth on the back of my neck, wee bites. Ooooh sir! Then easing me onto my knees, sideways on to the vast window, undoing the front of his trousers. Yes, oh yes please H, now that I *do* want. Yes please. And so he does. And that is how it is. For, like, *hours*.

Relentless.

And just when I think that that is it. That I can take no more. That that *has* to be enough. He gives more. And leaves me devastated .... Again.

*

Oh shit, I'm shagging a perve!

I mean, I got the domination thing, kinda, last time out. And I have no problem with that. I mean *absolutely* no problem! And the *other* thing really was no problem either. But handcuffs? He must've been carrying the bloody things with him all evening! Chatting away with all his mates, while all along they were sitting in his jacket pocket ready for our kinky little get together.

The little devil!

*

Have you ever cum and been able to remember it for days, if not weeks afterwards? OK, so maybe this is such a rare event that it's not that difficult to remember just one in a barren landscape and I guess I kinda know what you mean there. Once in a blue moon makes that blue moon a really special event. Even if it *wasn't* that special at all. But what if I was to tell you that it was one of several that happened on one occasion? Really. I'm not kidding here. So the actual number is not relevant. What *is* important is the intensity that went with one particular time. So intense, in fact, that it now seems to control your every waking hour. One that, no matter what you do, say or feel in order to distract your mind, is always there nagging away at you. Like an ache. An ache for more.

For weeks and weeks that ache stayed with me. After that time. The first time. Is it any wonder I was desperate for more? Desperate enough to behave a little stupidly. To *mis*behave. To almost ruin it – for us both. Letting your emotions run away with yourself, young lady. That was not clever. Look what you almost missed out on. If you thought the first time was great, the second time...........

I'm beginning to appreciate that there's more to this sex lark than I first thought. Alot more. OK, a *hell* of alot more. I've only just been playing at it really, haven't I? Treating it as a 'lark'. Like a little girl. A *silly* little girl. Would it sound too pretentious to say that there is an art to it? I heard someone say this once. Years and years ago. I remember thinking, oh, god, what a twat! Typical know-it-all, know nothing, stupid bloody student. Eighteen. I mean what would *she* know at eighteen? But now it's me who feels the fool.

An ebb and flow is the best way I can think of describing it. Like the crashing of waves on a beach, only each wave is bigger than the last and they keep getting bigger and bigger until one enormous wave washes you off the beach, drags you out to sea before dumping you exhausted back on the sand.

Well that was what it was like for me. Each time I thought that that was it, enough, really, I'm fine, but it kept getting more and more intense until it built to fever pitch and then, and only then, did I get my final release. Well imagine that, then double it.

Seriously! I'm not joking. I was already well on my way after the second, or was it third time? but Henry would not give up. He just kept coming back with more.

Like I said before – relentless.

I know that this all sounds a bit intense. Am I sounding like some pretentious twit too? Yes, I guess I am. Not like me at all, is it? But something has changed. Radically changed. I don't know what, exactly, I'm still trying to figure it out. I thought it was just a laugh. Just a 'jolly jape', but I'm just not my old self any more.

I don't think I ever will be.

I'll shut up now.

LXII

Pillow talk –

'Do you *really* think I'm a slut?' she asks and I turn to look into those deep, dark eyes.

All smiles, 'I think you're magnificent.'

'OK, so I'm magnificent. Now answer my bloody question.'

Nice one Sophe, no-one's fooling you these days. She's mainly curious, but there's a hint of hurt there too. 'It's just a game, hun.'

'I'll take that as a 'yes' then.' There's a long, long silence whilst she listens to my heartbeat thump, thump, thumping, her head now resting on my bare chest.

Then – 'I'll be your slut, Henry Blythe. I will.'

*

If I thought that the seachange in Sarah was remarkable, the transformation in Sophie is astounding.

Gone is that cheeky little lady who risked it all for the sake of a wee quip. No more larks. She is the very model of a professional. Efficient, polite and suitably removed. Distant. Maybe too distant? Oh shit, I haven't put her off have I?

Too much, too soon?

But no. She has given every indication that she wants more. Only now she is far more subtle about it. We communicate no longer by innuendo. No more 'so to speaks' ho-ho. Too obvious. Instead words are exchanged solely about work, plans, progress, prospects. Nothing personal. Once in a while a comment is slipped in that the casual bystander, should we be overheard, would find wholly innocent, but to us, and only us, has a fuller meaning. Sometimes it's more than the odd comment. No stresses on any of the pertinent words. Delivered straight. But we know. Oh yes, we both know..........

Sophie - 'Maybe we should press Harrington for more work. He knows we're up to the job.' (*Harrington = a night away and I'm up for it.*)

Henry - 'Yes, you think that you could manage that?' (*Can you handle another seeing to?*)

Sophie - 'No problem at all, Mr Blythe (*Of course I can, you silly man*). Just leave it in my capable hands. I'm sure I can work something out.', *(I can't wait to take you in my hands and make you .... – fill in the blank here with whatever takes your fancy.*)

Henry – 'Excellent. (*Yes. You give fantastic hand jobs!*)   See if you can tie him down to next week, sometime. *(Just wait til next week when I have you tied to the bed...)* We'll see what we can come up with. (*....and I'm shagging you every which way I can and making you cum and cum.*)

Sophie – Consider it done. (*Woo hoo!*)

We're winding each other up of course. I wonder if she realises why that *has* to be? Hardly an hour goes by when I don't imagine her bent over my desk or down on her knees. I think she's of a similar mind. But she doesn't bat an eyelid. Nothing. Even when we are alone, the veil doesn't drop. Not even an inch.

She's smart, this lover of mine. I'm impressed and more than a little humbled.

*

But next week is going to be out of the question. I have Sarah to deal with. I have gone from years of celibacy to having two lovers at the same time. Typical, huh? From drought to monsoon in a matter of days. And I should be jolly as hell. The sort of thing that most people, especially most *men*, would long for. A fantasy come true. But I'm not finding it easy, I have to admit. I guess I wouldn't feel so uncomfortable if Sarah wasn't trying so damned hard to make amends. If she was just carrying on regardless, not caring, it would be so much easier. But she's not. She is making an effort. And so should I, because it would be self-indulgent of me to put the blame entirely on her. If there was any drifting apart to be done, it was probably mutual. But is that so surprising? I mean, it's been well over twenty years. Let me repeat that, as much for my benefit as for anyone else's.... well over twenty *years*! Is it any wonder, really, under the circumstances? And then it hits me.

Longer than Sophie has been on this planet.

This depresses me even more but I cannot, I *will* not show it.

What makes it *easier* is that I'm actually enjoying the new attention from my wife. And I'm enjoying reciprocating too. We are re-kindling friendship, intimacy and even sex. After all this time. Who'da thought it? She is almost back to her old self. Her old, *bad* self. That self that got me hook, line and sinker all those years ago, that kept my undivided attention for so, so long. And when Sarah gets bad, she gets seriously bad. Lust has returned and I'm hoping that it's working wonders for her life, generally, in the same way that it is for mine. That wee spring in one's step. The tendency to smile more often than usual....*without* looking like a lobotomised fool.

Only for me it's two fold. If I spring and smile much more, I swear I'll put my back out.

So I resolve to give Sarah my full attention when at home and Sophie gets it (so to speak) when I'm away.

I just need a day or two break between the two of them to aid my recovery. All this *should* be getting me fit. It's not. Well, not yet.

So Sarah is Sarah and Sophie is Sophie and never the twain......

Well, not in my lifetime!

LXIII

I'm getting good at this. All this cloak and dagger stuff. All this deceit. Who'da thought that little Ms MacDonald could be so sly? Not me, that's for sure. But it's almost becoming second nature to me now. A new skill that I have no doubt will come in handy for the future. And I'm happy. Genuinely happy. I have something to remember, something to look forward to, something to yearn for.

Henry is appreciative. I can tell from the look in his eye.

And then he drops a bombshell.

No more trips away for the foreseeable future. I can't believe this. He says he has to crack on with a particular project. Simply doesn't have time. I'll just have to wait. But I can't. The thought of waiting, not for days, but weeks is crippling me. He suggests I go with someone else. There are plenty to choose from. If I really need a break. Is he taking the piss? No. All talk of visiting clients is off the agenda for the foreseeable.

And then I have a wee brainwave.....the mountain must come to....

So next morning I breeze into HB's office all smiles, settle myself down and – 'Listen, I appreciate that things are a bit hectic right now and we'll all have to knuckle down for a wee while, that clients will have to come to us if they need to meet, but I've been thinking – deep breath - why don't I help out by doing just that little bit extra?' H is non-plussed as to where precisely this is going. 'I have absolutely no problem with putting in some extra hours, maybe working late, taking work home even. Anything to help out really.' (Read – *I'm getting desperate here. No more trips away? Come on! Have you any idea what you're doing to me? Keep me behind after work and put me over this desk if you want. I'll do it. Take me back to my place. Do it there. I'll do anything. Anything.*)

'Well' he drawls 'I'm not sure that working late will help out much and I've *never* been in favour of employees taking work home. But thanks for the offer. It really is appreciated.' (Read – *I'm not shagging you in the office. I'm definitely not shagging you at your place* – OK. I don't blame you H, it's a pit! – *so, thanks anyway, but you'll just have to put up with it.* - 'It' being an ache that threatens to cripple me - *so tootle off back to your desk and don't bother me again.*)

For the first time in weeks, I crack and I'm angry at him, for the first time ever. 'Just book a bloody hotel somewhere. Just for the afternoon. Please H. I *need* it. Please.' And I can't keep the whinge out of my voice.

He glares at me. Muscles and sinews in his jaw twitch. Yes, I messed up again. I can't help it. Back to being a silly little girl. I bite my bottom lip so hard I taste blood in my mouth, trying to stop the tears welling.

'No.' Is all he says, then picks up the phone and starts dialling.

'Nick, mate, how the devil are you? Drink later ......?'

LXIV

Things are threatening to get out of hand. *Sophie* is getting out of hand. I blame myself of course. She's new to all this. So am I ... well, some of it. She's trying to adapt in a rapidly changing world and she's struggling to keep up. Is it any wonder she's angry.

Well, actually, she's *furious!*

But she has to appreciate that I can't just drop everything for her, much as I'd like to. I have to be careful. She doesn't. I'm the one with everything to lose and rushing at it like a fury is not the way to do it. That way mistakes are made. That way disaster lies. Be patient, Sophie MacDonald, take your time and savour all that comes your way. Every hour, every minute, every single, solitary second.

Tis the stuff that life is made of.

LXV

Am I going completely mad?

Yes, I think I am. Obsessive, that's what I've become, a bloody obsessive! Why else would I spend every waking hour thinking and thinking and thinking about one thing? Try as I might, I just can't shut it out. And it doesn't help that this ache is almost a pain now. It's like a toothache of the groin. And it hurts *so* much. I can't go on like this. 'No' was all he said. No. How bloody *dare* he treat me like this? Like some kind of object that he can just toss aside when it suits him. Pick me up, put me down. I'm a toy. I'm his toy. To play with as and when he pleases.

But what to do?

Well, if you got an itch, scratch it. I tried fiddling about, you know, down there, but it all seemed so pathetic. Each time I cum, it doesn't get *close* to doing the job. It's like a damp squib. Pointless and depressing. So, Friday night me and Emms are going out and this gal is getting laid, no matter what. I don't want to, I *really* don't want to do this, but I have nothing else. There *is* no choice.

I meet Emms in the usual bar but with a proviso that we are *not* hitting the Bozo Palace that we normally frequent. Come on Emms, why do we have to head for the usual haunts every time? In fact, why do we have to head for a club at all? There are plenty of bars that stay open late. Places that charge through the nose for a certain exclusivity. You don't have to slum it *every* weekend Emms. Not on my account, anyway!

So we find ourselves in some kind of Dude Palace instead. All background music and subdued lighting. What manner of wee beasties live here, I wonder? Well, never was there a more apt description of a beastie than 'lounge lizard'. Smooth, smarmy, shiny, scaly, slippery, slithering. Every time one opens its mouth, I expect to see a forked tongue flicker. It's the kinda place that John Smith would call 'home'. Well into the thirty-something generation. Too crap to have landed a woman in their go-getting twenties and now desperately trawling for meat at the local abattoir. I feel sick scanning the room and taking it all in. Ewww. I couldn't, I really couldn't. Not with *these* specimens. I'm already wishing that H was here to take me in hand. But that's defeatist. H isn't here. H won't be here. But if I want, no I *need*, this itch scratched......

So me and Emms settle for just one drink, coz I'm pretty sure that's about all I can take and I'm pretty sure that Emms is of the same mind given the way she's miming sticking her fingers down her throat, and all, but as we approach the bar we have to squeeze in past two guys who just won't give us enough room, gentlemen that they are, and they think that that's an excuse to start a conversation along the vein of - nice of you to rub up against me there, loverly lady, and what might your names be and do allow me to buy those drinks for you and, if you also let me fondle your breasts, I promise that I won't ooze too much slime all over your delightful body ......flicker, flicker.....

'Don't even bother' is what he gets from Emms, who was never one to take any bull from a bloke, but even as we wander off to find as seat, it's seconds out, round two and the next lizard slides into position beside me. Hi my name's Richard, 'Ricardo' to my friends, and I was just saying to my friend over there (*indicating lizard numero dos*) that I was pretty sure that I hadn't seen you two laydees in here before because, if there's one thing that old Ricardo never forgets, it's a bee-u-diful face.' I stare at him blankly. There's a long silence as even Emms seems lost for words. A whole crowd of responses are buzzing around my brain. 'Des bons mots' to lay this insult to our intelligence to waste, a witty riposte, some clever repartee. Which shall I chose? ..... Ah, yes, I know.....

'Why don't you just FUCK OFF!?'

Loud enough for many heads to turn. *Subdued* music. Oooops. Nice one Sophie. *Slight* over reaction.

He's shocked. Emms is shocked. So am I, a little. What came over me? I don't know. What I do know is that I am not taking this crap anymore. Treat me like an intelligent human being or don't bother.

But 'Fuck off' seems to work, and he wriggles off to join his fellow reptile. 'Couple of dykes', his predictable, parting response.

I turn to Emms, 'please tell me I'm hallucinating. *Please*.'

There's a guy standing at the bar with a big grin on his face. I guess he's witnessed the whole thing. I glare at him then stick my tongue out and the grin turns into a full blown laugh. There's something about him that seems familiar and he doesn't seem to fit in round here. He's with another guy who's more interested in the bottles behind the bar than what's going on on the other side of it. Not their usual haunt, is my guess. But he's caught my eye, so much so that even when I'm chatting with Emms, I'm barely listening to her and my eyes keep coming back to him. Sometimes he's looking at me, sometimes not. Not pushy, then. Not louche either, more 'laid back'. Casual. Nice looking, too. Fit.

What the hell, and I'm on my feet.

'Mine's a dry, white wine ..... if you're buying' I add with a cheeky grin.

'Really?' he looks pensive for a moment, then '.....looks like I'm buying then, doesn't it?'

YES!

'Brilliant entertainment' he adds after placing the order and turning back to face me. 'Must've taken alot of thought putting that little put down together' and he smiles again. He's not criticising me....seems like he understands that sometimes the right words will not come and that, in this case, wit really would've been wasted on the recipient anyway.

So I say, 'I'll think of something better, later. Never one to rush things.' Now at this point I'd expect some kinda lewd innuendo from the usual suspects – 'Like to take your *time*, do you, tee hee' ..but, no ..... instead 'Isn't that the definition of repartee....what you *wish* you'd said?' ... and I remember that one and smile at the memory. So he's smart too. I like.

'And I'm betting you're not a regular here, either' ...meaning he's not, too. Good.

'I don't have the requisite crocodile shoes.' I lie, coz I do. Thank F I'm not wearing them.

And so we're chatting away and time seems to pass easily, his mate still wedded to the bottles behind the bar and then he says –

'You've changed, you know? ....in the last year or so.'

I look at him blankly coz I have no idea what he's talking about now. 'And how would *you* know?'

'*Really* don't expect you to remember....but we've seen each other before.' Why does he look familiar?

'Ofcourse, it's the tongue I recognised first' oh yeah? here we go..... 'You must stick it out an awful lot.' Here's hoping I have my quizzical face on right now coz I have no idea where this conversation is going, but I've a nasty suspicions it's gonna turn crude. 'Because the last time I saw you, that's exactly what you were doing.... or was I just lucky?'

Now I'm racking my brains trying to place him. Then it hits me. The blind man... on the way to work....my first day .... then the guy that laughed at me. Oh shit. 'But that was *ages* ago. How could you possibly.........'

He shrugs. 'Some people you just don't forget' and I know that this is a come on, but I let it pass. He *did* actually remember, after all. That bit wasn't fake. 'I was late for work' I volunteer, without knowing why. 'First day.' First day, Sophie... and I feel maudlin again. 'Looks like you could do with another,' he hastens to add, catching my change in mood. I look round. Emms? Where's Emms? 'She left about half an hour ago.' 'You're kidding me?' 'Gave a wave and left...I guess she must think you're safe in my hands.' 'Am I? Am I really?' He looks me square in the eyes and says 'Yeah, I think so. Question is, am I safe in yours?' and he laughs again.

And so do I.

*

My flat. No messing this time. I want. He wants. My arms round his neck. He's tall. My legs around his waist. He's strong. And I'm whispering in his ear, come on baby, come on, I want it hard, I want it fast, just fuck me silly... and the clothes are coming off and he's got me down on the bed and we're playing with each other til we're both really ready, til we can't wait anymore and then he's on me we're going like rabbits, and shit that feels good, that's it, go deep baby, deep and hard, and oh yes, yes – god I need this and then I want me on top and god that feels good too, hmmm mm. Yes, indeed. And then I find myself instinctively holding my hands in the small of my back, as I ride and I ride, because deep down that's what I really want, I want to be .... restrained! Oh Sophie, what *are* you thinking? I'm thinking.....I want....I want..........

I want Henry Blythe.

'I'm sorry...I'm sorry...I'm *sooo* sorry...' and I'm standing in the middle of my bedroom, bent double, trying to cover my nakedness 'I can't, I just can't. I'm sorry.' And the look of total horror on my new lover's face, I'm scaring him and he doesn't deserve this. He doesn't deserve any of this. And he's trying to comfort me, his arm around me, with his cock still standing strangely to attention. All shiny. Oh dear. It's OK. It's OK. Really hey, come and sit down, he has both arms around me now and he rolls me onto the bed and curls himself around me and pulls the covers over us both.

Sleep doesn't come easily ..... partly due to the stiffy sticking in my back.

*

Bed has become my refuge. I spend pretty much all weekend there. On my own. My lover left first thing. I told him I thought it for the best. He didn't argue.

We didn't exchange details. We both knew we would never meet again.

I never even knew his name.

He never knew mine.

*

Monday morning and I'm not going anywhere. Work can go fuck itself, so to speak.

Tuesday morning I venture out. To the launderette of all places. Just sit there for hours watching the tumble dryers churning their multi-coloured loads.

Before I realise that all my dirty clothes are back at the flat.

Bugger!

LXVI

Oh god, what have I done?

Have I really done this? I want to reach out and touch her. To comfort. But I can't and she knows that I can't. So we sit with this chasm between us, neither knowing what to say.

A cold? Nice try, Sophe, but I don't think so. Red eyes. Sore nose. You could've got away with it. But I know you too well …. just not well enough, eh? It's that distant look in your eyes. This goes much deeper.

This damage is down to you matey, it's your responsibility. You have to make it better. Make it right. And bloody quick.

'Look, why don't you take some time off? Take some more sick leave, maybe tack some holiday leave on the end of it. You've been working hard lately, bit of R and R could do you the power…. Hell, we could all do with some for that matter.' I pause. Then say quite deliberately, 'Could do with a bit of a break myself.'

Sophie's head turns slowly to face me. There is a spark back in her roadmap eyes. Hope in her voice. 'Yeah?' 'Yeah. I don't know, a ….. spa break, erm….cottage in the country?' and even *I* can't keep the stress out of the first syllable of my final word. She bites her bottom lip. I want to bite her bottom lip too.

'Well, maybe……'

'Look, why don't I come up with some suggestions for you? Hey, I could even get *you* some brochures this time. That'd be a turn up…' and I'm already imagining a thatched cottage, miles from anywhere, with Sophe back to her old self, somewhere where we can make as much noise as we like, where Sophe can make as much noise as I can make her. Just her and me. I have to do this. I have been unbelievably careless with someone close to me, closest to me. I forgot that I have Sarah to fall back on and share my bed with. Who does Sophe have? For all I know, no-one at all. And let's face it, I don't know because I know next to nothing about her. And I *should* know, shouldn't I? So I just leave her to get on with it. But this is not a game anymore, Mr Blythe……

And I cannot believe my rank stupidity.

*

After Sophe has taken her leave, I have some serious thinking to do. Forget spa breaks. Hotels. Too public. But the cottage, miles from anywhere, now that really *does* appeal. A whole weekend, just the two of us. Weekend? Hmmm...maybe not. How am I going to explain to Sarah that I'm going away at the weekend...on my own. She'd only suggest coming too. And while the sexual connotations of the three of us together are somewhat arousing.......no! Get a grip. This is no time to joke. Those days are long gone.

What if I said I just wanted to take some time out? On my own. Go for a drive. See where it takes me. She knows I've been under pressure of late. But it still risks her wanting to come too. It's not like me to scoot off on my own. It'd be out of character. Too risky. No, it'll have to be mid week. A work trip. A *fake* work trip. She'd never know the difference. Except I can't really take real time off during the week. We're so busy. So back to the bloody weekend.

Hey, what about a lads weekend away? Yeah, me and Nick. Ermm .... fishing. Haven't been fishing for years. Which is going to look odd. And it'll mean I have to bring Nick into wee the conspiracy too. That is *not* a good idea. Too risky.

So we're back to the mid week work jaunt. On my own. I almost never go on my own. Will it look odd if Sarah finds out I've gone by myself? Maybe....but maybe not. Let's face it, her recent suspicions surrounded me going away with a *woman*. If I'm on my own, there's no reason to .... Yeah, but what if work wants to contact me and tries me where I *say* I'm going and finds I'm not there. No. Not much chance of that...and even if they did, I'll just make an excuse that there was some kind of cock up. Message never got through. I'll just have to risk it. And even though I don't like risk, in this instance I really have no choice.

And I find a fantastic place...late deal...Monday, three nights. It's expensive but Sophie is worth it. More than worth it. It's almost a damned castle, ferfucksake. She'll be thrilled.

And I wonder whether or not it has a dungeon.

*

As it always seems to do when you have something else to look forward to, the weekend dragged and dragged. Sarah had brought files home with her and spent most of her time engrossed in work. I whiled away the time browsing newspapers and daydreaming about times past and the week ahead. My recurrent reverie was of Sophie in an extended spanking session, bent over my knee. The sexual arousal that it caused, however, was less than welcome. Sure, Sarah was there and I'm sure that she would have been happy to indulge me, but I couldn't. I was saving myself. So I found myself making the age old excuse of being too tired and Sarah joked that

I had been burning the candle at both ends and I thought many a true word, my darling, picturing *my* candle with two ends .... in use at the same time.

*

    Rule one. Never write anything down. I broke it. I had to get a message to Sophie so I dropped off a note. Printed. Unidentifiable. Untraceable. But a broken rule nonetheless.

    'Monday. 10 a.m. Be there.'

LXVII

'Ohmygaaaaaard!' I say it again. And again. 'Like it?' 'Are you kidding me?' and I'm almost out of the car before it has come to a stop. And I'm running every which way, looking up, looking down and all around at the leaded glass windows, the tower, the battlements, the turrets. The *turrets,* ferfucksake. 'It has turrets! Where's the moat? Is there a moat?' 'Must have filled it in.' 'What, no drawbridge?' and then I'm bent double laughing and laughing and H has this grin as wide as a mile which just blows me away. So I run up to him, throw my arms around his neck and plant a big smackeroo on his lips. 'This is perfect.'

And I'm off again begging to be let inside, while H is unloading the car, dragging my bag out of the boot. Well, OK, my suitcase...well, OK, my *trunk*. Hell, I didn't know how long we were going away for. The note didn't say...so I spent all weekend washing and ironing pretty much everything I have and just packed it anyway.

All except my panties, of course. Those I will *not* be needing!

And then we are inside and there's this massive hall and when I say massive I mean, like, totally huge! And a huge staircase, too, kinda flowing around the walls in a great cascade of dark wooden steps with a deep red carpet and I can imagine myself gliding down them in a long, long ball gown and a diamond necklace and maybe even a tiara and all eyes are on this gorgeous, sophisticated woman and H will be waiting for me at the bottom of the stairs but we both know that I won't get that far because he'll come bounding up to me, hitch up that long, long gown and say....... 'What, no panties? You naughty, *naughty* girl!'

So I get the grand tour, the dining room with this long oak dining table that could seat twenty plus people, but just for the two of us, the kitchen with its range cooker that you could roast half a cow in, the drawing room ... with not a crayon in sight, and wafting up that long, long staircase to the bedroom with its massive four-poster bed which I leap onto and bounce up and down while H watches and smiles and I spy the four posts in turn and look at H, then look back at the four posts and I just know what he's thinking and I know that *he* knows what I'm thinking and I just say 'Oh, yes perlease!!'

And I bound over to him and throw my arms around his neck again and try to drag him over to the bed begging him to do me here and now. But he's not moving an inch, just looks down at me and says 'Wait'...but I can't....I can't wait Henry .... you've seen what waiting does to me – coz I want him to feel guilty – but the bastard's having none of it, 'You'll do as you're told young lady. Understood?'

'Yes sir.' I reply, then he just picks me up, throws me over his shoulder and marches off down the stairs.

So we're in the kitchen and all the goodies that H has brought with him are laid out on the kitchen table, loads of luscious food, fresh, tinned, frozen, chilled all of which I pile into the fridge or line up on the worktop and there's a whole case of different wines and a bottle of his favourite Napoleon and then he says let's go for a walk coz it's a lovely afternoon as we're now in the middle of a heatwave and the heat as we leave the cool of the big house fair takes my breath away, but I have a light summer dress on now and a wide brimmed hat made of straw, or something like that, and H is looking so fine in a white open necked shirt and he still has a wee bit of a tan, even after all these weeks. And we walk the grounds, our grounds, we hold and squeeze each other's hands, but that's all. Nothing more, coz H has said so, but I know it won't be long now. I know what's coming. Know that *I'll* be cumming.

Not long now.

We wander off the grounds immediately around the house, down a long path through some woods which then opens into a view from a picture book. Wide open fields sloping down to a small river all blanketed by heat haze. It's like a dream. H breathes in deeply and exhales loudly.

'Stand and stare', he says.

And I do. It's beautiful.

'Here' says H. 'We'll have a picnic here. Tomorrow maybe. And when we've finished...... Right here.' I look agog at H, but he's off into the distance. 'Outdoors? Naked?' My questions met by a slow nod. 'I've *never......*'

As he turns, '....then it's time you did,' and strides off, leaving me with that growing ache again, making me squeeze my thighs together. Mmmmmm...........

Getting down that long path with this ache was hard enough, getting back is going to be torture. And if you're ever tried walking with your knees tied together, you'd know.....

I shoulda brought some knickers, after all.

LXVIII

The timing is perfect. Not often we get stinking hot days like this. Have to make the most of them. It won't last. Never does.

I'm so pleased with Sophie's reaction to this place. Her excitement is intoxicating. It makes my heart swell. It also makes something else swell. I've been in a state of semi-arousal for hours, ever since Sophe climbed aboard the Country Express and started stroking my thigh and got carried away ... until I told her to stop. Added to that, she's been running around all afternoon in that flimsy, see-through dress with nothing on underneath. She doesn't think I *know* there's nothing underneath, but I do. It doesn't leave a whole lot to the imagination. And all I've wanted to do was tear it piece by piece from her body and then ravish her where she stands. And I know she wants this. But she will have to wait.

Not long now, my sweet.

*

The rest of the afternoon we are indulging in some cookery lessons and I'm showing Sophe how to chop and cut and whisk and boil and simmer and season and we're sampling wines by the large glass and getting just a *little* bit tipsy and I'm telling her how to aerate the wine and watch that ruby liquid swirl around the glass and the legs that hang down from the rim (*they're very skinny legs, H!*), then draw the aromas deep into the sinuses where all the receptors explode the senses and to recognise all the different nuances before even a drop has passed her lips and when that first sip reaches her tongue to draw in air to heighten the flavours and savour, Sophie, *savour* every drop before swallowing and leaving that lingering velvety texture in the mouth, still tasted long after it is gone.

So she lifts her glass to the light, then drains it in two gulps and says 'Mmmmm, nice. More please.'

Oh well.

And, for some reason, it occurs to me that 'pearls down fishes throats' can have two *very* different meanings. But more of that later......

There are also what Sophe calls 'moments'. Several of them .... when our eyes meet and I can feel the heat from her body and I'm drinking in her perfume and our lips are oh so close. But I let them pass and so does Sophe, because I think she now knows that this is part of the game. The prelude.

By six there is a palpable current, charged and sparking....and not just between the two of us.

For the last hour, an ominous rumble has rippled and creased and crumpled the air. Then large spots appear on the ground outside the window and fairly soon after that there is a steady fall of heavy rain. Sophie stands there, staring out of the window 'looks like someone wants to rain on our parade, H'. I join her, threading both arms around her waist, and peering out over her shoulder. 'Can't hurt us in here, hun. Take alot more than a little thunder to mess up this wee jaunt.'

Just then a huge flash and an almost immediate explosion. I feel a shiver run through her and she wants to turn away, but I don't let her, holding her tighter. 'That was close,' she breathes. And the rain rapidly becomes torrential.

As Sophie runs off to get changed for dinner the storm rumbles and rushes on. By the time she breezes into the dining room, all is laid out before her. She looks amazing in a dark blue, velvet mini dress that she must have sprayed on. Selfishly, I want her there and then but we both now know that that isn't going to happen.

'This is all very dramatic, H. Did you lay on the storm all special, like?'

'I try my best,' I admit.

'Oh, H, you're too, *too* modest.'

'I know, my sweet, I know.' And toast her with a glass of blood red wine....and she toasts me back from the other end of the long, long table.

The next hour or so is pure self indulgence, until I throw down my napkin and announce, 'Tis time, my child' then rise walk over to her side and offer her my arm. There is a sparkle in her eyes. 'Let me escort you to my bed chamber, my sweet, where I like to indulge in all manner of gross indecencies.'

'Oh sir,' she responds 'pray tell, what gross indecencies are these of which you speak? I am eager to learn of such things.'

'Patience, my child. Patience.'

*

She is standing in the middle of the room, close to the foot of the bed, and I circle her. 'Well well, young lady, I must say that you are looking most comely, tonight. And what manner of delights do you barely conceal beneath your outer garments? Hmmm?'

'Well sir, I have no further attire beneath....' I give a sharp intake of breath, '....save for my garter belt with which I retain my stockings, sir.'

'Well my lady, thou art well and truly a wee slattern, art thou not?'

'I do try, sir, I do try.'

'....and we both know what happens to little sluts, don't we my sweet?'

'I believe that harsh punishments are in order, sir. Severe and without mercy.'

'You are most astute, young lady......' and I'm turning towards a chest by the window and opening the top drawer, '....for punishment will indeed be most severe,' and I turn again to reveal a riding crop, gripped tightly between both fists, and I proceed to bend and unbend it slowly, then slap the leather keeper against one open palm. I restrain myself from giving an evil cackle.

'Oooh, sir.' And there is a slight quaver to her voice, as her eyes widen.

'But first, my child, I must inspect the recipient of tonight's chastisement. Disrobe....' and she does so. Quickly. '...hmmm, most comely, most comely indeed.' Comely, my arse, she looks simply stunning and I keep circling her, taking her all in, running the tip of the crop up and down her naked flesh, her breath coming in short gasps. 'I must ask you to recline in order to dispense my justice. On to the bed' and she's there in a flash, but sitting, uncertain what to do. I lean forward.

'Face down, my sweet,' my eyes widening, '....face down,'

On cue, there is another rumble of thunder.

LXIX

So, I'm lying there, watching H over my shoulder as he's back at the chest of drawers. The drawer is still open. He has more goodies. Handcuffs. *Please* let it be the handcuffs. But no, he has a handful of black things that I can't quite make out. Black tubes with red interiors. And then he has my wrist and is wrapping one around it and doing up a buckle and I see that it is some kind of leather bracelet with a padded interior, so I guess that I *kinda* got my wish. These look new. Never been used before. I'm the first. They are attached to chains which he then fixes to the four posters of the bed until I am spread-eagled, exposed and helpless.

I love it.

'Well, well, my sweet, do you feel suitably restrained?' I wriggle but can barely move.

'Why sir, I feel that you can now administer my punishment without any fear of interruption.' Nope. None whatsoever.

Woo hoo!

He drags the leather bit at the end of this whip thing up and down my back then over my bum and between my legs. 'Sir, much more of this behaviour, I swear that I shall become a veritable torrent!' Was that a whimper, Sophie MacDonald? Yes, I think it was.

'Enough, my sweet' and the first stroke comes down.

'Oh shit!'

And I let out a cry coz I expect it to hurt a bit, but that is a shock. And then the second. Shiiit! And I'm wriggling and writhing, fighting against my restraints but failing to avoid any of the blows, and on cue, the lightning streaks outside and the thunder rumbles on and after the next stroke, I start to get this warm feeling and it isn't just what's happening to my bum, though that has *alot* to do with it......

'Pray tell, young wench....' Wench? Hey, what happened to 'lady'? '...do my punishments suffice?'

'Sir, your administrations have been most plentiful....' I pant, barely catching my breath. Damned right they have! '....and indeed my cheeks must be fair rosy (fair rosy? They must be cut to bloody shreds!), but I think that maybe just a couple strokes more should complete the task at hand.' I'm not giving up *just* yet.

'Hmmm, maybe not....' What? I ask for more and you *don't* give it to me? What the.....

'You bastard!' and the words are out before I realise it. He leans in close, mouth by my ear, 'Didst I hear the lady correctly? That she is becoming ......' and his voice reduces to a whisper, '.....too lippy for her *own fucking good*?' And he pulls back and winks. Thanks for that H. Now I know he's onside with this and my stifled smile tells him I'm OK with it too. Coz then he's undoing my shackles and turning me over and fixing me to the posts again. Face up.

And his mouth is back by my ear, as he crouches over me like some bird of prey, in for the kill, and again whispers '...and it is said that, despite my copious strokes, the lady is *still* a complete slut. Do I hear the truth?'

'Prithee sir, I fear that your administrations have failed to flush the slattern from my being. I fear further punishments may be necessary to rid me of this affliction....' that *affliction* of needing a 'bloody good seeing to'. Oh please H, enough of the playing........ I'm fit to burst! 'I think maybe the ministering of a Right Royal Rogering would assist greatly, sir.' I want what you did to me last time, H, when you made my body explode and left me a gibbering wreck. That's what I want.

'The lady makes such *bold* suggestions...' and his mouth is on my neck, where he learnt, so early on, that I just squirm with delight, and he bites and nibbles and his tongue traces the contours of my throat, and I luxuriate in this, down onto my chest, onto my belly. Tongue and teeth. Then just teeth. Then to where my legs lie forcibly spread for him. And that's when I really start to thrash and scream, because I can feel the heat and humidity from his breath, so close to where I want his lips and his tongue. And I'm arching my back, thrusting my hips upwards, straining against my leash, begging, please, please Henry, pleeeeease. And he moves his lips further down.........yes, yes, YES!!

And then the world explodes.

And the lights go out.

And the sky falls in.

LXX

'What the FUUUUCK....?!

And I'm kneeling on the bed and I know that Sophe is somewhere on the bed in front of me, because I was just about to..... but now I'm crouching here in the dark and I'm covered in all sorts of crud and I'm dripping wet and there's a hurricane in the room as the windows have blown open and suddenly Sophie is screaming my name and she's thrashing around as much as she can and I'm trying to calm her down, kneeling over her, and she's wet too and covered in heaven knows what and it's OK baby, shhh, shhh, calm down it's OK. I'm here. Henry's here .... and though I realise that I sound trite, her fear subsides and she stops shaking and sobbing long enough to ask.....

'What the *fuck* just happened?'

I'm at a loss, but know I have to get the windows shut so I can get something lit in here as the only lighting is the lightning outside and that is barely enough to get me across the room to the window without crashing into something. So I tell Sophe what I'm going to do and try the switches first.

All circuits are dead.

Waiting for another flash in the sky, I head for the chest again. A candle, a torch? Nothing in any drawer. And then I turn and take in the whole scene and briefly see the gaping blackness where the ceiling used to be, as the sky lights up again and Sophie, oh my god, Sophie stretched out beneath, covered in crumbled plaster and water and I have to get her off of there, so I stride across the room and I'm so angry that it has come to this, this is just so *fucking* typical and I punch the bed post nearest me with the ball of my hand so damned hard and there's a crack and the sound of wood creaking and splintering and then ....

LXXI

'Henry?'

'Henry!'

'HENRYYYYYY!!!!'

And I'm shaking and screaming and struggling coz just after H loses his temper and thumps the bedpost, there's this god awful noise and a crunch and stuff falling and then this dead weight lands on top of me pinning me even more to the bed than I already am and then I lose it coz I just know it's H who's on top of me, even though I can't see anything and I'm screaming and screaming his name but no-one is answering. No-one is coming to help.

And then I freeze as the light flashes round the room and I take in all around me in that split second.

There's a bloody big hole in the ceiling. Most of the ceiling is on top of me. Henry is on top of me. There a big chunk of wood on top of Henry. Henry is not moving. Henry might be dead.

Henry might be dead.

.......and it's then that my hysterics switch from fear to sorrow and I just cry and cry .... oh, Henry, please don't be dead. Please don't be.... please wake up and I blub uncontrollably for I don't know how long until the reality of my predicament begins to dawn.

Henry might be dead. He might be alive. If he's alive he needs help. I'm the only one here that can help him. I'm underneath Henry and I can't move him off me to help him..... because .... I'm manacled to the sodding bed and can't move anyway.

Merde!

Merde and fuck!

Think, woman, think! I try to listen for his breathing but there's too much noise around to hear much else. The rain is still coming in through the roof and I'm getting cold. H is keeping me warm, just a little, but if he's dead he'll start to turn cold soon, won't he? I don't want to die under a corpse. I don't want to die here. Manacled to a bed wearing nothing but suspenders and stockings with a corpse on top of me.

What will mum think?

And I start to cry again, just small sobs, coz I can't see a way out, but I think better of trying to break my restraints again. I could bring the whole bloody house down at this rate. So I just lie there, trying to ignore the cold whilst straining to listen for signs of life. *Any* signs of life.

There's no blood that I can see. That has to be a good sign, doesn't it? I mean, at least he's not going to bleed to death. Internal bleeding? A blood clot. On the brain. That could kill him, couldn't it?

Oh Henry, please wake up. Pleeease.

Another age goes by...it could be ten minutes, it could be an hour. I don't know, but the storm has passed and the wind has died down and the night seems a little warmer, so I'm not so cold.

Just stuck.

I'm still close to tears, but too angry to cry anymore. I mean, come on, what was about to happen? His mouth was *that* close! I was *that* turned on. My bum was stinging like hell, but *that* was good, my wrists were tied to the bed and *that* was good too (who'm I kiddin'? It was fucking *glorious*!) and then what happens?

Nature dumps a ton of shite on me.

Well thank you *very* much!

Do you know, I mean, do you actually *know* how long I have waited for this night? Well, I'll tell you shall I? Five weeks and three days and about 4 hours, but OK, right now the four hours is anyone's guess.

And where do I end up? Writhing in restrained sexual ecstacy as my lover brings me off for the fourth time that night? No. Begging and begging and begging to be spanked or whipped or caned? No. Swinging from the chandelier with a nice, hard cock up my bum?

No.

Tied naked to a bed with half the roof and a dead body on top of me.

Yes.

Marvellous. Just sodding *marvellous*!

Then I'm shocked to realise that the whole of this tirade has been said out loud.

Oh well, who gives a fuck anymore?

I know I don't.

*

There's a faint glimmer of light in the room. An almost imperceptible lessening of darkness. I look up and the sky is no longer black. Now a dark, dark grey.

Dawn.

I look down at the body on top of me. Studying its outline. Oh Henry, I'd hold you if I could. Even if you're dead, I still would.

And then.....no? Surely not. My eyes strain so hard that I'm getting a headache, or is that from my arms being stretched so hard above my head for god knows how many hours? I can't tell...but I thought.....

Yes!

His chest is rising and falling. He's breathing! Soft sighs blending with the morning breeze. Come on, H, wake up babe...wake up! This is no time to sleep, damn you. I've been stuck here for bloody hours, not a wink all night. Alright for some isn't it? But the anger is brief. It's masking relief.

I try a nudge with my leg. Movement is restricted, and I'm numb with cold, but I get a wee shove in. A grunt. That's it babe. Another push.... a snort. Yes.....

Then another.

LXXII

Ooooooh.

Another bloody hangover! But this one's a killer. Dear Christ! What was I *drinking*? Wine and whisky? The grape and the grain. Must've been. Guaranteed brain damage. So I lie here concentrating on the thump, thump of brain against the inside of my skull somewhere near where the top of my spine enters my cranium. Thump, thump. And I feel sick too. A gentle rocking motion is doing my stomach no favours. Really don't want to throw up. Not now. And a voice... 'Henry? ...Henry....?' Sophe? Shhhh, Sophie, babe. Not now, hun. Feeling a bit nauseous. Terrible head. But the rocking continues, something pressing into my stomach. 'Henry, please wake up.' Time for breakfast? Hmmm....couldn't eat a thing babe, feeling a little dicky this morning.

Eh? Something wrong here. Waking up with Sophie? Can't be right. Where the hell am I? Work trip. Must be. Too much booze, back to her room for some serious naughtiness. Henry you bad, bad...... In which case, why have I got all my clothes on? Hmmm. Can't have been much naughtiness going on. Don't tell me we didn't get round to doing the dirty deed. With Sophie? Criminal waste that, matey. Criminal. But I seem to be a bit wet? And cold. Hmmmm, maybe we *did* do the deed after all. Wet sex? Oh, Henry, mate! Really? Been a looooong time since you last......

Thump, thump. Oooooooh.... and I hear myself groan. Shhh, Henry... got a bit of a head this morning. And there seems to be something on my back. Eh? Something heavy. Well that's going to have to go, head or no head. I try to shift it. Hmmm. Bit of a prob here. Doesn't seem to want to let me.

Best to get your bearings first. Open your eyes. That's not so bad. Still pretty gloomy. No bright lights. And I'm staring right into Sophie's beautiful eyes, which seem to be very watery, but she is smiling which is just a wonderful way to start the day.

'Morning babe.' She bites her bottom lip. I want to bite her bottom lip too.

'Morning.' she squeaks back me and a tear rolls down the side of her face and disappears into her hair.

'You got a bit of a headache, too?' She nods. 'Did we overdo it a bit last night?'

'Yes' and now she's quietly laughing, 'Just a bit!' and then she's jangling her arms and it takes a while to focus on what she means and then I see her wrists and the black leather and.... 'Oh Sophie, you *have* been a bad girl, haven't you?'

'Yes I have. And so have you.' and then she fills me in on last night's antics which explains the headache and this thing on my back and the fact that I don't remember an awful lot but it's all beginning to make sense. Slowly. Very slowly.

But I'm not moving an inch because everything hurts and I need to make sure everything's alright first. So I just lie there and talk as that's all I seem to be able to manage at the moment. I check that Sophie is OK. No bones broken. Need to get those cuffs off her. No sleep all night, poor girl. She's cold. I've been unconscious for hours. Probably got a huge lump on my head. No blood though...not that she can see. Large wooden beam across my back. Not too large to shift. Must have clocked me a right clout.

'OK, I'm going to try to move now, OK?' She nods, lips pressed tightly together. The wooden thing is actually not that heavy and, as I ease myself up, it slides down my back and clonks onto the floor. Suddenly the room is spinning and I slump back down again. 'Oh, shit!' You OK? Yes, I'm OK. Kind of. Concussion. Have to be careful. So I lie here and reach out and unbuckle a cuff with one hand. This lets Sophe release her other wrist. One of her hands is now on my back, the other stroking my hair.

'I can't reach your ankles right now.'

'I know. No hurry. I've had my legs open all night, which was a bit of a waste. A few more minutes won't make much difference.'

I pause, then say.... 'Don't suppose you fancy a sha......'

'Don't even *think* about it!' a pause, then she laughs. I smile. It's all I can do.

'Is that a 'no' then?' She doesn't answer. She doesn't need to. I could lie here for hours, relishing her face, her eyes, her aroma, listening to her soft, mellifluous gaelic tones.... but needs must. I slowly turn my head to face the foot of the bed, barely lifting it clear of the warm, soft belly that it's been resting on. Her waxed and perfectly trimmed mound is inches from my face. I remember now. Last night I was just about to....

Then I reach down, undo the last tethers and she relaxes, flexing her legs, easing them back to life. I close my eyes and try to rub some warmth back into her. Then I find my hand is stroking the fine hairs before me, following the direction that they lay to where they disappear between her slightly parted thighs. This lasts for many, many minutes. Nothing is said. Her breathing is steady and soothing.

And then I explore further. A sigh. A parting of the waves and my tongue joins my fingers. A gasp. Steady, rhythmic, hard breathing. She is close now. No escape, my sweet. No escape.

And it comes and comes again. And again. And then slowly dies.

Sex and death, Henry, sex and death.

She is asleep within seconds. I drag a blanket over the both of us, wrap myself around her and then so am I.

LXXIII

The sun is high in the sky by the time I wake. I have no idea what the actual time is, but I'm guessing around one. Getting out of bed is like prising an old toffee from its wrapping. Pulling myself free from Henry's arms and shaking lumps of broken and dried on plaster from my hair, face and body.

The room is a mess. The window is still open and the curtains hang wet and lank, barely moving in the breeze. My dress is on the floor where I dropped it. It's wet through. Ruined. Just like me, I think. I hang it up over the huge bathtub in the hope that I can resurrect it. Some hope. Maybe I could ask for a refund? I still have the receipt.

There's a large walk–in shower which I turn on to let it run hot. At least that works. After removing the vestiges of last night's excesses, I step beneath the steaming cascade. And just stand there. The heat easing back into my body, loosening muscles and tensions, washing all the crap away.

Later, I rummage through the selection of goodies in the kitchen, an overwhelming hunger hitting me hard. I need food. I need hot food. My core is chilled and I can't get warm. Not properly. Hmmmm.....quails eggs on toast with a caviar topping. Slumming it again.

Then I hear a creak on the staircase and I call 'Henry?' When there is no answer, I wander out into the hall and find him sitting halfway down, leaning against the banister rails, eyes closed. I rush up to sit next to him... 'I'm not well' is all he says.

'We have to get you to a hospital, H. As soon as....'

'You'd better drive me. Don't think I can. Might pass out.'

'I can't do that, H.' He opens his eyes and hits me with that quizzical stare of his. He thinks I'm abandoning him. 'I can't do that, Henry, coz I *can't* drive! I never learned.' I pause 'If we had a bicycle, I could sling you over the crossbar,' I quip, trying to lighten the load, but I know instantly that it's inappropriate.

'Or in the basket on the front?!' he manages, all the while I'm stroking his hair, then I feel this bump, this terrible lump on the back of his head, and although there is no blood, not even dried on, I know that this is serious and I have to do something.

'I'd better phone for an ambulance.'

'Can't. No phone. Miles from anywhere. No reception. No landline. No contact. 'S why I chose it. Isolated. Just the two of us. Nearest village is miles away. Take hours to walk. Make all the noise we want. No-one will hear.'

You're not kidding, I thought. I screamed the house down last night and no-one heard a bloody thing. Not even you, and you were on top of me!

'What are we going to do, H?'

'Nothing we can do. Stay here. Get better til I'm well enough to drive, then go and see a doctor. We should be OK. Bed's a write off, mind. Might have to sleep down here. Plenty of supplies. We won't starve.'

No, H, we won't starve, but you might just die of a brain haemorrhage.

H accepts my offer of food, hot food, and I guide him down to the kitchen and sit him at the table and make us a meal. It's not much, but my mum did teach me a few tricks. He eats. It's slow and deliberate. I can see that something is missing. Something is not quite there. He tells me that the first twenty four hours are crucial with head injuries. His friend, Nick, had a bad bang years ago when playing rugby and that's what *he* was told. I ask him if that's why Nick dribbles the way he does and he says yes, it probably is. 'You just have to keep an eye on me, that's all. Not that you can do much if things go wrong, but.....'

He said the nearest village is miles away. But I'm not going anywhere. Not now.

Not ever.

*

The rest of the evening is spent on the sofa. Most of the lighting is working downstairs but we fill the room with candles anyway. Henry is seated, I am lying flat out with my head in his lap. There is no other entertainment, which suits us fine, and we just talk and talk. Or rather I talk. H says he would rather just listen. He finds my voice soothing. A comfort. Henry has changed into some casual clothes. I'm in a bathrobe coz I couldn't be bothered to dress in anything vaguely formal and, again, that suits both of us fine, coz H has his hand between my legs and strokes and caresses me as I ramble on. Anything more energetic is out of the question, which is a shame, but what he is doing is lovely, unrushed, tender and it's over an hour before I cum.

LXXIV

Sophie's voice is lovely to listen to, but soon my mind wanders on to other matters.

I have a real problem here. Assuming that I am fit enough to drive tomorrow, I have to get to a hospital. X-ray, scan, whatever. I then have to contact the agent and report the damage. They will want to come and inspect the property and I'll have to explain what happened and try to cover up the fact that I was badly hurt. Why? Because injury means compensation. And compensation means legal action and that I cannot get involved in, and, oh shit, then there's Sarah from whom I've now got to conceal a bloody big lump on the back of my head and if she found out how it happened, or I *lied* about how it happened, she'd be the first to pull out the legal files and threaten to sue. Too many questions and all the wrong answers.

These things cannot happen.

*

I'm woken by a blinding headache at some time in the night, still sitting in the same position. My back hurts too. Most of the candles have burnt out. I must have dropped off. Sophie is still in my lap but she's now face down and all I can see is the back of her head moving slowly up and down, but the pleasure that she's giving me is over-ridden by the pain emanating from the back of my skull. 'Sophe, babe,' my voice a hoarse whisper, and I'm stroking her hair 'please, no'. Her face turns towards me, those dark pools for eyes and she's a little hurt, I can tell. 'Don't you like it?' 'It's great babe, but my head.......I don't know...maybe blood pressure or something? It's bad.'

She's horrified.

Suddenly she's up and straddling me, raining kisses over my face and saying sorry over and over and I just wanted to repay the favour and I didn't think that it could do any harm and ...... and somehow she lowers herself onto me so that my erection enters her, but I don't think it was deliberate. It just happened. Because she doesn't move on me at all. Just sits there, head on my shoulder and arms round my neck.

And falls asleep.

*

There's only a small supply of painkillers between us. I dose myself up on them the next morning before we set out because my head still feels like a well spanked arse. I have no idea if I'm fit enough to drive, but I have to take the chance. There is no choice. We have one night left and are due to go home tomorrow. Time is running out. Sophie is insistent that she comes with me, despite my reservations. I don't want to have to explain to anyone what our relationship is. Friend? Daughter? Niece? *Wife?!*

Or maybe 'my submissive-slut mistress, who's half my age'.

Yeah, that oughta do it.

We go to the doctor's first and he recommends the hospital, which is another half hour drive away. He suggests calling an ambulance, thinks under the circumstances that it'd be wise, but that'll take time that I don't want to use up. It'll also leave my car abandoned. I tell him I'll risk it.

Three hours are spent at the hospital before I get the results of my x-ray. Some good news. No fracture. I'm given stronger painkillers and told not to drive once I've taken them, so I keep them til we get back to the rental.

During that wait, I have time to call the agent and tell them about the damage and I can hear that they sound dubious, that I didn't cause it myself until I storm down the phone that unless they think I can conjure up 100,000 volts out of thin air, that maybe, just maybe, they should change their sodding attitude, and when exactly *was* the lightning conductor last checked? I have to bite my tongue to stop myself from telling them that I'd lain unconscious for several hours as a consequence and that perhaps a solicitor's letter might focus their minds...... Nope. Can't go there.

After I explain that I spent the last two nights on the sofa (a small, but necessary lie), they say that they'll be round later and open up another bedroom in the house for me to use for my last night and that maybe some financial compensation is in order, if I'd like to put in a claim. I'd like to tell them to forget it. No amount of money could compensate .... and I mean it. But then why should I make their lives any easier?

*

We're back late afternoon, but the day is not lost thanks to one of those glorious long, summer evenings where the dust rises on swirling, invisible currents and turns the air into a golden haze and the shadows take forever to draw long and jagged.

There's only one night left and so far it's been an unmitigated disaster. We haven't had one, single shag on this 'dirty (weekday) weekend' away, let alone furthered Sophie's training in the marvellous and mysterious world of submission and bondage.

I could cry, really I could.

But all is not lost. And so you find us packing the picnic basket full of the remaining goodies and wines (easy on the booze, Henry ... doesn't mix with the pain killers) in preparation for our trip down the wooded walk to the rural idyll. Although the heat of the day has long passed, there's a persistent, warm fuzz with not even a hint of a cool evening breeze. Sophie is in her light summer dress again. Naked underneath, I have no doubt ... causing definite stirrings in me, despite the opiates. A blanket is laid out beneath a tree and the food and wine arranged and Sophe settles down until I say 'and what do you think *you're* doing young lady?' and she catches my tone and there's a definite gleam in her eye?

'Just sitting down, sir.'

'And did I say that you could?'

'No sir' and she's on her feet in an instant. All coy and demure. Hands clasped behind her back, twisting back and forth like corkscrew..... and biting her bottom lip.

'Now, it *is* a warm evening, my sweet, so I think that we can dispense with the attire, don't you?' The look in her eyes tells me that she had been hoping that I'd say that. No hesitation. In well practiced movements, the dress has fallen to the floor and her sandals slipped off.

Oh, my.

From a shoulder bag that I've been carrying, the black leather wrist cuffs make a re-appearance. Just one pair. I see her falter. I see definite apprehension. She's not sure about this. Given recent events, I'm not surprised. I lean close to her. 'Do you trust me?'

Instantly. 'Yes, sir.'

'Then you have nothing to fear, my sweet.' And she holds out her wrists like the usual suspect. And for my next trick. A rope. She watches, fascinated, as I tie it to the chain linking the two leather cuffs. The other end I throw expertly over an overhanging branch and catch it on the way down. Easing her arms upwards as I pull down on the rope, holding back from raising her arms too far, as I'm sure that they must still be painful from two nights ago. The rope's end is tied to the chain link too. She is suspended. I turn her vista-wards and tell her, as before, to stand and stare, back concave as she leans forward and pushes back her hips, lithe and feline. She does so without a word. Heading back a few paces, I recline on the blanket, slip off my shoes, pour a glass of wine and take in the verdant hedgerows bordering a golden patchwork of fields, the distant hills, the winding river of liquid silver sewing them all together, the sun low and radiant on the far horizon..... and Sophie.

Arcadian perfection, all.

I have no doubt that I shall remember this sight for the rest of my life.

But she must be hungry...thirsty. It has been a long day for both of us, so I rise again and offer her the wine. She accepts and I place the glass gently to her lips and tilt it, the chilled liquid emptying into her mouth, her eyes on mine throughout. When she's finished, 'thank you, sir' in soft, soft tones. 'Hungry?' A nod. A plate of various comestibles appears before her and I feed each tiny piece to her, then more wine and some spills, I think deliberately, onto naked breasts forming tiny rivulets on her pale skin. Her nipples stand proud as they catch a cooling breeze, tiny bumps appearing on once smooth skin. A shiver as I move behind her. She cannot see me, but senses my immediate presence, then feels me as I press myself to her. She can feel my arousal, even through the material, and pushes in tiny movements, goading me on. Slowly I brush her raven hair to one side, exposing the nape of her neck. My mouth descends to where neck meets shoulder. And I bite. Hard.

A stifled scream from deep in her throat, then breathing hard. My tongue follows the contours of her spine, tiny undulations, as I ease myself back to allow my lips to reach the hollow that is now her lower back. And then down between perfect cheeks, still pink with tiny fading welts, as I kneel behind her.......

LXXV

Henry Blythe is a bad man.

Well, I knew that from the *first* time. But frankly if being bad is this good, then that's fine by me. No, let me rephrase that. If being bad is this good, it's bloody brilliant.

Coz I'm standing there, well half standing, half hanging, while this lovely man is doing the most amazing things to me. And it *is* just perfect, coz not only am I *so* turned on, but the summer sun is now low enough in the sky now to hit my naked body and the warmth just adds to it all and the restraint thing just gives me goose bumps coz, try as I might not to, it does actually do it for me. Turns me on even more. And then the view just fades out as I close my eyes, let out an almighty scream and cum.

Wow.

Then I hear H standing up behind me and I think, hmmmm he's gonna hit me with the big stuff now, but instead I hear this kinda of slapping noise and so I struggle to swivel round a bit and see, over my shoulder, H slapping hard at his trousers and I think, hmmmm, that's not right, if there's any slapping to do he should be doing it to *me*, not himself. I never would have had him down as a masochist. That's *my* job.

By now I'm getting a little tingly in the legs, like pins and needles. Must be post-oral sex stress syndrome or something or maybe I've just been standing still too long. And, as I'm watching H doing this little dance, the pins and needles really do start to feel like pins and needles. Owww! Just as I spot H taking his trousers off (yeah!) I look down to see all these little brown specks on my legs and shit these little buggers are *biting* me and it bloody well hurts! And now H is waving his trousers in the air, giving them a damned good shake and then he's slapping his legs like some manic German in leather shorts and a trilby and I start screaming for H to get these wee shites off my legs too, coz they are biting the buggery out of me.

Then H comes running over to me with his cock at half mast and it looks kinda sexy and kinda funny too, but I'm not really in the mood anymore coz I've lifted myself up off the ground to stop anymore of what I'm guessing are ants getting onto my legs and I'm swinging on the rope like a kid on a big rubber tyre. H has come to the rescue and is holding me round my waist and lifting me up so that he can untie the rope but he tells me that me putting all my weight on it has only tied the knot even tighter and he 'can't get the fucking thing undone'.

But he wipes the last of the little buggers off my legs, so at least I'm not getting bitten anymore but I can see that H is, coz he must be standing right on top of the nest and he doesn't even have any trousers on as he's naked from the waist down, the poor man.

He's got his teeth onto the job now and I think the rope is coming undone but then there's these buzzy things around H's mouth, just where all the evidence of what he was just doing to me is. I guess I really must taste sweet, like he says I do, coz I realise that these buzzy things are wasps and I know that wasps like sweet things like jam and that. So he now starts swatting at these wasps whilst trying to get the rope undone with his teeth whilst holding me by the waist whilst being bitten by ants.....so he really has got his hands full, hasn't he?

LXXVI

And just as I finally get the rope off the wrist restraints, I hear this cough. Now I know immediately it's not Sophe because it's not a girly-like cough, it's more of lady-like cough. Well, more like a *man pretending to be a lady*-like cough. So I wheel round just as Sophe falls onto my shoulder so I'm holding her in a sort of fireman's lift.

And there's this woman standing there. Well, harridan would be more accurate. All tweed and brown brogues and straight, grey hair cut like an open-faced crash helmet. And she's carrying a clipboard and on the clipboard is this symbol which suddenly clicks as that of the rental agency and, oh fuck, she's come about the damage and opening up the spare bedroom and I'd completely forgotten about all that.

So my mind is racing.

Damage limitation exercise.

Here I am, standing naked from the waist down with a completely naked, very young woman hanging from my shoulder. In a field. Miles from anywhere. This woman in front of me doesn't know who I am. Not for sure. She can see the rope hanging from the tree and, depending on how long she's been standing there, may well have seen the leather wrist restraints that Sophe was wearing and that the rope had been tied to them. For all I know she may even have been there while I was giving Sophie a damned good lick......

Shit!

She can't see how *old* Sophe is, though, because she's draped over my shoulder with her face halfway down my back. So it *could* be my wife I'm holding on to and the whole situation may not look *quite* so dodgy.

Really?

Then I see that the battleaxe is not looking at me but appears to be examining my right shoulder and so I turn my head to follow her stare and find Sophie's naked bottom an inch from my face....and, on full show, her perfect and recently waxed.....

Oh my!

My first reaction is to hide Sophie's exposed parts, so I put my hand in front of them, blocking off the old bag's view. Only it ends up as more of a slap. On her bottom. So Sophie being Sophie waves her legs in the air and squeals, 'Oooo Mr Blythe, that's it, give me a *really* good spanking. I've been a *very* naughty girl.'

Damage limitation? Who am I kidding?

I'm fucked.

'Mr Blythe, I presume? Mr Henry Blythe?' All I can do is nod. The ants are still biting and a wasp is showing an abnormal amount of interest in my top lip. I'd try to blow it off only, knowing my luck, I'd blow it straight up my left nostril. 'Couldn't help but hear the screaming, so I thought I'd better investigate.' She positively bristles.

'Ants and wasps,' is all I can say in response, through narrowed lips, rubbing the back of one leg with the front of the other, then hopping from foot to foot to emphasise the point.

'Ah.' A pause. 'That will explain the use of the manacles, then?'

Bitch!

'Well your new bedroom is ready, if you'd care to vacate the old one. I've brought a claim form for you, but....' glancing at Sophie's bottom again '......I'm guessing that you *won't* be needing that now.'

Double bitch!!

She turns to go, then 'Oh, and err, if you've no further need of the rope..... erm..... *and* the restraints.....I'm sure that *I* could .... err....' A twitch at one corner of her mouth and off she stalks.

*

The quicker that we get out of here the better. Throughout our little contretemps, I've been standing on the bloody ants nest and reckon that they've gnawed me down to the bone. Sophie, thankfully, seems to be free of the little blighters but can't put her dress back on as it's crawling with them. And I can't put my trousers back on for the same reason. So she's back off up the path, stark naked except for a pair of sandals, swinging her dress around in the air, her lovely little bottom jiggling up and down ....

Oh god, I could cry.

And I do. But it's down to the pain more than anything else. Not only have I got ant bites all over my legs (though, thankfully, not as far up as my crown jewels) but that bloody wasp stung my top lip and it's starting to swell.

I couldn't feel more stupid if I tried. Following Sophie up the path, naked from the waist down is bad enough. Doing it with a raging hard-on makes it doubly so.

But you can't keep a good woman down. Sophie will not be disheartened. She's back at the house and into the kitchen and sorting through the remnants of our food and wine and she pours me a very large brandy, and one for herself then sets about making up some grub. She's being kind. No, she's being lovely. And she's being lovely whilst being completely naked. Most men would give their right arm to be in my position now, but reality is beginning to sink home and all the cosseting in the world is not going to make it right.

We go home tomorrow.

Whilst Sophie goes back to her little single-person bedsit, I go back to my wife. I go back to my wife with a bloody great lump on the back of my head, both legs covered in ant bites and a swollen lip courtesy of a wasp sting. Now the wasp sting I can just about cover. Shit happens, right? The ant bites are going to take a bit of thinking about ...... and the lump on the back of my head??? Frankly, fuck knows.

What the hell am I going to do?

LXXVII

Oh, poor Henry!

The man's miserable. And is it any wonder? He's spent a small fortune in an effort for the two of us to have a three day kinky shag-fest and the most he's had is one prematurely ended blow job. And I reckon we're running about three-nil on the orgasm scoreline too.

And as if being knocked unconscious wasn't bad enough, both of us have legs that have the appearance of some deadly tropical disease and H's top lip looks like he's been clocked by a heavyweight. I can see his problem, too. I could be covered head to toe in red stripes courtesy of a nine foot bull whip (I wish!) and no-one would be any the wiser ('cept H, of course!), but Henry....well Henry has a hell of alot of explaining to do to his darling wife when he gets home tomorrow night. I can't think where he'll start. 'Well, the wasp just came outa nowhere. Zap! ... and the ants' nest? well .... nope can't think of a reason for that one, especially as I was (supposed to be) in the middle of a large city at the time ... and as for the large bit of bed that fell on my head, well you shoulda seen the expression on the face of the girl who was tied naked to it!' For once, I'm glad I won't be in *his* bedroom tomorrow night.

So I'm trying my hardest to put that out of his mind on this final evening and I'm determined that we'll get some satisfaction from our wee holiday. I'm treating him like a lord, coz I guess that's what he is ..... at least for one more night. While he reclines on the sofa and sips a soothing Napoleon, I'm down on the floor, in front of him giving, him one of my Sophie Specials, which he hasn't had before .... on account of the fact that I've only just made it up. Basically, it consists of 'oral cock worship'. Hmmmm.

That's about it really.

I mean, what more is a bloke going to want when he's feeling a bit down and in no condition to get energetic? Tell me you wouldn't, and I'd call you a liar. It works for me...and it seems to be working for Henry too, coz I give him my eyes as I'm doing it and he's loving every second. Then, when he's good and ready, I climb aboard and lower myself on to him. And I bet he thought that last night was an accident! Silly boy. And we just stay like that, moving slowly, 'savouring the moment', as H likes to say and I'm hoping that, in more ways than one, I'm taking the pain away.

In fact, it seems to be doing alot more than that. It seems to have brought H back to life. Well, for about the next hour or so, anyway. The dining table certainly gets put to good use. It stands in for Henry's desk, as it turns out that we've both had this fantasy about him giving me a good seeing to bent over it. And to think people are going to have to eat their dinner here. Possibly even tomorrow night.

LXXVIII

I know I'm a lucky man.

But it wasn't until tonight that I realised just how lucky. I have had the worst few days of my life and yet...and yet this darling woman brings me back to life with one of the most glorious hours of rampancy that I have ever experienced. Her resilience is remarkable. *She* is remarkable.

And not a hint of kinkiness in sight. Well, maybe just a small one. A small and really rather cute one.

'Oh bum', as Sophe would say.

I may have the headache from hell, have legs that itch like a hooker's hosiery and a lip like Sophie just bit it, hard, but she made it all go away. I resolve to sleep on my quandary. Sleep can solve a million problems. I have just the one, so I reckon I'm in with a chance.

*

'Pyjamas!'

'Eh?'

'Pyjamas.' .

It's the first thing on my mind when I wake up. The first thing on *me*, is Sophie. Somehow she's managed to get kitted out in *the* sexiest black lingerie; has raised my morale, so to speak, and has climbed aboard. Again. And to top it all her hands are behind her back and it wouldn't take more than one guess as to what's keeping them there.

'I hope you've got the key.' She says as she keeps up that slow, luxurious rhythm '...coz otherwise I'm almost as fucked as you are!' And she sinks down hard on me, just in case I didn't get it. 'So what's with pyjamas? I've never seen you wear any, or are you just an old fashioned guy at heart?'

'Nope. Well kind of, as you well know...' and she wriggles on top of me, the little minx, '...but so is Sarah. She bought me these silk pyjamas for my last birthday.'

'Oh yeah? Romantic, huh?' a hint of jealousy at my wife's name.

'I guess. Thing is, I need some way of covering my legs up over the next week or so, until these damn bites disappear. So the answer is ....' I pause for effect. Sophie yawns for similar effect. '.... to *finally* get round to wearing my birthday present.'

'Hmmmm, might work. And what about getting into and out of them. Won't she spot the problem then?'

'Shouldn't do. Not if I change into them in the bathroom and then surprise her by wafting in wearing my new togs. She'll just think I'm being 'romantic', as you put it.'

'I don't think I've ever seen you 'waft'. Is it sexy?'

'Abso-bloody-lutely!' and then I realise something 'Those are *silk* stockings, aren't they?'

'Erm, yeah.'

'There you are then. You were on top of me while I was still asleep, yes?' She nods and winks, '...so, *subconsciously* feeling your loverly thighs rubbing against me, I thought 'silk stockings' then 'silk pyjamas'. Pure genius.'

'Yes, I am, aren't I?'

'Yes you are.' And he pulls me down and kisses me. I break off...

'...only if it'd been me, I woulda thought 'silk stockings' then 'great legs' then 'excellent arse' then 'fantastic shag'.... and then I woulda fucked me silly.'

So I do just that.

LXXIX

Holidays, even brief ones, are supposed to be relaxing, aren't they? Oh, unless you holiday with Emms, in which case a subsequent two week rest cure and then rehab might be more in order.

And if anyone looked in need of a complete rest, it was Henry Blythe. I mean, I had tried to make things better for him, well, better for both of us really. There was no way I could have had a good time with H being in such a state. But what should have been three whole days of unbridled lust and kinky exploration, was reduced to just one night interrupted by regular scratching. We might as well have been on one of our work trips. At least I managed to get the orgasm score line up to a more respectable eight for me and four for him, albeit still wildly in my favour, thanks largely to H's swollen top lip.

So we have a leisurely drive home, most of which is interrupted at regular intervals by H's swearing and cursing whichever god he can think of for ruining his holiday, 'thanks a bloody bunch', and 'if ever there was an argument for atheism.....' and how he's 'never, *ever* going to the country again', as long as he lives!

But me? Well, I'm not so sure, coz I'm thinking of that tree and that rope and those black leather wrist cuffs and hanging there naked with that beautiful view and the summer sun on my body and what H was doing to me when the insects attacked and what he would have done if he hadn't been bitten and stung and I'm thinking what a wonderful thing to think up for me and I *really* want to do it again. Yes please, sir. Just security check the venue next time.

At my suggestion, we stop at a small country pub coz neither of us is in any hurry to return to our own domestic lives. I'm having a good go at getting Henry aroused under the table, as we sit alone in the deserted garden at the back. I don't know what it is about this man, but the more we shag, the more I want. This is not normal for me. Normal is 'once was enough, thanks mate.' Maybe it's the serial orgasms? Yeah, that'd be it then. However, my handiwork doesn't seem to be having a huge amount of success, coz H seems more interested in his beer. And then he has what I believe is called a 'eureka moment'. 'That's it! Wasp.... *in* the beer glass .... *then* get stung on my lip ... then tip back, then *fall over* backwards ....then bang head! Brilliant!' he turns to me, 'brilliant idea of yours to stop here, babe. Just brilliant!'

'Like I said, I'm a genius,' but I think that this is stretching it all a bit far. It's hard to ignore his enthusiasm. If he thinks that I'm brilliant, then who am I to deny it?

It's late afternoon when H drops me at home. He tells me he won't be in in the morning. He's gonna feign a cold or something. There's work he can do at home. Besides, it probably wouldn't be too clever for both of us to return to work on the same day. People might put two and two together......

'.......and get eight?' I add.

LXXX

So I'm sitting in the car. The engine is still running. Not sure I have the courage to go indoors just yet. Sarah's car is parked outside, so I know that she's in there. I've decided that the sympathy vote is the best one to go for. Appeal to her maternal side. Oh dear, look at my lip and my poor, poor head. Ouch, yes it does hurt. Perhaps I need a lie down. Not sure that I should have any alcohol though. Painkillers – the ones that are no longer in their prescription marked box. The ones that are now nice and anonymous. Yes, maybe I should take two and then have an early night. An early night in the silk pyjamas that you bought me. Might make me feel better. That way I can change into them long before you come to bed and I'll have to take them off long after you have left in the morning. Yes, I'll be staying at home tomorrow. Not quite up to going to work.

Engine off. Bag out of boot. To front door. Key in door. Door open. Inside. 'I'm ho-ome.' Pouting swollen top lip, for effect.

In the kitchen. Sarah. Chopping. Knife in hand, pointing it towards me. Angry.

'Where the *fuck* have you been?'

Oh, shit!

LXXXI

It's strange being back at work after so long. Not quite like being back from holiday, at least nothing like being back from the holiday me and Emms had. I do actually feel alot better. I mean, I know the last three days have been pretty awful, but there were some great times and as for the sex...... if that's not enough to put a smile back on a lady's face, well......

Nothing seems to have changed much, though. Carla is being extra nice, which is a little scary. I still don't trust her. Jeff is still filling one paper hanky after another (he was probably just the same as a pubescent teenager) and John keeps slip-sliding along. Hollie just sits there like she has a broom handle shoved up her bum, scowling at me over the top of her horn rims every time I walk past.

It seems strange without H here though. I'm reminded to start calling him HB again on account of the last three days. Or maybe 4H on account of how hard he was the first night ..... or 4B on account of yesterday in the pub garden. At about eleven, I broach the subject of H's absence with Carla. Gotta make this look all innocent, after all. 'Got a bit of a cold after his trip this week. Strange time to get a cold though. Right in the middle of a heatwave. He can't have had enough clothes on.' And she gives me a knowing smile. She can't possibly...... can she?

And, as ever on the first day back, everything drags. I'm tempted to give H a ring at home, just to hear the sound of his voice and to make sure that he's OK but think better of it. Knowing my luck his wife would answer and besides, I'm under strict wotsits never to phone him there, even under the pretext of work. 'Orders is orders, sir!'

I work late coz I'm meeting Emms straight from work and won't have time to go home and get changed. The office is empty by five, being 'Fuck Off, It's Friday'. It gives me a chance to regroup. To reminisce. To question. And the big question right now?

'What the hell do you think you are doing, Sophie MacDonald?'

You see, it's very easy to get caught up in things and get carried along by them without even querying the rights and wrongs and stuff. But given times like this, times when I get a chance to draw breath, doubt creeps in. Balling a man twice my age is one thing. Balling a man twice my age who is *married* is one whole lot worse. Mum would be horrified. But she'd also take one look at H and be ever so jealous too.

I'm like a teenager at the fair ground on a ride that's so fast that I couldn't get off, even if I wanted to....but when the ride does finally come to a halt, I just want to hand over my cash, all of my cash, and brace myself for another go.

*

When Emms arrives, a little late for a change, I'm in a pensive mood. I know that she'll want to hit the clubs later, but I'm not really in the mood tonight. My mind is elsewhere.

So I'm a little thrown when Emms seems a bit off too. Normally she's full of life and raring to go from the outset. But tonight she just plonks herself down and says she could murder a G and T, waves a twenty at me and asks would I be a dear?

As I'm standing at the bar waiting to line them up, I'm looking back at Emms and she's not even moving. This is bloke trouble. Has to be. I'm not gonna pull any punches here, so...

'OK. Who is he and what has he done?'

'Not beating about the bush then, Sophie?'

'So to speak,' I add for good measure. It gets half a smile. I can see it's a struggle.

'His name's Guy,' she dives straight in. 'Guy de Giverny' a look of disbelief flits across my face, '*Seriously*' she insists. 'He's a marquis.' At that, my disbelief reaches mega proportions and my chin hits the floor. 'But that's not the half of it...' and I can tell she's building up to it ..... downing the G and T in one is a pretty good indicator.... 'He's a friend of my dad.'

'Is that it? You have a bloke that's a friend of your dad?...and that's a *bad* thing?'

Emms nods... 'it is when he's the same *age* as my dad.'

I sit stock still. Am I hearing this right? Emms is shagging a guy twice her age?

Oh, glory hallelujah!

Emms I could kiss you! I could hug you to death, you absolute darling, you! But I stay stock still coz I know that I can't show any emotion other than the shock that is expected. If I tell her what I really think, I'd have an awful lot of explaining to do.

So she gets, 'Oh my gaaaard. You're shagging a wrinkly?!'

Emms looks at the floor and nods. I've never seem her looking so sad. '....and that's not the half of it....' she goes on, '....he's asked me to marry him.'

I'm dumbfounded. A whole range of emotions flood through me, happiness - yes, doubt – absolutely, but most of all pure joy for my best friend.

And, not least of all, *envy*. I could never be jealous of Emms. Never in a million years, but envy seems about right.

And it hurts.

LXXXII

First rule of defence – say nothing.

Second rule of defence – find out as much as possible whilst saying nothing.

Third rule of defence – do *not* forget your wife is a lawyer. As if.

So I just stood there, staring blankly, giving her my best 'what the hell are you talking about?' look. Do not show guilt. Just don't. It didn't seem to help much.

I didn't like the way that she was waving that knife around either and in twenty odd years I was pretty sure that I had never seen her quite so angry. If my balls were still attached to the rest of me at the end of the evening, I would consider myself a very lucky man.

'What *is* the problem?' I persisted.

'I repeat my question, where the fuck have you been?' So this was what it was like to face my wife in court. Direct eye contact. No deviation from the subject at hand. No answer to the question, you get the same question again. And again. Until she got the answer.

The answer that she already knew.

Somehow I doubted that His Honour Judge Cunningham would have allowed the F word in court, but I guess you never knew these days.

'Away on a business trip...' and I held my hands out, palms up, to prove I had nothing to hide. 'What's the big deal?'

'The 'big deal', is that I have spent the last two days trying to get in contact with you, only to be met with a blank wall. I can't contact you. Your office can't contact you. Where you're supposed to be, no-one has seen you. So I repeat my question, where the fuck have you been?' There it was again. And I could tell by the look on her face that she knew where this was going. She already fucking knew. But I saw a glimmer of hope here. She knew where I *hadn't* been, or at least she thought she did, but she didn't know where I *had* been. She couldn't do. She may be a lawyer, but she was not Superwoman – at least, not without the costume on.

Diversionary tactics – 'And what exactly is so important that it couldn't wait until I got home?'

She was torn between pursuing her initial line of enquiry and answering a perfectly reasonable question. What *was* so important? 'Your mother's been taken ill. She's in hospital.' Diversion success.

Bingo! Line of defence supplied. 'Really? Well that's a coincidence. Because that's where *I've* been.'

I could see that this threw her. 'Visiting your mother in hospital? But how could you……?'

'*I* have been in hospital thanks to a rather unfortunate accident involving a beer glass, a wasp and a bar stool,' and I hoped that she noticed the swollen lip at this point. I was trying to dribble just to reinforce the point. What *I* noticed was that Sarah had gone awfully quiet. My deliberately oblique reference to the circumstances of my accident had thrown her into a quandary. These were *not* the answers that she was expecting. She couldn't renew her attack with the 'where have you been' because I'd just told her where I'd been. And why. But she was not finished yet.

'So why didn't you call me?' and she folded her arms as a sign of defence herself.

'Well mainly because I was unconscious for some of the time...' she looks suitably aghast, '... partly because my phone was broken (quick thinking, H! Thank fuck the thing is still turned off!) and partly because I didn't want to worry you. As it turns out, it was nothing serious. X-rays showed no fractures. Painkillers prescribed and discharged.' I was on a roll now, 'And what could *you* have done exactly? Come running to look after poor old Henry coz he hurt his ickle head? No. Not likely, is it? Not with your work and all (that's it H, go for the jugular), so I dealt with it without causing anyone else any distress. Only, right now, I could do with a strong drink, as I have a rather painful headache although, unfortunately, I can't have one because I need to take some painkillers (producing them, magician-like, from my jacket pocket), painkillers that I have had to lay off of today, due to a rather long drive home. OK?' I drew breath. Finally.

Sarah was still angry, but I was hoping it was self-directed anger. I knew I had the upper hand now. She was on the back foot. Running out of steam. But she was still not finished.

'And the hospital didn't call me because…..?'

I just gave a shrug and held my hands out, palm upwards again... 'Why ?' is all I said. Keep it brief H. Less chance of talking yourself into a corner. 'By the time I got to the hospital, I was conscious again and could deal with it.' Nice one!

Last gasp.

'And your client didn't know where you were because.....?'

Making great show of still not being believed...exasperated and emphasising each individual word. 'Because I never got there!' And time for a change of direction .... 'Is this about Carla, again?' Knowing full well that it would have been Carla that Sarah would have spoken to at the office. Sarah just shook her head. What could she say?

'So can we get back to the important matter? My mother is ill but you seem more concerned that I've been off shagging. Is that right?' That's right. Make *her* feel guilty. 'So where is she right now? Which hospital? because, even though all I really want to do is lie down, I guess a visit is in order.'

'She's been discharged,' barely audible. A silence descended. It was going to get milked for all I could get from it. Yes, Sarah, accuse me of having an affair. Accuse me of lying to you. When, in fact, I had been unconscious in hospital. And the emergency that prompted all of these accusations?.....was no longer an emergency at all. Brilliant.

Time to defuse.

'Do we have anything to eat? I'm kind of hungry.'

She puts the knife down, walks over to me, put her arms around my neck and kisses me on the lips. Stroking my hair 'Sorry' was all she could manage.

Then, 'Ow.'

'Oh my god, what *is* that?' and she tentatively stroked the back of my head again, feeling the large lump and banging the final nail in the coffin that had been her suspicions and allegations.

After a light meal, we retired to bed where I donned my new silk pyjamas. Sarah was suitably impressed .... although she wasn't quite sure about the socks. I was, but didn't elucidate. Just muttered something about still being in shock and that my extremities might be feeling a little cold. She was so impressed with my attire, in fact, that she insisted that I chastise her in no uncertain terms for being such a 'bad girl' which, of course, I was more than happy to do. She then treated me to an exhibition of her extensive oral skills, mumbling something about warming my extremities up and then insisted (again) that I chastise her *whilst* she demonstrated her extensive oral skills.

So, far be it from me ending the evening with no balls at all, there wasn't that much left of them, that was for sure.

Maybe there was a god after all?

*

So as I lie here, a whole day later, reminiscing about my oh so narrow escape the night before, I know that things are going to have to change. That was too close for comfort. And knowing Sarah, she's still not one hundred percent convinced, despite all the evidence to the contrary. The fact that she still suspects Carla is testament to that. Will she check up on the facts? Yes, probably, but medical confidentiality should put a halt to that. She might approach the hospital, in the unlikely event that she can trace it, might even get confirmation that I was there, but I doubt it.

I'm just going to have to cool it with Sophie. I'll explain. Hopefully she'll understand. She *has* to understand. Much as I'd love to see more of her, further diversionary tactics are called for. I absolutely cannot risk Sarah catching me out again. Any further trips are above board and without my young lover. Much as it pains me. We need, no *I* need, to put some space between us. And lessen the space between me and Sarah.

And with the bites all but disappeared, I can now recline in sock-free comfort, whilst Sarah picks up where she left off the night before, lessening that space to absolute zero.

LXXXIII

By about ten thirty, things have lightened enormously. Emms's gloom has well and truly lifted but neither of us fancies going to a club, so we've settled on a Friday night just boozing and chatting.

Emm's changed from the gin to rum about two hours ago, which is probably a good sign, if not a great mix. All I've done is so far is calm Emms down, then tell her it's actually a pretty good situation to be in, the guy's a *marquis*, fergodsakes, landed gentry, and so what if he's old and wrinkly (at forty seven!), if he wants to marry you, is that so bad? And I'm sure her father will come round, coz this Guy is a pretty good catch whichever way you look at it. Of course, the whole time I was thinking of me and Henry, wishing it was me that H'd asked to marry. Wishing it was me who only had the problem of telling my dad and not having to keep the whole thing hush-hush from absolutely everyone, even Emms, on account of him being married and all.

It all comes out that she met Guy during her week in the country. When she was staying with Uncle Seymour, him with the villa in Capri. What Emms didn't let on was that Guy spent most of the week in *her* country, so to speak, as well as a couple of other places too. He's part of the horsey set. Polo and show jumping and the likes. He has a stable of about twenty horses ... and he's hung like one too, Emms couldn't resist telling me, and has an 'appetite' to match. They pretty much became an item, albeit on the quiet, but never missed a chance for a roll in the hay, and pretty much anywhere else the fancy took them.

He's a widower, his wife was a heavy smoker and died of lung cancer a few years back. He was devastated. Has been out of circulation since and has only just got back in the saddle (Emms' term, not mine).

And there are so many times that I just want to say to Emms, I'm having an affair with a much older man too, so I *do* know what it's like, but it's so much worse coz I can't be seen with him and no-one must know, not even you and it's like I have another life that's separate from everything and everyone else. A life that's just two people.

But I say nothing. Coz I can't.

And it's me that ends up feeling a little low.

LXXXIV

Saturday – me and Sarah visit my mother. Always a difficult occasion at the best of times. Ma's OK. Possibly a minor stroke, but certainly not life threatening.

The rest of the weekend is spent fending off Sarah's maternal instinct, which is sweet but becoming a little claustrophobic. She's trying to make amends after making such outrageous accusations. Anything I can get you, are you feeling alright, are you hungry, comfortable????? No mention of another blowjob, I notice. That lady needs to get her priorities right.

Sunday – and I'm just chilling out. My legs are pretty much back to normal, the fat lip has gone and even the bump is noticeably reduced....and so, thank god, are the headaches. No codeine means a fine bottle of rouge with the Sunday roast. It gives me time to work on plans for me and Sophie. I don't want to stop seeing her. She is so good for me, makes me feel alive, young, excited ... and, err, horny as hell, and I hope I'm good for her too, despite evidence to the contrary a week or so back. I'm hoping that she's over that after our week away. A week, I might add, that would have finished off most relationships, whatever their status, but Sophe, bless her, just keeps on going. I find her resilience remarkable. Sure, her sensitivity is a little scary too. But I'll just have to keep reminding myself that this is a young woman whose emotional maturity I should not take for granted. I still have to tread very carefully. If she goes off the rails again, there's no telling......

But there is no way I'm going through Friday night again.

Not in a million years.

Monday – back at work and after a restful weekend I'm raring to go .... almost. My first contact with Sophie is going to be interesting. I've already worked out that I'm going to be all smiles and pleased to see her, remembering that I'm not supposed to have seen her for nearly two weeks and completely forgetting the fact that only three days ago she was trying to give me a handjob under the table in the garden of a country pub.

Yes, best to forget that bit.

Completely.

......only the thought of it is having the reaction that she didn't get at the time. Bugger. So that when she breezes in in a figure hugging skirt, with what I am assuming are stockings on underneath and I start imagining what she looks like without the skirt, I just know I'm not getting up from this desk for at least another thirty minutes.

So I ask her to sit, and ask her how she is and is she feeling better now and how was her week off (just *wonderful*, Mr Blythe – really?!) and that she heard I was unwell last week and how am I feeling now? ... just fine thanks and then I lower my voice and say that she should just keep smiling, no matter what I'm about to say, just in case anyone walks past the office and looks in through the window. There's a flash of panic across her face but I move quickly to dispel any fears. I explain briefly and quietly what happened when I got home and how I talked my way out of the situation. That she must realise that it was a very narrow escape and that I can't afford for it to happen again.

'Of course, HB,' she interjects, 'that's not a problem. Not a problem at all. I fully understand.'

'So, I'm going to have to cool it for a while. Take a few trips with other people. It's no reflection on you. I want you to understand that. I *need* you to understand that.' And throughout, darling Sophie has this plastic smile painted on and, like a real trouper, carries on as if everything was normal ...... which clearly it isn't. And when I add 'But if *we* are to carry on ....then....' her smile widens even further.

LXXXV

Oh merde!

Henry hasn't half been through it recently. As if the three days away didn't turn out bad enough, he gets home and finds that events have conspired against him and dumped him even further in the shit!

No wonder he wants to cool it. But at least I know it's not for good. For one horrible moment there, I thought that that's what he had in mind. Phew! Thank heavens it wasn't. I don't think I could handle that. Not now.

So work muddles along and we have a few drinks after work on the odd occasion but it's in a group of us so no suspicions are raised and I'm being a good girl (for a change) and keeping my distance. All very professional. And H goes away on a couple of trips and it's nearly a month before there's even a glimmer of hope that we might get together, even for a night, but I know that it's doing good coz when H is away his wife calls the office both times, so I know that she's checking up on him and checking out who is still in the office and I know that H's caution is justified and now H knows too, coz I tell him as soon as he's back and he's grateful and I know that we are OK.

But after over six weeks (!) I've had just about as much restraint as I can handle, that is, I've had no restraints at all, so to speak. And the old ache is coming back with a vengeance and a couple of times I catch H looking at me and then at his desk and I know just what he's imagining.

Bad boy!

At last I think, maybe it's *my* turn to take the initiative. A holiday is clearly a non-starter. Not after the last time. At least not in the middle of nowhere, coz he needs to be contactable, just in case there's another emergency. And, with his mum ill, that's a definite possibility. And what with H's declaration of war on the countryside, I wouldn't bet on him wanting to go anywhere rural anyway. Not without a crash helmet and a barrel of insecticide. Hey, what about the seaside? Fresh air, sunshine, seafood.....hmmmmm, crowds of pissed up tourists, seagulls crapping on you, sand getting everywhere (yes, and I *do* mean there!).

Nope it has to be a city centre or nowhere. He can't hack it anywhere else, poor dear. Civilisation or nothing. I just keep coming back to getting a hotel room for the afternoon. It just sounds so cheap though and H isn't like that and I'm not sure I want to be like that either. It's just that I'm getting desperate now and anything will do. Even the odd couple of hours snatched in the afternoon between meetings.

Except that I know (coz he did explain it to me) that the two of us absent from the office at the same time might just raise suspicions and that's assuming that we can find somewhere remote enough not to be spotted without having to travel for hours to get to.

Oh bum!

There's always my place......

Yeah, right. I'm obviously losing touch with reality here.

I'm at a loss. Really I am. I guess I'll just have to wait for the next wee work jaunt and hope that it's just the two of us and, if it isn't, that we can still get together .... somehow.

Why can't I just have a normal relationship instead of putting myself through this all the time?

Ah yes, I'm a masochist.

I guess that explains it.

LXXXVI

This is possibly the happiest day of my life.

No, that's unfair on Sarah. My wedding day was the happiest day of my life. And a few others with her are up there too. Like that first time ever that she produced the handcuffs and we .... but, and it's a big but, this is gonna take some beating.

It's said that everything comes to he who waits, but given my run of bad luck lately, I'd kind of given up on that old chestnut. And there I am, just muddling along and out of the blue a client says, 'Hey H, how do you fancy going international?' I look at him askance, over a very fine ale, and ask him to elaborate. Well it turns out that a sister company of theirs is looking for a new avenue as far as creative work is concerned. They've had enough of the people that they work with and just fancy a change, have noticed our work and liked it. Stoke the creative juices. Could only be short term, but let's see what we can come up with and, if it impresses, then who knows. Could become permanent. So, with my approval, he'll pass on my contact details and arrange a meeting at their offices and we can see what develops.

Sure I say, and where exactly would their offices be?

Paris.

I leap out of my chair and punch the air above me. Repeatedly. And shout yes, yes, yes, yes, YEEEEES!!!! At which point everyone around me bursts into spontaneous applause and several people slap me on the back. At least that's what I *want* to happen. Deep inside. Instead, I sit there with a widening grin and say 'Sounds good' How soon can we go?'

Because Paris means France.

And France means French.

And French means Sophie.

YES, YES, YES , YES ..... indeed!

*

No way was I going to count my chickens on this one? Imagine her reaction to being told about the plans only to have them all fall apart before we could act on them. Too risky. Potentially extremely hurtful. At the very least, I was going to wait until we had that very first meeting firmly arranged.

And now that I have.......

Team meeting – everyone there, well maybe twenty or so.

'Ladies and gentlemen, today I have a very special announcement to make. There is a possibility, and I stress a possibility, that we will be going international. A short term contract has arisen with foreign clients that could well lead to bigger things. I'd very much like this to happen (*no kidding*) and it's an exciting opportunity for this company. I'll be putting a small team together to work exclusively on this project and our first meeting is due to happen in two weeks. The company is French and we will be going to Paris.'

I let this sink in. There's a general murmur in the room. I deliberately don't look in Sophie's direction. I'm hoping that she picks up on what this means. Hell, of course she does. She's way too smart to have missed it.

That team will consist of myself and Carla Ventura and Sophie MacDonald , who as some of you may know, is a fluent French speaker. There may be room for one extra, at a later date. In the meantime, John will be taking over my projects, so that I can concentrate on working up this side of the business. ('Working up this side of the business?' Nice euphemism, Henry Blythe.)

LXXXVII

At the mention of our names, myself and Carla turn to face each other. Her eyebrows shoot up before mine do and we're gawping at each other like two paralytic owls. Paris. A trip to Paris! And I thank heaven that I'm perched on the edge of a desk, coz if I'd been standing up I'd be collapsed on the floor right now. And I know I'm shaking, so I grip the desk firmly with both hands.

I'm going to Paris.

I'm going to Paris with Henry Blythe.

Ohmygaaaaard!

LXXXVIII

It's a treat to see Sophie's face when I make the announcement. Carla looked pretty amazed to, which is great. We should make a good team, the three of us and, of course, I have an additional reason for asking Carla. I need her for cover. Although I'm still not convinced that Sarah believes me, I need to carry on regardless. Let her know I'm not afraid to associate with the woman she still seems sure I'm having an affair with, even if it does make a mockery of Carla's sexual proclivities. I guess Sarah hasn't got round to checking out my story, though I'm not sure how she would. Phone our office and ask to speak to the dyke and see who she gets put through to? It *could* work, I guess.

And the real danger of course, is that she changes her suspicions to Sophie, if she hasn't already. I guess that she reckons that Sophie is way too young for me and therefore out of the running. By all accounts she would be right .... only she isn't.

*

So the team gets to work. Henry, his lover and the lesbian. You couldn't make it up, could you? But, for all that, we get on really well. We gel. And after some liaison with the French, we set about a mock project for a presentation in two weeks. Sophie can barely suppress her excitement and really throws herself into the job. It's even given Carla a boost. Maybe it's the thought of Gay Paree?

Sophie only has to hang on for another twelve days. I'm hoping that with something to look forward to, it'll put her mind at ease. No, who am I kidding? By the time we get there, she'll go off like a firecracker. Same as ever.

Roll on Paris.

LXXXIX

Two weeks actually whizzed by. I can't believe that we are off already. I expected the usual. Clock and calendar watching until the fateful day. But no, work was so busy that time just flew. It's been great. I've had a ball. Just a pity that I haven't had Henry. But that's all about to change, isn't it?

*

We make our own way to the airport. H and Carla are already there when I arrive; H tapping his watch in remonstration. Oh dear. I've been a bad girl already. One nil to Henry. There's an hour to wait so we hit the executive lounge and feast on coffee and croissants, just to get us in the mood. Lucky really, as I had bugger all in the flat this morning, except for some rather lumpy milk.

But before you know it we're touching down in Paris and running the gauntlet of what could be an airport terminal or a large, industrial greenhouse. And then out onto the chaotic roads, Paris-bound, following the signs for *centre ville*. 'Looks like you'd be right at home here H,' as an upturned skip on wheels cuts up the taxi we're in and we hang on for dear life. But he just smiles and shakes his head and looks out of the window. No, you're right H, let's just enjoy it while we can.

The hotel has a suitably historic French façade, is large and anonymous, just as I'd expected. No point in staying somewhere small...not when you intend to bring the house down. I mean, where would you look at breakfast?

Having dumped all our gear, we meet in the foyer and head out on foot. No work today, just travel and sight-seeing and relaxation. Purely by chance, I'm sure, we seem to have ended up in the boutique area of the city. When I say boutique area, I don't mean it's all twee and chic, I mean it's jam packed with boutiques. Woo hoo. Me and Carla are in seventh heaven. Rushing from one shop window to the next, but at Henry's insistence we stay out of any shops coz he says we'll have plenty of time for that later. We are here to get our bearings and work up an appetite for dinner ..... and something else, I hope.

We pass the Louvre, home of the Mona Lisa and her crooked smile. Maybe it's the strange glass pyramid outside that's got her so flummoxed? I can't say I warm to it. Henry just stands and stares and then asks me what I think of it. I give a gallic shrug and pout, but he continues 'I like it's daring, it's challenge...but it's an anachronism.' He turns to me and says 'do you know the word?' I'm not going to give him the satisfaction of me saying no, even though I have no idea what an anchorism is. After a period that I guess he judges as long enough not to expect an answer, he goes on 'an anachronism is something that is ...... out of time. Something that is out of kilter with something .... or someone,' he adds, then pauses. 'A bit like me ..... with you.' And he saunters off, head down, leaving me alone .... and worrying again.

We then wander through a park, tour back through some back streets with more designer gear shops and back to the hotel by five.

'Right, dinner at eight. There is a table booked here. It'll save us having to search out a restaurant elsewhere. So three hours to relax, have a soak and put your glad rags on so you can both sweep in looking bloody gorgeous.' And with that, he's off.

Three hours *just* to relax and soak and dress? Who's he kidding? Not when I find out which room he's in.

Uh-uh..... no sir.

XC

I've not even had chance to run a bath when the phone rings. No prizes for guessing who this is going to be.

'Henry, I seem to have a bit of trouble with my plumbing. Can you come and have a look at it for me?'

'Really?'

'Yes,' she says, and then breathes 'something keeps dripping and I'm hoping that you can sort it out.'

Incorrigible.

But I'm having a bath first, whatever state the young lady finds herself in right now. Wash the grime of the day away ..... just so that I can go and get all dirty again.

So to speak.

*

Carla is only on the second floor; Sophie on the fifth and myself on the seventh. I hadn't foreseen having to visit Sophie's room. I'd assumed that we would be using mine. The one with the four-poster bed. The four-poster bed that I've just spent ten minutes checking the sturdiness of.

Once bitten.....

So here I am, fifth floor, tapping lightly on the door, it opens a crack, and then I'm left to make my own entry. Sophie has moved to the middle of the room, her back to me. She's in this flimsy black gown kind of thing. She turns to face me and lets it fall apart and off her shoulders.

Oh shit!

... or maybe merde! ..... under the circumstances?

She hits all the panic, or maybe emergency, buttons at once. Heart rate up, increased perspiration, shortness of breath, weakness of legs, swelling of my ....

She smiles. 'Didn't you bring your plumbers tools with you, sir?' *So* coy.

'I don't think I'll be needing them,' is what I want to say, but it comes out as ' I da fee I be nee em.' Please, someone, tell me I'm not dribbling.

'Well,' she says, producing a nice, shiny, new pair of handcuffs from behind her back. '...luckily I brought my own,' and she slips the cuffs back behind her, from where I hear a familiar ratcheting sound as they close tight. And just for a split second I recall ....

'And today, you get to do ...' her voice lowers to a whisper, 'whatever you want. And you don't get the key ..... until you have.'

And so I do.

XCI

Well I asked for it. And I sure got it.

At nearly a quarter to eight, I'm still lying in bed. I know I need to get up. I just don't seem to be able to summon up the energy. My bottom is sore and so is my bum, if you see what I mean. My jaw aches and so does my throat (again). There are slight marks around my wrists which I have no idea how I'm going to hide. My hair looks like it's been through a blender. I feel as though I have been bent every which way that's possible. Which, indeed, I have. It was brutal at times, relentless (as ever), sometimes scary, exciting throughout, exhilarating even. My head is still spinning and my body seems to be tingling from top to, err, bottom, but I know that I couldn't give it up, even if I wanted to.

Which I don't.

He called it 'breath play'. God knows how they're gonna get the mascara and lipstick stains out of the pillowcases. Not my problem. My problem right now is getting vertical, getting showered and dressed and somehow putting on a normal face and being 'just wonderful' for the rest of the evening. All in fifteen minutes.

It's not going to happen, is it?

But I manage to slide off the bed and crawl on hands and knees to the bathroom and sit on the shower floor whilst the water cascades over me and pitter-patters off my shower cap. I must look a right state. No 'must' about it.

Five minutes later, the cool water seems to be bringing me to my senses And I, at last, get to test the strength in my legs. I towel and decide that the only way I'm gonna do this is to stay simple. After all, I am in the capital of chic. Understate it all. Barely any make-up, simply dressed, hair in a pony tail. All it needs is some way of untangling this bird's nest and I think I can do it. Did I pack a rake? It would help. In the end, I'm about half an hour late. Well, it's s'posed to be a lady's prerogative, so it's about time I make the most of it.

At eight twenty five the phone goes and I know who it'll be, but I let it ring out as a sign that I'm no longer here and am on my way down. Which I am, just as soon as I've checked that my cardigan sleeves are long enough.

*

Plastic smile re-applied, I breeze in to be met by Henry looking suitably (post-coitally) relaxed and Carla looking simply stunning. Who the hell is she trying to impress? Not me, surely?

'Apologies all round. I dropped off. Must have been the journey.' In a quieter voice.... 'wiped me out', avoiding eye contact with H and picking up the menu - 'So, what's à la carte tonight?' still avoiding eye contact. 'I fancy something big and juicy.' Pause. 'Filet mignon, maybe? How 'bout you, H?'

'Sole, I think. I haven't had fish for a while,' and I choke a little on my water.

Nice one.

And the rest of the evening goes like a dream. Somehow I've worked up a ravenous hunger. So, I notice, has H. Little wonder. He has protein reserves to replenish. My tiredness ebbs away with the intake of food and fine wine and by liqueur time I've brightened up no end. Carla takes her leave, soon after, claiming to need an early night for our big day tomorrow. That suits me. It leaves H and me together. Alone.

I'm easing out of my cardy now, coz I figure enough is enough, and make great show of rubbing the red marks around my wrists 'So babe....' after Carla's out of earshot '.....ready for round two?' Out of the corner of my eye I catch H looking at me, smiling and then slowly shaking his head. I keep my eyes on my wrists.

'Not had enough, then?'

A sip of wine, swirling it in my glass, then 'just getting started, me. I seem to have developed a taste.' And I turn to face him, 'Any more tricks up your sleeve?'

'Not tonight, my sweet. Not tonight,' and I struggle to hide my disappointment.

'But can't we just....?'

'.... spend the night together? I'd be mortified if we didn't.'

So would I.

And don't think for one moment, Henry Blythe, that that's an end to it.

XCII

The following morning I'm looking forlornly at the breakfast offerings. If ever a man was in need and a damned good fry up, it was this man. Instead, I'm faced with wee pots of yoghurt, croissants, and cheese slices (for breakfast?!) and insipid looking bits of spicy meats. *Cold* spicy meats.

Where's the big, fat, juicy sausages, the rashers of thick cut bacon with crispy fat along one side, mushrooms fried in high cholesterol butter, fried eggs still runny in the middle and thick slices of buttered toast??? Proper toast.

Croissants. Fucking *croissants*!

Good grief.

But Carla is happy at least. One dry crescent of flaky pastry and an espresso you could stand a spoon up in and she's well away. Well, my dear, one of us here has been emptying the contents of one's testicles and prostate for the last twelve hours and needs something a *little* more substantial than pastry, thank you very much. I'll be cumming fresh air at this rate. For all I know, I already am, given Sophie kept her mouth well and truly clamped this morning, preventing me from checking out my current status.

So I just pile into whatever I can get my hands on and dose up on high strength coffee by the bucket load. Maybe it'll keep me going, though I doubt it.

No sign of Sophie until we are just about to vacate our table. 'No breakfast?' I enquire. She just shakes her head and adds, 'not hungry. Must've had my fill last night,' .....*and* this morning, I'll warrant.

We get a limo ride out to the offices of Herzoot SARL. An ultra modern glass edifice in an ultra modern 'parc industrielle' on the outskirts of Paris. We are greeted by the MD, or whatever that is in French. He insists we call him Michel (pronounced Me-shell) and his English is way better than my French. I introduce him to Carla then Sophie. He doesn't know which one to look at first. Like a kid in a sweet shop. Good start. He introduces us to his assistant, Françoise, a cute little number that would have most guys' tongues hanging out. Petite, lithe and very pretty. What are the odds on her and Michel....? But I can feel Carla's eyes boring into her, so if Françoise is not sorted in that respect, then......

But Michel has no qualms at all with respect to my two ladies. I lag behind and follow his eyes. Bad man, huh? We have something in common already. He guides us to a conference room and we are served coffee whilst a number of other individuals drift in, are introduced and are seated. Their air is casual and distant. The men have all eyes on the two new women in the room. The two additional French women (one fluent in English) just stare into their coffee cups.

Thanks ladies.

Carla appears to have no interest in either of these two. I can't see why.

The meeting is fairly brief and cordial. We discuss our past projects, awards (evidently of no interest to our hosts), current projects and Michel runs through what he needs from us, much of which we have discussed on the phone already anyway. Sophie and the French woman (Mimi) assist with translation, where needed. They seem to be competing with each other. Again, I can't see why.

By eleven the meeting breaks up with the hangers on (who seem to have no other purpose than to make up the numbers), drifting back the way they came. There is a look of regret and lingering eyes on some of the male faces, as they take their leave, but the MD has given his orders and they are sent packing. Monsieur Le Directeur has designs there, mateys, so scram. We have yet more coffee (I'll be flying home under my own steam at this rate) and some more bloody croissants, when Michel announces it's time for lunch ..... at eleven thirty. Well, given the paucity of brekkie, I'm all for this early and (hopefully) long lunch break thing that the French do. I need a serious protein intake or this trip is going to be totally shattering. So I'm more than happy to indulge, especially as this means that the working day is pretty much over.

Seven thirty til eleven thirty. However do they manage? Easy. Two people, one job.

*

The limo is back and ferrying us even further out of the city. What I'm expecting is a twee country house with ivy on the walls and a menu on a blackboard outside. What we get is a bloody château. With a moat. And turrets. Sophie's eyes are on stalks and she looks at me all knowingly and surreptitiously rubs the thumb and forefinger of one hand around the wrist of the other. I pretend to ignore her. Not an easy job. But, I go with the flow, determined not to be overtly impressed by this display of wealth and prestige.

Carla couldn't care less, as she's ensconced in conversation, in broken English and French, with Françoise. And I thought that she was in a relationship back home. Must be something in the water ... other than bubbles.

We are treated to a tour of the rose gardens and then the interior area that is open to the public. Michel is greeted like an old friend by the maitre d' and we are shown to what is clearly the best table in the room, overlooking the gardens and moat. I'm still not impressed .... and won't be, unless I find that this place has a dungeon.

Michel has cornered Sophie and is conversing only in French. I'm not sure if this is a deliberate ruse to keep her all to himself, but let him try. He has no hope there and I'm comfortable with his attention. All good for the old *entente cordiale*, I guess. Just don't try touching her up or you *will* get your fingers broken. I smile at Sophie and it looks like she's trying to raise her eyebrows in exasperation, but I just raise my glass in response. If she could glare at me without being noticed, I'm sure she would. I resist the temptation to wink.

The meal itself is the perfect antidote to a measly breakfast and I make the most of the heart attack cholesterol and coronary calories. The wine, as ever, is superb and as for the brandy, well, I'm beginning to see the attraction of France, albeit through rather blurry rose-tinted specs. So, by the time we pile into the limo back to the city (via M's office), I'm well on the way to cordon bleu heaven. We've been in the restaurant for nearly four hours. Incredible...or should that be '*incroyable*'?

I've spent most of this time in the pleasure of my own company. Carla and Françoise and Michel and Sophie seemingly paired off. No problem. It's good to see people enjoying themselves. And I have great fun winding Sophe up. Taking my watch off and rubbing my wrist, running my tongue around the inside of my cheek, licking the red wine off the outside of my glass.

She'll be steaming by the time we get back to the hotel.

XCIII

'Why did you let that old letch corner me like that, H?' I'm not happy.

'What 'old letch' would that be, my sweet?'

So, OK, I coulda chosen my words a little better. 'You know what I mean,' not to be diverted from the accusation in hand, '*and* he's a groper. Kept pawing my arm and even my leg once, under the table it was.' We are standing by the lift now, waiting for a ping and the doors to open.

'What happened to the 'I can handle any bloke you chuck at me' Sophie?' I scowl in response. 'You did a brilliant job, babe, had him just where you wanted him, where *we* wanted him.'

'You're making me feel used, H, and I don't like it.'

'Don't knock it, hun, it's a skill to be envied by us chaps. Womanly wiles. Something we men could never do. And it's a skill you need to learn. You'll find it invaluable, believe me. Just watch Carla. She's a bloody expert.'

'But she's a .....'

'Yes she is, which is just possibly why she's so damned good at it. And whenever she wants to, she'll just switch allegiance. Like tonight for instance.' I'm not keeping up here. Something I don't know? 'I don't think we'll be seeing her again today.'

I, for once, am lost for words. 'You mean she....?' H says nothing. 'With....?' H *still* says nothing. 'You *are* kidding me?' I get a slight shake of the head from him. 'Well bugger me!'

And as the lift doors open, he says, 'don't worry, my sweet, I have every intention of doing just that.'

*

It started as soon as the lift doors closed. Pushed roughly against the wall, lifted bodily from the floor, my legs dangling then spread, arms tight around his neck, skirt hitched up, telling me I was his to do with as he wanted, and the word 'slut' and 'little' *may* have been mentioned...... yes, yes, yes......

It ended some hours later with him in my mouth, my throat was too dry to swallow and me dribbling, just like his friend Nick does. God, it went *everywhere*, but Henry said that it only added to the fun. It's supposed to be good for the skin, so H tells me, so my boobs should feel all soft and smooth by tomorrow morning.

But it was the perfect ending.

Simply perfect.

*

You know, I could get used to this afternoon delight stuff. There's something very appealing, decadent even, about taking time out from the day, *during* the day, and getting shagged stupid. And then convening at an excellent restaurant, after working up a huge appetite, and stuffing yourself silly all over again. I'm not sure that today's lunchtime banquet was such a great prelude though. H was teaching me some oral techniques that he was keen for me to learn and I very nearly puked on at least two occasions. Got there in the end though. He can't stop smiling now.

One more string to my bow.

*

Sure enough, seven sharp the phone goes. 'Oh hi,' says H, all chirpy, 'how's things?' a short pause and he mouths 'Carla' at me. 'Sure that's not a problem. No, no, no, really, we'll be fine. You go ahead and have fun. All good for Anglo-French relations.' There's a stress on the word 'relations' and I'm not sure if he's using a euphemism or reacting to the fact that I've now got his cock in my mouth. His next few words are 'uh, umm, ermmm, yeah, yeah' and I'm still not sure either way. Now desperate to get off the phone before he gives the game away, he keeps trying to wind up the call, but Carla is having none of it. My guess is she's over compensating for bailing out on us. Suits me. I have H exactly where I want him, which makes a change.

And then he takes me by surprise and switches. Now, *he* wants to keep the call going as long as possible, (asking all sorts of stupid questions) as he has me by the hair and is making good use of my mouth. And throat. The bastard.

I shoulda know better, shouldn't I? Oh well, live and learn.

XCIV

Last full day in Paris.

Breakfast is a cordial, if predictably lacking, affair. 'Les Trois Anglais', all looking well and truly fucked, I would say. Post coital glows abound all round. You can almost taste the sexuality in the air. And it tastes way better than breakfast.

Carla can't keep a smirk off her face and keeps drifting off into a dazed reverie. She obviously got what she wanted last night, but is back in time for her usual minimalist nosh. Her and Françoise. Doesn't bear thinking about. Or rather it *does*. In great detail. Those were the days, eh Henry!?

I've been smiling so much the last twelve hours that my cheeks ache. Sophie's new found skills, and the enthusiasm with which she approaches learning them, have just blown me away. Literally.

And as for Sophie herself? The happiest bunny in the bunny farm, I'd say. She's going through all the places she wants to visit today. A list more suited to a whole week than a single day. The usual touristy things, as well as every designer boutique in the city.

'We'll have to come back then, won't we?'

'Ooooo, yes!' and even Carla snaps out of it long enough to agree.

*

First stop, the Eiffel Tower. Sophie's idea. She must have something on her mind. 'His name was also Henry, you know?' I inform her.

'Who?'

'Mister Eiffel. Monsieur Henri Eiffel,' trying on a French accent for size. And she scans the edifice, slowly, from the very base to the very tip and then all the way back down to the base again, as she does so letting out an elongated 'Wooooow!!'. She then turns to me, raises her eyebrows and adds, 'I can *see* the resemblance.'

'Really? I doubt it....' and I sniff '....... because I just made all that up,' and I get a 'you bastard', before she narrows her eyes at me and thumps me on the arm. Carla, who has deigned to join us today, has a good laugh at that.

'I knew that,' says Sophie …. and I'm rather betting that she did.

And it's race you to the top. The ladies opt for the lift and join the queue. I've always fancied doing it on foot, but those steps look a little intimidating. What the hell. You only live once. It's easy to start with, but I flag around the half way mark and am met by a couple of giggling schoolgirls, as I grope up the final few steps. A couple of schoolgirls named Carla and Sophie.

Phew! And this is only the first floor. We stop for a rest and some refreshment before I venture out on the next leg. 'Are you sure you can manage it, H? I mean, at *your* age!' She gets the evil eye from me and then I'm off. Slow and steady this time. Not going to rush this. But two steps at a time. Needless to say, I'm beaten again, but find my second wind halfway up, so I don't feel too bad by the time I spy Sophie at the top of the steps ….. leaning on the railings and doing a pretty good imitation of someone having a chronic asthma attack.

There's less room here. It's more crowded. Sophie is buzzing around like a frenzied fly, but then I see her freeze. There's a look of horror on her face as she's looking at her feet and she's rooted to the spot. I follow her gaze and realise that she's standing on a glass floor. A glass floor with a view straight down to the road below. Maybe a hundred metres below. She doesn't look at all well.

'Problem, Sophe?' all innocent, standing right in front of her.

'Feel sick,' is all she can manage …. then she sways a little. I scoop her up and virtually carry her to a more solid looking area, where Carla joins us. 'I think I'm going to have to get this one back to ground level, before she makes a mess,' and tell Carla to carry on without us. No point in spoiling her fun. Only another hundred or so metres to go. So she's queuing for the lift up as we're queuing for the lift down. We wave good-bye first. Once on our way, Sophie sinks into me, stands on tip toe and whispers, 'honestly, the things I have to do to get you alone.'

So I draw back, look her in the eye and say - 'Oooo, you little bugger!'

'Right on both counts, baby!' and she bites her bottom lip. No, that's *my* job, I think and lean forward to do just that.

By the time we get into the next lift for the ride down to ground level, I'm amazed at how much you can get away with in a one minute ride. OK, so we've been here before, but that lift only had two occupants. This one is nearly full, but it doesn't stop Sophe from airing my assets and rubbing me up the wrong way, so to speak (to quote the lady herself). Her slender fingers feel amazing, wrapped so tightly around my cock. Luckily, I have a long overcoat on, so that when we vacate said metal box I'm not doing my own impression of the Eiffel Tower for the hordes of tourists to admire.

Not to be deflected from her task, I'm marched unceremoniously to a distant corner (one eye on the lifts awaiting Carla's return), where Sophie's handiwork is resumed with gusto and I resume biting her bottom lip. After five minutes, I decide that enough is enough and tell Sophie that she'll have to wait for the rest. She does what she usually does in these situations. Pouts.

I've been able to soften to a manageable size by the time Carla rejoins us and we then traipse along the south bank of the Seine and cross to the Louvre to see the Mona Lisa, as Sophe wants to find out what 'the old tart has got to look so bloody pleased about'.

And then, as we just *happen* to be in the area, it's hit the boutiques time and I leave the two ladies to spend a small fortune or just oooh and ahhh at the lovely goodies and then marvel at the price tags. A lonesome stroll through the gardens to the Orangerie fills an hour and then I head back to the hotel.

Time for tea? And no, I don't want a bloody croissant. But the other pastries and cakes are excellent. As the tea is bound to be crap, it's yet another milky coffee. It's straight down the gym when I get home. In fact, I'm going to have to take up residence there for a couple of weeks to burn these calories off. Either that, or spend the next month shagging Sophie silly.

Yeah, that gets my vote.

*

I tell Carla it's OK if she wants to slip off this evening and see Françoise. In fact it's in my interest on several levels. Apart from the obvious, one new one is that I know that Carla has a long term, live-in partner back home and that this little affair means I have something on her. It's now fairly obvious to her what's going on between me and Sophie, which is careless, I know, but at least now the secrets lie both ways. I can probably trust her, but you never know. So we now have an unspoken pact between us, the 'what happens in Paris ...... et cetera et cetera,' except that my transgression won't stay in Paris, will it? Not by a mile.......

XCV

A life lived behind closed doors. That's what we have. Even the smallest of intimacies happen in private. Out of sight.

Can you imagine how wonderful it feels just to be able to walk down a city street with your lover's arm around you? ... your head on his shoulder? Or, simply, hand in hand? It's never happened before. Ever. The perpetual fear of discovery. But here, just for once.... freedom.

Carla has seen fit to leave us to our own devices again this evening. She didn't waste any time there, did she? Strangely, my respect for her has actually increased. She's away from home, saw something (or someone) that she wanted, and went for it. No harm done..... Sensible.

Unlike me.

But, hey, I'm not complaining. Really I'm not. I'm making the most of it coz we go home tomorrow. Savouring every last moment, as H would say.

So we find an out of the way restaurant. Nothing flashy, just quiet and intimate and have just enough food and wine to be merry, but not too much coz H says I need some more oral lessons (of course I do) and he doesn't want me being sick, coz it's a bit of a passion killer, apparently.

So it's a long and leisurely few hours of passion before lights out, which seems to suit us both well, variety being the spice of, and all that. But in the morning I wake him with what has now become a regular going over, demonstrating my new found expertise. He's most appreciative. My skin is going to be like silk by the time I get home.

My souvenir of Paris.

*

Friday morning and back in the office. Paris seems light years away. It's almost as if it never happened, except for the fact that H is absolutely right and that my breasts have never been so lovely and smooth. Someone should bottle that stuff. I'd volunteer to lend a hand....or two.

XCVI

Last night's homecoming was a little tortuous. Sarah was congenial enough, but it spoke volumes that her first question after enquiring about my well-being was to enquire after Carla's. And then Sophie's. Maybe if she had posed those two questions the other way around it would have been more poignant. But then, maybe, it was quite deliberate. Which way would you play it? Get annoyed that the same old subject was cropping up, yet again? Attack being the best line of defence. Or just play it cool? Cool implying guilt? You never can tell with Sarah though. She's almost impossible to read at the best of times. At the *worst* of times....well, you've got no chance. The temptation was there to tell all on Carla, in an attempt to put Sarah's mind at rest, but I decided against it. For one, it really was none of Sarah's business whose pants Carla was currently exploring and the fewer people that knew the better. Secondly, it could put the spotlight onto Sophie .... if it wasn't already. Far too risky.

*

This morning, however, all is brightness and light in the office. Sophie seems to be on cloud nine, or maybe even twelve. She is most thankful for the body lotion that I gave her. She says it's worked wonders and could I get her some more? And maybe some face cream too, please?

Sometimes, she really does go too far.

Funny, sitting here this morning, watching the staff flitting by my window. I'm wondering where my priorities lie. I'm also wondering where the future will take me. Yes, a pensive mood.

So, where *do* my priorities lie? Maintain my marriage. Maintain my lover. Maintain my business. Sounds easy, doesn't it? Never is, though. So, number one – marriage – that'll be fine just as long as Sarah doesn't cotton on to what is actually going on. It's a must have, though. Number two – lover – lost for words right now. Paris was a dream. Sophie is just magnificent. Mere words cannot express. Three – business - can pretty much look after itself. Positivity breeds success. And we are going places. Let's face it, if we can drag the French out of their own territory, we have to be doing *something* right.

It's numbers one and two that I have to be mindful of.

*

I'm almost grateful when the closing bell rings and I'm heading for the exit. A night out with Nick. Haven't seen the old bugger for ages. At least it seems that way. I know that I should be spending some time with Sarah, having been away all week, but she didn't seem too bothered. After all, she has me all weekend. She can do with me what she will, then. Let's hope so. My wind is up!

*

My drink with Nick comes as a bit of a shock. He's not his usual congenial self. Sat slumped at a table staring soullessly into his pint. Barely acknowledges my arrival. 'Work, money or wife?' No point in pissing around.

Nick lifts sad eyes to face me, 'try all three.'

Ah, not a great time to be going out for a drink, then? But if best mate has problems, it'll have to be a counselling session for the next hour and, let's face it, I've sounded off at him on more than one occasion. It's time to return the favour.

Work - It seems that redundancy is in the offing. Hence no money coming in, hence wife is going to be seriously pissed off....*when* she finds out. My advice – once it's certain, tell her straight away. If she complains that she should have been told earlier, just say what would've been the point? Might never have happened.

Nick knows I'm right, as it's the conclusion he'd already come to himself. He was just looking for someone to endorse his thoughts.

By the end, I'm thinking, this could have been me, not so very long ago. Lost my company, lost my income...maybe even lost my wife. Now the first two are no longer a problem, but I've made number three even more likely.

Best get home and make sure that's not going to happen.

But I don't. I end up on a pub crawl with Old Nick. He's in no hurry to go home and persuades me that I'm not either. What are friends for, eh? Seven pints. Jeez, I can't remember the last time I had *seven* pints. Seven pints *and* a curry.

I pile into a taxi around midnight and by the time the door falls open in front of me and I've picked myself up off the floor, it's pushing twelve thirty. Sarah's long since retired, so ever the thoughtful husband, I crash on the sofa.

Fully clothed. And reeking.

XCVII

Weeks and weeks go by, and as the memory of Paris fades I can't help but hint that maybe we should go again. Henry's not so sure. It was a bit of a treat, he says. Expensive, if not productive. And, after all, the work to be done is to be done here. Not there.

I pout, stop short of stamping my foot, but it makes no difference.

Emms is seeing her bloke most weekends, so I don't even get to go out on the piss. Daddy still doesn't know about her relationship, let alone the proposal. I'm sure all hell will break loose when he finds out, if what Emms says is anything to go by.

So life got lonely all of a sudden. No Henry. No Emms. Just me in my crap bedsit at weekends, with nothing and no-one to do.

*

It's now been five weeks and four days and about seven hours since Henry last left me unable to walk properly. I never thought I'd long to be disabled, but under the circumstances......... It's alright for him. He has the wife option should he feel the need. The only options I have are a four fingered shuffle and an aging vibrator whose batteries, the last time I looked, were leaking a sticky liquid.

I long to do the same.

It's not fair.

Emms suggested I go down to Guy's place for the weekend. See if she can't sort me out with one of the stable lads ..... or maybe a lord. There was a certain appeal to this, given the liberal use of riding crops in and around stables, but it wouldn't be the same without Henry administering my punishment. Him I trust. Anyone else, forget it.

And, in the same way that Emms' dad doesn't know about Guy, Emms doesn't know about Henry, no matter how much I'm tempted to tell her. I mean, the way things went in France, it's not as if it's a major secret anymore. Carla clearly knows something is going on...though maybe coz she's strayed from the straight and narrow, she's now *more* likely to keep schtum? So Emms still thinks I've been pretty much celibate for the last year, except for that poor bloke that I scared the crap out of at my flat that one time. No wonder she's worried about me.

Hell, *I'm* worried about me!

I guess I'm no good at making my own entertainment. I need other people to help me out. Unfortunately it's just the one person that I need to help me out, and he ain't coming out to play.

XCVIII

Sophie seems to think that it's only her that's desperate to get together again. It's not. Ignoring the obvious reason, I'm putting on weight and getting seriously out of condition. I've been back to the gym, working out, not just to sweat and work off those extras kilos, but in an attempt to work off some sexual frustration too. A vain attempt, I might add. How the hell is running a couple of miles better than a bloody good shag? Exactly? I mean the scenery isn't exactly inspiring, is it? Twenty sweaty blokes. Might do it for some people, but I'm not one of them.

Then a client wants to talk on Friday. Frankly I've had enough of being stuck in the office for the last few weeks, so I suggest that I drive down, just for the day, to see him. Day trip. No overnighter. But I mention it to Sophie anyway ...and she wants. Sure, it's the same as me. Trapped in the office. There's no implication of any playtime. Just time together. Which is no bad thing, because it's one thing spending the working week with someone, in a crowded office, it's entirely different from being on a one to one.

So Friday, I pick Sophie up from her place and we are off. I think that we are both acting like a couple of kids. It's like the first day of the summer hols. First I have to apologise. I haven't been avoiding her. It's just been so busy. She knows. She's exhausted. Needs a holiday. Some chance I jest. Yeah, some chance she echoes.

For once, I'm not so pleased that I have such a wide car. It's comfortable and luxurious even, what with the leather hide, but when it comes to getting friendly........ Because Sophie is getting restless and it's like a previous trip when she couldn't sit still for a single minute and ended up resting her head in my lap and........ Only this time, we take it in turns so that, by the time we reach the client's office, the washroom is my first port of call. Sophie has no such need, having swallowed the evidence long since.

But on the way back, neither of us are in a mood to compromise, what with Sophie practicing her manual skills for the first forty miles. We *have* to do something. There's plenty of countryside en route, so when things start to get seriously sticky, I pull off the road into a lay-by. She's out of the car. Not under her own steam. Under mine. By the hair. It's some time since we played that little game and I can tell by the noises she makes, and what she says, that this is exactly what she wants.

But this is to be a quickie, no time for formalities here ..... so she's bent over and we are just loving the spontaneity of this and there's no sensuality, no passion, just pure lust.

It's over before we really know it started but that's OK, as that's when we get to savour the moment, however brief.

'Got caught short, did we?' I turn, horrified, to see a middle aged woman with a bulldog. There's a passing mutual resemblance. I realise my trousers are round my ankles, Sophie's panties are halfway down her legs and her skirt up around her waist. My groin is pressed hard against Sophie's bare bum. Whilst the woman can't 'see' anything, as such, there's little left to the imagination. I turn to block her view so that we can compose ourselves, sight unseen. That accomplished, we make our excuses and leave. Those excuses being mainly – 'for fuck's sake', 'nosey old trout' and 'I should have known better than to try another shag in sodding the country'.

At least I didn't get bitten this time though, by the look on the face of the bulldog, it was a close run thing.

We had a bloody good laugh about it on the way home, but inside I was fuming. Reduced to a quick shag behind the bushes on a major highway. Is that what we have come to? Good grief. It all seems so sad and pathetic.

*

I stop by at Sophie's place, so she can drop off her bags, but I just sit in the car with the engine running. I'm actually quite pissed off now.

The same old questions keep nagging me. 'What the fuck are you doing?' being the foremost in my mind.

I need a piss, so off goes the engine and out I hop. It'll only take a minute.

But almost as soon as I step through the door, I know that it is a mistake. I have never trespassed into Sophie's world before and that is exactly what it feels like now. Trespass. Her accommodation is tiny. Not just by my standards. By anyone's. Just one small room. A single bed in one corner, a tiny fridge, sink, two ring cooker, microwave, a chest of drawers with a mirror on top. And that's it. There's a bathroom with a toilet and shower off to one side, which is where I can see Sophie through the open door. Her back to me.

The place is a mess. There are clothes everywhere. On the floor, on the furniture, hanging out of drawers, draped over some kind of clothes rack in the corner. And from the odour, I'm guessing they're not exactly clean either.

The walls are adorned with posters and postcards. Pin ups, I guess you'd call them. Movie and TV and music stars, the names of whom have never entered my orbit. They are hunks, lean faced, square jawed without a hint of jowl, tight skinned with no crease or line in sight, bright eyed with no bags, prominent cheek bones, full heads of hair and no touch of grey, their torsos the very model of those whose metabolisms can burn off every last calorie and more without even trying, skin tight, fat free, rippled and fine.

Time was, I looked like that. I catch sight of myself in the mirror. Now look at you. Who are you trying to kid? Her...or your own self?

Welcome to Sophie's world, Henry Blythe.

She is barely out of her teens. Little more than a child with juvenile desires and longings and an adult life new-birthed from chaos. Is that it? Is that the attraction? The child I never had?

I ask again, 'What the hell do you think you're doing? Eh?'

Seriously.

She wanders in. 'Oh hi. I thought that you were staying in the car.' I wish I had. 'Sorry about the mess. It's been a bit hectic, as you know.'

There's a brief lull as I struggle to think of something appropriate.

Finally - 'Do I not pay you enough?'

She gets my meaning. Instantly. 'The money just seems to go. You know how it is. Clothes mainly. Have to look gorgeous for my man!' and she smiles, wide.

And I guess that that's it. All that finery. All that money. For me. And she lives like this.

Good grief.

There's a framed certificate of some sort on the wall by her bed and I sit to examine it more closely. It's a degree. A university degree. A 'very good university' degree. 'Sophie MacDonald, B. A. Hons.' I read out loud. 'You're a *graduate*?'

'You really *do* still think I'm thick, don't you?' but I'm shaking my head in disbelief.

'What on earth were you doing working as a *receptionist*? As *my* receptionist. With a *degree* to your name?' I'm beginning to sound distressed, but can't help it.

"S no big deal,' she shrugs 'I'm fluent in French. That was easy. The rest I just muddled on through.' You do *not* 'just muddle on through' to go to *that* establishment, young lady, I think, but say.....

'And ended up answering phones with a Jamaican accent?'

She's shocked. 'Oh fuck, you heard that one *too*?' she says through her fingers. The smile I attempt is pathetically weak.

'Why were you wasting your *time* like that?'

A shrug. 'It all worked out OK, in the end. Didn't it?'

Yes, I guess it did. Kind of.......

'We *have* to get you somewhere better than here....' This is awful, I'm thinking, and almost say – no child of mine is living in a place like this. But I don't. Instead it's '...even if I have to help out. A deposit. Rent in advance.' Whatever it takes.

'Ya don't have to H. I can manage.' Clearly she can't. Not at all.

'Sophe. You are a professional woman now. You shouldn't still be living like an impoverished student. Not anymore. Time to grow up, hun. Really.'

This gets a reaction. She sags, 'I've let you down, haven't I?' and she can't take her eyes off a small area of carpet about a metre in front of her. Something stops me from contradicting her. All I can think is 'I shouldn't have come here.'

I have to get out.

Suddenly I can't breathe.

*

I leave Sophe just standing there. It is not kind. It is not me. I just know that I can't stay. I tell her to take the rest of the day off. I'll see her Monday.

All the way home these thoughts are careening around my head and I need time and space to think them through.

First thought. What the hell do you think you're doing? Well we've had this one already. No real answer yet. I'm having fantastic sex with a bright, smart, vivacious and wonderful young woman. Someone I could happily spend every minute of every day with, sex or no sex. But, I'm also being unfaithful to my wife. Someone with whom I've had well over twenty fantastic years.

Second thought – what now? Where *exactly* do you think this is all going? Worst case scenario – Sarah finds out the truth. The definitive truth. Her sixth sense has already told her there's a problem here. She even knows what the problem is. She just hasn't quite got to the heart of the matter. Yet.

And, when (not if) she does? There will be absolute hell to pay. Will she forgive and forget? Somehow I doubt it. She's not one to take it lying down, despite her sexual proclivities. Revenge and spite will rear their ugly heads. Hell hath no fury..... like Sarah Blythe. And who could blame her? After all, I promised.

So divorce and a relationship with someone half my age .... who is also an employee. Is that my future? In ten years I'll be retiring. In ten years Sophie will be in the prime of her life. At the height of her sexual appetite. Insatiable. No, *more* insatiable, if that's possible.

She'll fucking kill me!

There'll be young bucks like bees round the proverbial. Younger, fitter, better looking. While I get older, weaker, saggier with each passing year. Is she going to want to hang around? I doubt it. And who can blame her? Do I want to head into my old age as a lonely man?

And then there's children. There's a reason women hit their sexual peak in their early thirties. That one last opportunity, if they haven't already. Their last hurrah. Get up the duff now. It may be your final chance. Do I want to become a father at sixty? Would she want the father of her kids to be a pensioner? Having a kickabout, with the boys, from behind a Zimmer frame?

And what if I stay with Sarah? I lose Sophie for a start. I'm not sure I could take that right now. I already feel as though I've just left part of me behind in her chaotic flat. One more piece of flotsam to add to her collection. There'll be more, I'm sure. Someone like her won't stay single for long. She could have the pick.....

And what pain am I going to cause? I've already seen what she's like at the merest possibility of us not seeing each other again. If I finish it all, will it finish her? I can't do that to her. The distress would cripple her... and me. I just can't. And to cap it all, she works for me. She relies on me to give her an income. What will happen to her if that's taken away? It couldn't get any worse. Could it?

Third and final thought – How the fuck did I get into this mess?

I can't even bring myself to answer that one.

I remember, years ago, someone at a dinner party saying that to decide which of two women you should stay with you had to ask yourself one question. Which would you rather spend the night with...tonight? And whichever you decided upon was the one you should spend the rest of your life with. It didn't really sink in at the time. I had no reason, then, to consider it in any great depth. But now that question *is* relevant. Directly relevant. So who would I chose. The beautiful, young woman – my lover - or the beautiful, older woman – my wife?

I can only conclude that the question is unfair ..... on the wife. The young lover is novel, exciting and has youth and vitality on her side. And time. However content you are in the long term relationship, by comparison it is bland. Novelty and excitement are both long gone. As is youth.

Which would you choose?

*

Somehow I find myself lying in bed staring off into the blackness. I have come home, said hi to the wife, zombied through dinner and hit the sack early complaining of a headache. Which I really do have. Sarah is beside me. I think she's asleep, but can't tell for sure.

I still can't blot it all out. There's still a maelstrom in my head. It lasts for hours. Until, finally, I'm swamped with fatigue and sleep takes over.

My mind made up.

XCIX

Well the last person I expected to see on a Saturday morning is Mr Henry Blythe. Maybe he went out for a jog and got lost? He's certainly looking lost. Firstly he apologises for rushing off like that last night. It's not a problem for me, I say, very few people seem to want to hang about my flat for too long .... Eau de Pussey or no Eau de Pussey (but I don't mention that bit).

He tells me he didn't sleep much. He had alot of thinking to do and it kept him awake most if the night.

First off, he says I've got to find new accommodation. I absolutely cannot live in a dump (his word) like this. I know he's right, but I'm buggered if I'm gonna let on that he is. So I shrug and leave it at that. This weekend is gonna be spent flat hunting – no, not with him, he can't be seen out with me, so I'll have to do it on my own. A decent place, one bedroom, separate lounge, bathroom and kitchen. Maybe even a small garden. Space for a washing machine would help. I like the sound of that. The garden, that is, not the washing machine. Can't think why I haven't done it before. Lack of cash mainly. I've spent on stuff like there is no tomorrow and maxed out every line of credit. Up to my eyeballs in debt with just a few designer clothes to my name.

I mean, it's hard keeping up with the likes of Henry Blythe. Company director. Barrister for a wife. These are wealthy people. Well, wealthy compared to me. H is paying me well, he takes me on expensive trips, albeit mainly business trips, there's no criticism there, but come on H, I'm kinda outa my league here. I remind him what I said last night – '....clothes mainly. Have to look gorgeous for my man'. He says that I'd look gorgeous in a sack with a bit of rope tied round my waist. I say, that could be arranged, but I'm not sure the rope would stay round my waist for very long.

He doesn't laugh. This worries me.

He's sitting on my bed and I'm kneeling on the floor in front of him. His hands are clasped on his lap and he's gazing off into the distance.

'What's wrong, H?' He says nothing...at first.

'I ....err, I just don't think that I can.......I mean, I can't ......' but whatever he wants to say won't come.

So I say it for him. 'This is where you dump me, isn't it?' and I'm squeezing his hands so tightly in mine, gritting my teeth. Trying to stop the inevitable. There's an empty space where my guts used to be. And I can't breathe.

The lines on his face are looking deeper. Those sparkling blue eyes look watery and sad. But he still won't look at me. Please look at me, H. Please look into my eyes. I know it makes you melt. I've seen it before...that way you won't be able to do this.

But he doesn't.

'I've created the most godawful mess here, Sophie. Whatever I do, someone, somewhere is going to get hurt.'

'And that someone has to be me, right?'

Then he looks at me, '...and me... not sure that I can ... I want to keep .... but I *have* to do this.' And he's back staring out the wall opposite him, 'I stand to lose everything if I let this continue. Sarah, will find out about us, you know. It's a bloody miracle she hasn't already. She's come *so* close. And then what?'

'You leave her for me, H' and it seems so weak, even as I say it. Why would he? Lose his wife, lose his home, for some young bint half his age, who doesn't really know what she's doing and is still living like a pauper. What do I have to offer him, exactly?

'So this is the pay off, is it H? New flat. Dead relationship. Buy me off, then just walk away.'

He's horrified. So he bloody well should be. Anger and hurt are jostling for position and I'm not sure which one is winning.

'You think that this is easy? You think I *want* to do this?' I'm sitting there tight lipped now. 'What would you suggest?' he counters, smashing the ball back at me. 'Where exactly do *you* see us going with this?'

And of course, he's got me there. I've considered the consequences even less then he has. He might as well be asking me for a solution to world hunger or poverty. Forget asking him to leave his wife. Even through the tears I can see the folly in that.

I don't know H, I'm just enjoying being together. The sex, the luxury hotels, the food, the wine ..... the handcuffs. Not that I say any of this, of course. It all sounds just a teeny bit shallow. So I just shake my head. I'm defeated. I know I am. What the hell am I gonna do now?

'And then there's work, of course.....' Now it's my turn to look horrified.

'You're not going to *fire* me too? Surely? ......H?'

He's shaking his head 'no, I'm not going to fire you ....' and there's a 'but' coming, I just know it, '...but do you think that you could carry on, at work, just as before?'

Course I can, H, sure. I'll have tears streaming down my face all day, smeared mascara, I'll wail and I'll bawl like a banshee, but no-one will notice. So, yeah, no problem.

Who am I kidding. It wasn't so long ago that I locked myself in the loo to have a quiet cry coz of what was (or wasn't) going on between us. What chance am I gonna have of covering up my whole life falling apart?

'God, this is awful. I lose my bloke, I lose my job. At least you don't wanna make me homeless, too. Or was that an empty promise?'

'This is my fault, Sophie. It's up to me to make this right ......'

'As the only responsible adult here, you mean?' He lets this go.

' ....to do whatever it takes. Look....' and he's looking down at me again, 'if you honestly think you can carry on at work, then I really do want you there. You make the world of difference to the place. It'd be like a morgue without you.....' and there's that *but* coming again, '...but the last thing I can afford to happen is histrionics.....' That's a word I don't know. '...have you throwing a wobbly when things get tough.' Ah, got you. 'I'm just not sure that you can carry that off. Are you?'

Shit! I *so* wish he wouldn't keep doing that. Asking me a bloody question where I can't give the answer that *I* want to give. My forehead on his knee now. 'You already know the answer, don't you?'

Defeated.

That's when I give up trying to keep it all in.

That's when the levee breaks.

C

It was over twenty five years ago that I last did anything like this. I swore then that it would never happen again. Couldn't stand the distress it caused. Yet here I am watching Sophie collapse before my eyes.

I feel like banging my head against the wall over and over and shouting 'stupid, stupid, stupid!'

I mean, what have I left her with, eh? Broken heart, no job, no income. I promise everything I can to her and I'm kidding myself that it's ever going to be adequate compensation for my disaster. Apartment - we'll get you somewhere nice to live, job – look I know loads of people, they'd only be too happy to have a bright, intelligent woman like you to.... and references will be no problem........

Oh, will you shut the fuck up!?

And then anger takes over and she's accusing me of all sorts. Using her, is top of the list. Just picked on poor innocent little Sophie. She's cute but not very bright. She'll be good for a shag, the little slut. Give her a good seeing to then dump her when you've had enough, coz I'm sure there'll be another silly wee tart along in a minute. And do you know what? You're probably right, Mr Blythe, and I should have seen it coming coz you know what I always thought? That I'd be the one to dump you. I mean, let's face it, you're no spring chicken are you? Not exactly a young stud, but do you know what the really galling thing is? You beat me to it!

Bastard.

So I rise to go, because there's no use arguing with her, even though none of what she has said is true, but then she's hanging off my neck saying sorry, sorry I didn't mean it, honest, please don't go, please don't. Please.

We just stand there. Just about holding on.

This *is* killing me.

CI

I have my Henry back.

I don't know what has happened. Where he has been. And I don't much care.

Because he's back...

>........ and I'm grateful.

PART TWO

END OF TIME.....

WEEKS LATER.......

I know that I shouldn't be here...and I'm scared. Scared of who I might meet. Scared what they might say, or think.....or do. But I can't help myself. I'm drawn. When I heard, my heart leapt into my mouth and I felt my legs go weak. It'd been a while since that'd happened. And the same person was the cause then, too. It's amazing how the mere mention of a name can have that effect on your whole body...as if it was draining the life out of you.

I had to sit down. My head buzzing with the million thoughts that his name had let loose. When did this happen? Why didn't I know sooner? What is it that's the problem? Where is he? Who is he with?.....and most of all, the one thing that I tried not to think of...just how bad is this?

There were just shreds of Carla's phone call embedded in my brain. Seriously ill....collapsed...hospital.....unconscious......ICU.

The nurse is pleasant enough when I stop to ask the way, but I struggle to get the words out. Not like me, I know, but my mouth seems so dry and I have a terrible sense of foreboding. Don't want to seem upset. Want to appear together, composed. Not sure I succeed.

Nothing has prepared me for what I find though. I know roughly where I'm going but had already made my mind up to keep walking, even when I get to the right spot. Just in case....just in case there is someone else by his bed. You see, I didn't think that it would be right to be seen there, under the circumstances. It was slightly irrational, I know, but I'd learnt to be cautious in such situations. I'd learnt that from you. There really was nothing to fear. Not really. No-one had ever known, not really.

And then there he is....alone in a room. But still I keep walking, taking in as much as I can in that one brief glimpse. Unconscious? Asleep? Wires, tubes, machines, all the paraphernalia of modern medicine. His lifeline? But I stop a few paces on. Making sure the coast is clear. Pause, a deep intake of breath, turn and march straight in.

Unconscious, yes......resting. I'm standing in the doorway, not sure what to do. Nothing, but nothing, has prepared me for this though. I had expected him to be sitting up in bed, reading some intellectual tome which he'd lay on the bed, smiling as I walked in. Pleased to see me. I'd wanted to cheer him up by my very presence, see that smile that used to melt me. But I could see that that was not going to happen. What could I do?

I almost walk away, not being able to bear to see him like this. I am rooted to the spot for maybe a minute before I slowly move across the room to the far side of the bed where there is a chair. Sitting with my back to the window, my bag on my lap, my eyes dart around to the room, tubes and gadgets of all sorts. He looks like he's wired into the wall. A constant beep beep beep. Then the bed, then his shape then, at last, his face. It is a full minute before I realise that I really am shaking. I look down at my hands than back at his face. What am I supposed to do, Henry? Tentatively I reach out, scared to touch his motionless hand. And then the comfort of warm flesh on mine, but my comfort. Not his. Me taking strength from him, when it is clear that it is him that needs it. He that needs me when I had been so used to it being the other way around.

'I'm here, Henry' I struggle to say. My own voice almost startles me. Was that me talking? I try to snap out of it.....take a deep breath.... 'a right bloody mess you've gotten into here, Henry. Took your eye off the ball, didn't you?' It just doesn't seem adequate. Words won't come...at least not what I should say. Levity sounds crass but I can't bring myself to be serious. It seems equally inappropriate.

'We had fun, didn't we?' Oh, do shut up woman! Is that really the best that you can do? 'Miss you babe' ...well that's a slight improvement. At least it's true. My thumb strokes the back of his hand, careful to avoid the harsh needle piercing his vein. I sigh. If you can't think of anything to say, best to keep quiet. But all I can think of is really crap stuff like 'remember when we....I used to love it when you....' and every other cliché in the book that you're supposed to say in such circumstances when someone seems to be close to death and they need to hear the familiar, the routine to bring them back to life...but I just can't do it. You were familiar to me but never, ever routine.

And still the machine, marking out the heart beat...beep, beep, beep........

And I'm not sure why, but suddenly after a slow minute of silence, it all comes flooding out. 'remember when...I used to love it....you never guess what so-and-so.....last week I nearly....' some of it trivia but then lapsing into 'affaires du coeur', if you'll pardon the expression...and, after a quick look at the door, I lower my voice and start reminding you of some of the things that we used to get up to.... 'oh, Henry, that time in the lift...I spent the whole evening trying to get your attention, trying to see if things were all right between us, after several weeks of nothing but professional contact, whilst not appearing too keen in front of all those other people until, at last, I'd had enough. I'd held on as long as I could, tempering that ache that I had, and just kind of .....drifted away.

When the lift arrived I slouched in and slumped against the wall. Head down. And then, at the last minute, you just appeared in front of me. 'Almost missed it!' you said. 'Oh, hi Mr Blythe....' trying my damnedest not to sound pleased to see you, trying to forgive you for ignoring me all evening. And I'll never know who made the first move...I hoped that it was you, but I really didn't care coz as soon as those doors closed we were on each other, mouths, kisses, hands, gropes grasping, bugger, I wished that we were staying in the tallest hotel ever, I just wanted that ride to go on and on..... But the lift lurched as it slowed and I thought, Please don't let anyone come in, not now, not like this!

But the doors opened to reveal that couple standing there. But you dealt with them, didn't you? In your own sweet way, and as the doors slid shut, 'click'...it took a moment to sink in...I couldn't move my hands...Oh Henry, you *were* being bad! And then the doors opened straight into that huge room and you practically dragged me out of there, the cold of the steel around my wrists behind my back, teetering on high heels, a little bit drunk, an awful lot as horny as hell.

I know things got more complicated after that night and it was just the beginning but it's a night I'll never forget. I can remember it now, almost every detail as if it was last night....I so wish it was last night H, wish you'd given me such a night to remember only *last* night.

I miss that, miss that ....mastery...that command...yeah, alright, I admit it, that skill! No-one has ever come close. They lacked your acumen, Henry.

Hell, they just *lacked*!

And as for our few days in the country....possibly the best and the worst few days of my life.

Swinging from that tree while you were being eaten alive....after you'd eaten *me* alive! Honestly, when that woman turned up, I'd have given anything to have seen the look on your face. All I had was a view of your naked bottom. Upside down. Which was *probably* preferable. What is it about rural old bats and us trying to have a shag in the great outdoors?

And then I remember your head injury and look at the bandages around your skull, white tape covering your salt and pepper hair and I'm thinking – is there a connection here? Is this something to do with what happened that weekend? H, I do hope not. That would be awful. I only want good memories of that weekend even when I was staring a slow and painful death in the face and I thought that you were dead, I'm sure that I wasn't actually taking any of it seriously. It's how I cope.

Like now. Lying there looking like something that escaped from an Egyptian tomb. Come on H, don't ya know you've got a company to run. It won't run itself you know. Well, it probably could, but it still needs the main man to keep an eye on it.

I've almost run out of steam now. Struggling to find anything else to say. Some people keep this up for weeks, months, years even. Trying to bring back what they have lost. Never giving up. I can't help but admire their dedication. But I'm not sure that I can do this. No response is hard to take. Talking to myself feels stupid.... slightly mad even.

Come on H, a cup of strong coffee and two ibuprofen'll soon sort you out.

It occurs to me that talking about our sex life might not be such a great idea. I mean, I'm trying to get a reaction here. That reaction being Henry stirring, waking up even, talking to me, saying 'Hi, how are things?' What if I got a reaction ....in the wrong place? What if poor old H (OK, less of the 'old') was lying here unconscious with a bloody big stiffy sticking up under the bed sheets like a tent pole? And then the nurse walked in? What *is* she going to think? That I've been having a quick fiddle with him on the quiet? Or maybe even practising my oral skills? And, let's face it, this man needs his blood elsewhere in his body right now. Coursing through those parts that need healing, not those parts that need a bloody good........

So, OK H, no more sex talk...we don't want you getting all excited, do we? Not in such a public arena, anyway. There's bound to be an old trout around here somewhere, keeping an eye on you.

Don't tell me I've got nothing else to talk about? I mean, I know we had an affair but it wasn't just sex. Was it?

OK. I've been fine, thanks for asking. I mean, I've been walking around like a zombie since I last saw you, but .... My friend told me I was bereft. I didn't really know what she meant. She had to explain it to me. Bereft as in bereavement. As if someone had died. Ooops, sorry H, no offence! But she was right of course. We'd both been there before. Chucked by blokes that had got under our skin. This is just worse, is all. Harder to bear. I spent the whole weekend crying in bed. Didn't know what else to do.

Then my mate Emms came round and I explained it all to her. She was stunned. Not sure if it was coz of what I had been doing (yes I told her all the juicy details!) but also who I'd been doing it with. And there was her thinking that she was the only one into older men! And there was her thinking that she was the only one getting laid. And the fact that I'd kept it secret for god knows how long....... That absolutely *killed* her.

Oooops, sorry again.

She said that getting somewhere new to live was a great idea. Turn over a new leaf, she said. A new beginning. So I called in sick on Monday morning, as you must know. Hollie took the message. She sounded as smug as ever. I'm betting she thought I was just taking a long weekend. I'd loved to have told her, H, just to wipe that conceited smile off her face. I had no idea whether you were in or not. I wouldn't have wanted to speak to you, anyway. OK, maybe I would.

Emms bunked off too. We found a great place which was newly decorated and furnished. It even had a garden. Big enough for a few friends to enjoy. And a tree to play under. And not an old trout in sight. I know it was expensive, H, but you did say whatever it took. I can afford the rent pretty much, especially as the new job you got me pays even better than the old one. But thanks for the deposit and rent in advance...and the bonus you gave me when I left. Well, I was Ms Sensible. All my debts paid off. And some left over. What do you think of that, eh? The new me.

Still a bit fragile though. It'll take time, Emms said.

There's barely a moment of the day when I'm not thinking..........

The new job is great and the Boss seems like a nice man, but then you'd know that, what with him being a friend of yours. I don't know what you told him about me, about why I left, but he seems to be treating me like the bees knees. I'm not taking any crap from anyone there. No-one, but no-one is going to push me around. It's probably helping that I'm still bloody seething about what happened, but I think I'm getting a reputation as a ball breaker.

If only they knew!

Henry, I didn't really mean it when I thought, Oh my god, I'm shagging a wrinkly and oh my god I'm shagging a perve. Not really. I mean, yes, I *was* shagging a wrinkly perve, but I really didn't care. I was only joking...honest. It was all so new to me and I wasn't sure what I was doing. I wasn't bothered about what I was doing, actually.....I even *marvelled* at what I was doing, being with you. I mean, who'da thought it? A gorgeous young babe like me with an old fart like you! It's not like I have a father complex or anything.

Would you believe that I read some poetry the other day? No, seriously. Three words caught my eye in a shop window display. 'Stand and stare'. And that's what I did. Just stood there, and stared. I thought, bugger me, now there's a coincidence. But then I saw what else was there and there were two lines of what I guess was poetry underneath. And I read them out loud, to myself, then over and over until I was sure that I would remember them. You shoulda said it was from a poem. I would have liked to have known the rest. Because I finally understood what you meant.

And, do you know, I never regretted a single, solitary moment. Nope.

Not once.......

And....then there is, I don't know, a blip, just something that jars me out of my train of thought, my ramblings, something cold, intangible, a squeeze of the hand? Maybe a spasm...

Beep, beep, beeeeeeeeeeeep....................

And suddenly all around me is chaos, from the calm waters of comfortable reminiscences to the maelstrom of well rehearsed emergency procedures...in a heartbeat.

Someone, a nurse? is shouting something in my face, but I can't understand. I stare blankly, stare too long until I am man-handled out of my chair and ushered out of the room as others rush in. So I stagger to the window so that I can watch until I find myself pressed hard against the glass, the heat of my palms draining away into it as my eyes flit from face to face, at all the new arrivals, serious in their task, and I'm taking in the odd word, crash, adrenalin, and someone has both hands on Henry's chest and is pushing down, hard, and all I can think is, stop that, it must hurt even though I know it is for the best, it *has* to be for the best.

And then that thing that seems at once familiar but also alien, two flat pads, and coily leads and they are placed on his chest, now naked, and someone shouts 'CLEAR!' and his back is arching and I grit my teeth as I feel the pain and the stress in his body, but still beeeeeep.....and I'm thinking come on Henry babe, come on, as the pads are placed again and 'CLEAR', but still beeeeeep....... and I find myself thinking, no, not like this, it can't end like this, not like this Henry, you're too good for it to end like this, no, please no, but all I'm able to say is 'No, no, no.....'

Come *on* babe. I now realise my entire body is shaking and my breath is coming in short sharp bursts and then I hold my breath as....

.......his body arches again in one final lunge for life,

but beeeeeeeeeeeeeeep..........

And there is suddenly an air of defeat in all of those in the room, shoulders slouch, heads hang as if something has been lost and a man in a white coat with pens in the pocket, like some kind of lab technician, is looking at his watch, as I move to the open door, and he's saying something that doesn't quite register, just the odd word....

Time .....

..... ten a.m........

....dead.

PART THREE

TIME WAS......

SEVERAL YEARS LATER........

'Mummy, mummy, what's a organism?'

Uh oh. Alarm bells are ringing. An *organism*. What he really means is.......

'An organism? Weeeeeell,' think, girl, think... 'An organism is something that is a living thing. It can be very big, but usually it's really quite small.' There, that should just about cover both bases. 'So, why do you ask?' I enquire, stroking his hair.

'Weeeeeell,' he says, mimicking me, the little sod! 'I heard Auntie Emma say that she'd just had the best organism *ever*. Can I have a organism, mummy? Can I?'

'Probably not just yet, darling.'

'Maybe for my birthday?'

'Maybe' is all I can say.

'Yeeeah,' he cries as he runs off down the garden, 'I'm gonna get a organism.'

Yeah, and I'm gonna have to have words with 'Auntie Emma'........

*

Oh how times have changed. It all seems so long ago now, but it's gone in the blink of an eye. It could almost be just yesterday that I stood there and watched it all come to an end....... That day still so fresh in my memory. What I saw, the sounds, the smells.....what people said. I have no doubt that some things stay with you forever.....

It happened like this........

All I could do was stand there, in the doorway, as they removed the pipes and wires. Disconnected him. A nurse asked me if I needed anything. That it must have been a terrible shock. Would I like to sit with him for a while? What for? I wanted to ask her, what the hell for? He's not here anymore. He's gone. But she was trying to be kind, so I just shook my head.

I made it halfway to the main door before my legs gave way. Someone helped me to a chair. Some hard plastic thing. The shakes had taken over and I was fighting for breath. The person left me, saying something about getting water. Then they came back. But it wasn't them.

Through the tears it was hard to make out who I was looking at. Then I saw.

In that one split second – a look of recognition (both ways), a look of realisation, (from her), then a look of sheer horror and she clack clack clacked off down the corridor as fast as her stiletto heels could carry her.

I had to get out of there. Feel the cold air on my face.

And as I stood leaning against the exit door, in the distance behind me, I heard a woman's primal scream .... of despair.

*

I hadn't spoken to anyone for days. Hadn't eaten for as long either. I must've still been in shock. Traumatised. I just lay on my bed trying to blot it all out.

Then the door bell went.

Who the hell can that be? No-one would call round. Never have, 'cept Emms and she was away visiting her bloke. She didn't even know. But she'd be round when she couldn't get in contact with me. What do I do then?

Door bell again.

I wasn't bloody answering. How could I have, like this? I was a mess.

Door bell.

Go away. Please go away. But whoever it was, was not giving up. If anything they were getting more persistent. Then I heard a voice. 'Sophie? Sophie? It's me .... Carla.'

It took my brain a while to comprehend what was happening. Carla? Here? What the hell.....? I looked at my door. Should I? It was going to take alot more than that to rouse me.

Door bell .... long and hard. Then ring ring ring .....

Please go away Carla. Please.

'Sophie, please answer. I need to talk.' *She* needs to talk? Well go find someone else to bleat at. 'Sophie, please!' I was getting angry now. Who the hell...? Coming round here uninvited. So I stormed to the door and shouted through it. 'Go away, Carla. I don't want to see anyone.' She won't give up now. Stupid move. And so it went on. God knows how long for. Until I resigned myself to open the door. She flooded in. Arms around me. Hugs. Didn't seem to notice the state I was in....or didn't care. But I just stood there rigid, unresponsive. It was down to her to guide me back to my room. It was a mess, but not unusually so. She sat me on my bed and she settled next to me. She was making soothing sounds but I took little or nothing in. Telling me I've had a terrible time, and what could she do for me, have I eaten, I'm still in shock. Nothing I don't know already.

'Why are you here? Really here?' and I wasn't even looking at her, this friend from the past.

'Henry asked me to keep an eye on you....some time ago. When he thought that you were ..... struggling with things. He just wanted to know that you were OK. Coping.'

'Well I'm not, am I?' And I attempted a contemptuous laugh. It didn't work. 'Bit bloody late, isn't it?'

'I know, now, it's way too late, but he would have wanted me here. I know that much.'

'What can you do? You're not me. You can't feel what I'm feeling. Can't take this grief away.' And I felt the tears welling up again but refused point blank to let them fall. And I certainly wasn't doing that thing where my chin wobbles uncontrollably either. That just looked silly.

But Carla, to her credit, was not to be dissuaded. I guess I would never have expected her to be so. She was buzzing round the room like a hyperactive bluebottle, picking things up and trying to find where to put them. She must have been mad. I wouldn't have known where to start. And all the while she was talking to me and trying to glean some kind of response.

'Things just weren't the same after you left, you know? Truth be told, after .... well, things went into decline pretty quickly. Henry looked like someone had knocked the wind out of him. Big time. Pretty soon after, we started noticing things.... things that weren't quite right. He kept, I don't know, doing clumsy stuff, dropping things, stumbling. Some days he just didn't seem to be there at all. It didn't mean much at the time, but....... I'd guessed what had happened between you when he announced that you wouldn't be coming back. I just put it down to post relationship blues. But then, one day, he just went. Flat out. Well he was rushed to hospital. Something about bleeding on the brain. Scans and all sorts. The whole office was devastated when we heard the news.....'

I wasn't really listening and then I heard the word.

Funeral.

And it jolted me out of my daze and I found myself staring at her open mouthed.

'You must come.' I heard her say. And I'm stunned. Start shaking my head, more and more violently,

'No, no, no, I can't.'

'You *have* to, hun,' she was squatting in front of me now, holding my hand, 'I know it's hard, but it's part of the grieving process. You need to say goodbye.'

And then the tears were falling. 'I can't sit there and watch them *burn* him. I just can't do that. It'll be awful.'

She was downcast. I heard her say, 'Yeah, you're right. It will be. Awful.' And I seemed to have got her going on the crying stakes.

'Besides, his wife. She knows. She was at the hospital, when........' and I can't say anymore.

'I know, Sophie. She told me.'

'You .... you've spoken to her? About me?' A nod. 'She must hate me.'

'That I can't answer. She's a hard one to read, that one.'

'So I can't go, can I, even if I wanted to, which I don't anyway, so ....'

She tried, she *did* try.

Later - 'You must think I'm a silly little girl, messing with people's lives like that?'

'Me? Sophie, I'd be the last person to judge you ....or Henry, for that matter. People have judged me all my life for who I am..... I wouldn't,' she said, slowly shaking her head, '..... I just wouldn't.'

Finally – 'I'll say one thing, though...I've never seen Henry happier than when he was with you in Paris. Never. That's gotta be worth something, hasn't it?'

I laid my forehead on my knees and said nothing.

*

Days and days later, I'd lost track of time by then, the whole rigmarole starts again.

Doorbell.

I was guessing it was Emma, this time, coz I hadn't heard from her for ages. More to the point, she hadn't heard from me. I was up and about a bit more, so begrudgingly headed for the door. But it wasn't Emms....

.... It was Sarah.

I made to shut the door in her face. Pushed hard as she pushed back and I'm hearing 'please Sophie, I just want to talk.' What *was* this? The Sophie MacDonald Counselling Service? ..... but I wasn't listening, I wasn't listening to any of this, 'please, I'm not angry, please don't be angry with me for coming to see you like this.' And then I just gave up, slid down the wall and collapsed on the floor and the tears came yet again.

And she was in my face, squatting down like Carla did days ago. And she gathered me up and guided me into my little room and I ran to sit on the bed, pulled my knees up under my chin, wrapped my arms around my legs and stared off into that safe place called the middle distance where nothing was in focus and nothing bad had ever happened and never would.

'I just wanted to say sorry. Sorry that all this has happened to you. It's been dreadful, I know. And I .... I guess .... I just wanted....someone to ... to talk to.' She was rambling, coz even though it all sounded rehearsed, it all came out at once and probably in the wrong order.

'You .... ?' Is all I say without even giving her the courtesy of looking at her.

'No-one else knows what it's like, do they? To lose him like that? All I get is platitudes, deepest sympathy, but no-one *really* knows. I just lie awake at night, wishing he'd come back. Wanting.' Then she changed direction with 'do you have anyone? Anyone you can talk to?' I waited, then nodded. 'Good' she went on.

'But she doesn't know yet. Doesn't know he died. She's away.'

'Call her Sophie, you need to talk. I need to talk, too. But I have no-one. No-one close enough. That's why I came here and I'm sorry if it's upset you but I just knew that you'd be the only person to understand how much.......' and I heard a sob. 'I'll go' she carried on, 'but I just wanted to show you this,' and something was put in front of my face. I paused, then took it, but didn't see what it was. I was still in the middle distance. 'Please look.' A deep breath and I tried to focus. A photo. A photo of a woman with long, dark hair cut with a fringe. Dark eyes. Slim, pretty. Smiling.

Me.

'I don't remember Henry taking this. Where is it?'

'Sardinia.'

'Can't be. I've never been there.' The photo slipped in my hand.

I heard a sigh. 'It's not you, Sophie, it's *me*.' And I looked again. The hair was the same, long, dark, fringe, large, dark eyes ..... but the nose and the shape of the face .... and the clothes.... Oh god, I wouldn't be seen dead in those........

For the first time I turned to face her, looked her in the eyes. Eyes red raw. She was tired, I could see that. No. Exhausted. But I was still holding this small piece of card. 'You?' and she nodded.

'Don't you see? He had no choice, Sophie. Not really. What he saw in you, was me. Me, twenty odd years back, when .....'

'So he never really liked me then? Is that what you're saying? Not *me,* really?' and it's a mix of distress and anger.

'If his behaviour way back then was anything to go by, nothing could have been further from the truth. And yes, really. That's why, after the initial shock, I couldn't blame you. That time in the hospital, was the first time I'd seen you. Properly. It was like looking into a mirror in time. I'd known for months that something was going on. I'd kept harassing him, even accusing him of having an affair .... with Carla......'

'Carla? But she's a ....'

'Yes, yes, I know that *now*, but back then.......' She shook her head. 'I was *absolutely* convinced you know?'

'I wouldn't put it past him.' I couldn't help saying.

'No. No, Sophie, he never would,' and then it all came out about how years and years ago, from just before they were married, that they both promised to each other that they would never, ever be unfaithful to each other and that Sarah knew that he had kept that promise, until just lately when she realised that something was wrong and when she finally found out the truth, it all made sense. Henry, reaching back into his past. Reliving his youth. Infatuated. For such a brief time. 'It must have seemed priceless to him. That time with you. So I just decided that I could blame you as little as I could blame him. Because you were me.' She paused for breath. 'Does that all sound a bit crap?'

'Yeah, totally crap' but my laugh was the first one for weeks. 'You didn't *really* think that he and Carla....?' but Sarah nodded in a way that said, yeah, I was a complete twat. It happens.

We both managed a little laugh at that.

More seriously - 'He finished with you, didn't he?'

I gave a nod. Then, 'how did you know?'

'Same way I knew that he was seeing someone else. Call it a sixth sense. Those little things that make up a whole. Paying more attention to his appearance, new clothes, smiling more, hitting the gym. And the bloody humming! He said it was down to saving an important account, but it wasn't was it? It was another woman that.....'

'You're wrong, Sarah.' I cut in, 'When those things happened, it *was* about winning an account. I remember, coz he was a different man. Overnight, pretty much. He suddenly had a spark. But there was nothing going on then. Really.'

She looked stumped. 'Really? Wrong again, eh? I must be losing my touch. I wasn't wrong about you splitting up though, was I?' I was shaking my head... '.... because one day, I just knew that it was over and I had him back.' She exhaled a deep sigh. 'All too briefly' she muttered, eyes falling to the floor.

Sarah stayed on for hours. We even adjourned to a local bar for food and drinks. The first time I'd been out or eaten or had alcohol for yonks. It all seemed alien to me somehow. All those people, smiling, laughing. But I persevered. The food was tasteless and the alcohol went straight to my head. I still didn't even know what day it was. It didn't seem important anymore.

But as we chatted some, just a little tiny bit of the tension eased and, after a while, I couldn't shut the bloody woman up. You should have heard the things that Sarah and Henry got up to when they were my age. Honestly, it made what we did look tame by comparison. It was strange that Sarah felt that she could share such intimacies with me. Maybe because we shared the same man....?

And as we parted late that night, we both said, 'Thank you,' simultaneously, and then laughed. And we knew we both meant it.

But as I turned to walk away, Sarah asked, 'do you have anything? To remember him by? A memento?'

I was about to say – 'no', then – 'just one thing. He sent me a note. I kept it, but it's not personal. Not handwritten. It's printed. It could be from anyone – It just said

'10 a.m. Monday. Be there.' And I felt myself well up again and only just managed a choked 'How did he know, Sarah? How did he know that that was when he would die .... *and* that I would be there?'

After a pause she just shrugged then shook her head. 'It's just coincidence, Sophie. Nothing more.'

'Yeah, I know, but it's kinda spooky, isn't it?'

She nodded and it sent a single tear down her cheek. In a hushed tone she said, 'yeah, kinda spooky.'

*

When I got home, I found a business-type card on my chest of drawers. Sarah Blythe – home address and phone numbers. Hand written on the back was a single word ......

ANYTIME

*

'Oh, YES!'

My lovely little friend Emma Tomkins was sandwiched between two hunks of guys, one was playing with her ample bosom and the other had a hand between her legs, coz she had seriously struck lucky on her hen night what with the rugby boys we ran into about half an hour ago. These poor chaps just didn't know what hit them coz Emms was making free with her body tonight because, as she said, she was 'gonna eat, drink and make merry, coz tomorrow I diet.' 'Making merry' she had already explained, meant she got to 'fuck whoever I want tonight, coz it ain't happening again. Ever. OK?'

OK, Emms, whatever you say.

So she was indulging in what she called a 'tuna sandwich' and I *thought* I got the reference. I was just hoping it stayed as the type that was vaguely allowed in public and is not pursued in private.

But Emms had other ideas and she invited 'the lads' and all her posh girlfriends back to her place for a 'proper party'. We were not home long before I spotted her disappearing into her bedroom with two blokes in tow. Same old Emms. Some things never changed. Then I saw another guy disappear bedroom-wards. Then another. And *none* were coming back out again.

Ohmygaaard, she was eating the poor sods alive.

*

Around nine the next morning, I took Emma a cup of tea. There were only two guys left by then, but both were unconscious, naked on her bed. They looked too shagged out to manage a hot beverage. Poor boys. Call yourselves fit?

Emms was sitting up looking as pleased as punch. 'I have *always* wanted to try that!' she beamed. 'So, bin there, done that!'

Enough said.

*

Sarah sent me one of Henry's scarves. It still had his scent on it. It became my most prized possession.

*

God knows what time of night it was. I was barely conscious and all I could hear was this trilling sound. There was a pale glow coming from the far side of the room and it took a good few seconds to realise that my phone was going. And it wasn't going to stop. So I squeezed my eyes tight shut for one last time, took a deep breath and hauled myself out of bed. The best I could do was make a grunt in response to answering. There was nothing but silence on the line. 'Hello?'

'Zat you Sophie?' Despite the obvious effects on her of alcohol, and probably tiredness, I still recognised Sarah's voice instantly.

'What time is it?' I managed through the grogginess.

'I'm so sorry to call at thiz time. Really. But .....' and then she broke down. A woman in distress. It could have been me at any time in the last eight weeks. 'Shouldn' 'ave dizturbed you .... sorry ....panicked....scared of bee on my own...in the dark...'

'Is OK' I said, 'I had to get up anyway. The phone was ringing.' The old ones are often the......

And she laughed through the tears. 'How do you *do* that? Make a joke when you must be feeling as shit as me?'

'It's what keeps me going, Sarah.'

What else could I say?

*

It was an inspired choice and I'm really not sure why it didn't occur to me sooner. I was thinking, who the hell could I.....? No-one really seemed appropriate. Not *really*.

So it was Sarah, of all people, that accompanied me to Emma's wedding.

You have to understand that things had moved on in the interim. It's fair to say that we had become friends by then. Not the kind of friend that you go out on the piss with, go clubbing and pull some gangly lad who likes a dildo up his bum... Not *that* kinda friend. That wasn't really Sarah, as you could imagine. At least, not these days, anyway.

I reckoned Sarah could do with meeting a few of the landed gentry. She'd feel much more at home in that kinda company than I would, that was for sure. Sarah was Dutch courage for me and it probably worked both ways. We both admitted that it was the first time either of us had put on any glad rags since Henry was around. She'd taken some persuading, as I'd expected, but I played the sympathy card – 'I *can't* do this on my own. Besides, we're gonna find you a Duke to shag!' She knew I was joking. I knew I wasn't.

Emms met me at her new front door. 'New' in the sense that it was new to her, not new to the house. To the house it looked about three hundred years old. It was no surprise to Emms that I was bringing Sarah. As I've already said, I'd let her in on my little secret ages ago. She was absolutely stunned. It's not often I can do or say anything to shut her up. I did that time. Once the whole story was out, she was nearer to tears than I was.

So when I introduced Sarah to her it was a real hoot to see Emms point to Sarah, then to me and then to herself and say – 'The wife, the mistress and her slutty little friend?! Now that is *so* weird.' Then she shrieked, 'isn't that *wonderful*!?' and gave Sarah a massive hug, much to the latter's confusion and delight.

*

Emms' new house was enormous. Almost beyond comprehension. I couldn't believe the space that just one room provided. I mean it was bigger than my flat. Just one room. And there were dozens of them. All I could think was that my best mate was going to become a Mrs Marquis. A bloody marchioness fergaaardsakes! And here was I, a lowly commoner, playing hunt the bride so that I could get her to the altar on time. Not really my job, I know, but Emms' dad had seen fit to become best friends with a bottle of malt and was currently in no condition to do much at all. But with the agenda's next item fast approaching, I ran down corridor after corridor shouting her name, almost to the point of hysteria.

Time was running out.

Finally, I heard a noise coming from one room on my right where the door was slightly ajar. 'Emms?' another grunt, so I pushed the door. And there she was. In all her finery, like something out of a fairy tale. The princess. It brought a lump to my throat. Really. 'Oh Emms,' I said making to give her a big hug, but my arms were still open wide and I was a good three feet away when she held up both her hands to stop me coming any closer. She pointed down at the flowing train and gave another grunt. So we kissed each other's cheeks, at a distance, and I told her she looked stunning, simply stunning, which she did.

'Hmmm......,' said Emms. Not like her to be tongue tied.

'You OK, hun?'

'Yeah, just a bit........hmmmmm.'

'Nerves?'

'Yeah.... and.... yeah.'

'I'd offer you a drink, but under the circumstances....it's probably not.... Besides, your father's drinking enough for the two of you already.'

'Yeah .... drink ....f – f – fine.' Great, now she'd developed a stammer. 'Yeah .... hmmm ... yeah ... oh fffff.......' This was worse than I thought. And not only was she talking complete drivel, but she was shaking too....*and* hyper-ventilating.

'Oh fffuuuuck!' and I was panicking now, coz she seemed to be having some kinda fit and both her hands were on her belly, but lower than that and there was this lump down there that she had her fingers wrapped tightly around and then her face contorted, her eyes rolled back in her head and it's 'oh baby, oh baby, oh baby....uh uh uh' and her whole body was convulsing and then, *and only then,* it clicked.

'That was ..... aaaawwwesome!' she gasped as the final shudder subsided.

And I was looking from Emms' face down to the bulge in her dress and then back at Emms and I slowly started shaking my head. 'Honestly, Emms!'

At that point a head popped out from beneath her dress and said 'Hello! I'm Guy. You must be Sophie. Pleased to meet you' and he proffered his hand. His fingers positively *glistened*. He spotted this and said 'Ah, maybe not, eh? I'd kiss you on both cheeks instead, only ermm... same problem.' And he smiled .... and his face glistened too.

'This is supposed to be unlucky, Emms. You *do* know that, don't you?'

'Sophie... do I *look* unlucky?' and with that she guided Guy's head back beneath the taffeta folds.

'Right-ho!' said Guy.

Right-ho? Good grief. He'll be saying 'Rather' next.

'Oh, rather!' said a muffled Guy.

See what I mean?

*

So it's at least one more orgasm later that Emms serenely glided down the aisle, more relaxed than I've seen her in a long time which, under the circumstances, was probably no great surprise. She was supported by, or rather was supporting, her father, with me in close attendance acting as a kind of ball boy. The knot was ceremoniously tied (Do you, Emma Persephone Tomkins ....? Persephone?! And Emms turns to me and glares at my snigger) and it all brought a tear to my eye, partly coz I couldn't help but think who was missing from this happy gathering and that that coulda been me up there in the princess dress with the coital afterglow.... but that passed as I got caught up in the festivities and there was nothing like a glass of champers to cheer you up, was there?

The whole affair was really quite formal. I wasn't sure it was really Emms. It was too staid. But she just smiled serenely and I had to keep checking on Guy's whereabouts just in case he'd decided that slipping under the dining table and resuming where he'd left off earlier was a good idea. Rather! But he stayed put at Emms' side and they both really did look great together.

Then it was time for the bride and groom to lead the dancing, so there was polite applause as they took to the floor, stood opposite each other waiting for the start of the waltz.

There was a loud click, followed by static, as the orchestra's sound system was switched off ...... and then Emms' favourite club sounds were blasting over the PA and Emms broke away from Guy and started leaping around the floor on her own, looking for all intents and purposes like an epileptic tea cosy .... with Guy looking on with his jaw around floor level. And he wasn't the only one. Half the audience had the same facial expression. They could've been clones. They probably were. Well, inbred at least.

So I didn't waste a second, coz I wasn't having my Emms dancing on her own on her wedding day and I was up and at 'em and then Guy, bless him, saw the funny side and even he was trying to join in, even though he did look a bit of a twit. And pretty soon anyone under about thirty five was up and dancing....anyone over that just sat and watched, some smiling, some scowling.

Anyone over *sixty* five was having a quiet coronary in the corner.

Sarah, to her credit, was sticking to the sidelines but making as much noise, whooping and clapping and stomping, as a rugby team with a free firkin of ale between them.

Two hours of dancing, topped up occasionally with bubbly, seemed to fly by and the sun was low in the sky by the time we got to vacate the marquee and head indoors to a light supper and some quieter chat.

There was this guy who'd been talking to Sarah on and off for a while. I was hoping that he hadn't latched onto her coz she probably didn't want that. I sidled up and got introduced to Josh. 'And what title do you have? Earl? Duke? His Royal Highness?'

'Only a lord, I'm afraid.'

He's 'afraid'?

'Looks like we're slumming it today, then, eh Sarah?' who smirked and took her leave. Toilet break. 'So Josh, I couldn't help noticing that you've been showing my good friend Sarah some attention this afternoon.'

'She's a very attractive woman...' he offered.

'Yes, she is and she's also a *very* good friend of mine, who happens to have had a *very* hard time of it, of late, in case you didn't know. And if you didn't, then I'm not going to be the one to tell you, that's up to her not me, but I'd hate, and I mean *hate,* to have anyone, lord or no lord, taking advantage of her, coz if they do, they'll have *me* to answer to. Understood?' and, to emphasis the threat, I found myself waving a fork under his nose. A threat that was *slightly* dampened by the cherry tomato stuck on the end of it. So I shoved it in my mouth and chomped down hard, just to make sure he got it. That could've been your testicle, mate.

'Loud and clear,' and he even saluted. The cheeky wee shite.

My new found assertiveness just had another outing.

I could get to like this.

*

By five, it was time to wave good bye to Emma and Guy, off on honeymoon to some place in the Caribbean I'd never heard of. It had the word 'Virgin' in it, so it didn't seem very appropriate. Emms glided down the staircase, on Guy's arm, in her landed gentry day garb, caught my eye in the crowd below and slowly ran her tongue over her glossed lips. Oh Emms. Not *again*?! But by the dazed smile on Guy's face, it wasn't difficult to guess who was on the receiving end *this* time.

Tradition stated that this was where the bride chucked her bouquet over her shoulder and the woman lucky enough to catch it was, supposedly, the next one to get hitched. Emms, grinding tradition under her stiletto heels, just carried on down the staircase, walked straight up to me and handed me her bouquet. Then she hugged me, whispered 'Miss you', and then headed for the door, Guy in hot pursuit.

OK, so now *I* was lost for words.

*

Given the distance we'd travelled, me and Sarah had decided to make a weekend of it. We had the run of the house (I use the term 'house' loosely) and there were several other house guests to keep us entertained. Josh was still around but seemed to be keeping his distance. He flinched every time I got close.

It was Sarah's idea, a drive in the country, find somewhere nice to stop for lunch. Food wasn't exactly high on my agenda though. I was feeling more than a little queasy after yesterday's excesses. Unfortunately, it was becoming a bit of a habit for me, feeling queasy. I'd actually been a bit sick that morning, and not for the first time, so I resolved to cut down on the booze from here on in, although I wasn't sure that booze was the reason. I hadn't drunk *that* much yesterday. And nothing at all the day before. More to the point, though, I'd already decided that a diet was in order. After starving myself to near oblivion for a month after Henry's death, I now seemed to be over compensating and was piling on the pounds. Nothing seemed to fit anymore.

But besides all that, Sarah said that she had something that she wanted to discuss.

So I nibbled on a salad while Sarah, regaled me with stories of you-know-who from times past. God, that woman can talk! I wasn't about to stop her, though. There was as much a *need* there as anything else. A cathartic chat. It was anybody's guess who was still the more fragile. I knew that it wouldn't take much to set me of again. And I could see that her flow of conversation verged on desperation at times.

And so to the main topic...at long last.

'I have to decide what to do with the company, Sophie. My first reaction was just to get rid....the last thing that I wanted was to have that responsibility too. I have enough to do as it is. Trouble is, as a going concern, I'm not sure that it's that sellable. Without the main man there, is it really worth that much?'

Well, it turned out that she'd been talking to Carla. Not what I'd call going to the top man, given that John was supposed to have been Henry's second in command. But Carla had put in a good word for me and reckoned, with everyone pulling together, that we could all keep the company going with Sarah as a nominal MD/CEO type person but with the rest of us actually doing the productive stuff.

Part of the reason for contemplating this path had nothing to do with commerciality and everything to do with sentimentality. She wanted to keep Henry's name alive even though he no longer was. I empathised. I'd have liked to have done that too.

Besides, the remuneration package, as she called it, was far too generous to refuse. It would've meant letting down my new boss, who had been so kind since Henry died, but something about this felt right. I was sure that when I explained it to him, he'd understand. The bottom line was, he'd have to.

One thing we were both agreed on. Jeff would have to go. Sarah would see he got a decent severance payout. I suggested monogrammed handkerchiefs. Once I explained, she saw the funny side.

So, yes, I would soon be back at Blythe Enterprises. All guns blazing. I couldn't wait to see the look on Hollie's face. Jaw around basement level, I reckoned.

The conversation (for 'conversation' read monologue) then veered into the extremely personal. I've already mentioned that what her and H got up to when they were younger was .... shall we just say 'adventurous'? Well, she seemed to be determined to go into more and more detail and it reminded me of Emms when in full flow, although Sarah did have the good grace to lower her voice a tad. But in the end, I had to call a halt. I was beginning to feel a little jealous. I was also beginning to feel a little horny. I could see that Sarah was too. And I wasn't about to go there.

Sex and death, Sarah. I get it, but enough. Really.

*

And I never did tell Sarah what I thought might have caused Henry's death. Some things are best left unsaid.

*

'Mummy, mummy, can you eat words?' roused from my daydream, it takes me while to understand what I'm being asked.

'Words? Can you *eat* words?' He has something in his outstretched hands. I dread to think what. 'Well,' I continue, 'yes, I guess you *can* eat words....' but I hesitate, not wanting to have to explain what 'metaphorically' means, '..... but why would you want to?'

'Because...' and he draws the word out for effect, 'they look like spetty, and I like spetty.' And he opens his hands to reveal a wee wriggling beasty.

It clicks. Spetty equals spaghetti.

'Worms, Harry, *worms*! Not words! And no, you can't eat worms. They'll make you sick!'

'Ohhhhh ..... but they look like spetty, mummy. Are you sure?'

'Quite sure,' disgusting creatures sometimes, boys, aren't they? But I guess he didn't mean any harm. There's a twinkle in those sapphire eyes of his that tells me he wasn't exactly being serious. Cheeky wee sod! It reminds me of his father, like when he sits and eats his meals. Slow and deliberate. Taking his time.

Meet Harry. *He's* now my most prized possession.

*

Nearly three months since that fateful shag in the country, and I was fit to burst. Largely over the downside now, life was getting back to as near normal as it was ever going to be. Work was back on track, although that seemed to be the heart of the problem. I'd thrown myself into work. Work was life and life was work. The company was solid and we were all working our socks and shoes off and, if I was perfectly honest with myself, I was doing it as much for H as anything. Something inside refused to let go. The best I could do was submerge it.

But one thing wouldn't be submerged though.

Sex.

Sarah's wee chat at Emms' wedding didn't help one bit. It only served to put the subject right back at the top of the agenda. What with her tales of bondage and submission and threesomes and foursomes and .... oh, shit!

Was that where things were going with H? I hoped not. I never did like crowds, *especially* in bed. Centre of attention, that's me.

Anyway, in the end, it all got a bit too much.

*

The poor buggers didn't know what hit them.

First off was Ian – Ian I picked up in a pub. Yes, it was me that did the picking. Since all the grief, I was in no mood to pussyfoot around, so to speak, so I went for the best looking guy there. I was surprised how easy it was. Pick and choose. Forget the night club, I told him, whose place is nearer? I got the honours. In reality, of course, it was always going to be my place, but I felt that I had to go through the motions. Which was just as well, coz I had a pair of handcuffs that were just *asking* to be christened....just sitting there in my bedside cabinet, all shiny and new. Needless to say, carrying my accoutrements around with me on an evening 'on the pull' might just have been seen as a wee bit on the presumptuous side. And, for the blokes, just a tad scary too.

So we were back at my place and I was plying us both with booze, coz remember this was the first time since H and I was more than a wee bit nervous, and we retired to the bedroom and actually he was a pretty good snog and I was a little surprised to find myself in the mood now. Eager, even. Clothes were coming off and I was pleased to see that he was in the mood too. So I climbed aboard, and was savouring every last inch, when I felt that old familiar urge to have my hands restrained behind my back. I reached for the drawer and the manacles see the light of day (well, OK, *night*) and I was waving them in front of Ian, whose eyes lit up when I said, wanna play?

Well, he grabbed them off me like they were some kinda lifesaver and before I knew it he'd slapped them on his wrist, fed them through the headboard bars (bought especially for the purpose) and fitted the other end to his other wrist.

'Now you're talking' he rasped. 'Do with me what you will, baby.'

I'm mortified.

'Not you! ME! You pillock! Fucksake!' And I started beating the wee twit on the chest, ordering him to take the bloody things off.

'OK, OK' he kept protesting. 'Just give me the damned key, will ya?'

'Key? Ah, key. Riiiight. Now where did I put it?' And I could see the look dawning on the poor boy's face...

'You do *have* the key don't you?'

'Yeeeah. Hmmmm. Somewhere.' So I rummaged in the drawer, looking for the packet that the wee lovelies came in. 'Key, key, key, key, key,' I kept saying, as if this would magic it from nowhere. I was probably annoying the hell outa the guy now, but I really didn't care anymore. He buggered it all up, so he was gonna sodding well pay for it.

Then my hand landed on a plastic bag and I remembered that that is what the damned things came in and that that must be where the key was. So, taddaaaa, 'here we go' I said, as I produced the bag.

Only it's empty.

It's empty coz I just caught sight of the key flying out of the open end of the bag and down the back of the bed's headboard.

Oooops.

Well, now I knew *where* it was..... just have to go get it. Hmmm....problem here. My nice new bed was quite large, (no prizes for guessing why) and it was also quite heavy. It was even heavier with the weight of a fully grown man on it. Me? I was only a wean. Tiny really, by comparison. The bed base was almost at floor level. The only way to access the area where the key must have landed was between the headboard and the wall. A gap of about two inches. And six feet across. I took a peek.

'Hmmmm,' I said out loud, coz I was milking this for all I could get now. 'No sign!'

Ian was beginning to panic. Just a little. Wherever it had gone, it was well out of my reach, I told him. 'Just do something,' he pleaded. 'They're *your* handcuffs!' 'What?' I asked in all innocence. '*You* put the bloody things on. Why blame me?'

'Try shifting the bed a little' he suggested.' Oh yeah, that's really helpful. Half a ton of man and bed and you expect me to move the lot?

'Well at least try!'

'Pointless,' I told him and, judging by the way his cock had shrunk in the meantime, I'd say it was *un mot juste*.

'You didn't bring a saw with you, did you?' Now I really *was* taking the piss. Ian rattled his chains.

'Cup of tea?' I suggested, helpfully. 'It might be as well to sober up at this point.' He just shook his head and whimpered.

But then he's up and at 'em and has twisted himself around, has fed his feet through the bars and was pushing with all his might, trying to inch the bed away from the wall. And bit by bit, it worked. Until there it was. In all its shining glory.

The key.

Of course, once he was released, there was absolutely no way that we were going to get into a passion thing once again. I think my exact words were –

'Fuck off!'

Just my luck, eh? To find *another* submissive.

*

Friday night and number two was a guy called Phil. Or 'Philip' as he insisted on being called. (Yeah, I know, the alarm bells really shoulda started ringing! Must've been on the blink.) Well, 'Phillip', was a little more promising. He was sort of a blind date set up by Emms. Philip was ex-Army. Captain. Hmmmm, I couldn't help thinking .... officer class .... used to telling others what to do......maybe one for 'strict' behaviour ..... discipline .... *maybe* we'd have something in common.

Well, it started off quite well. We went to a very pleasant restaurant. He was a nice enough chap, but I couldn't help thinking that he wasn't exactly concentrating on the matter in hand. He was just too easily distracted by others in the restaurant. Hey, stop looking at the waiter. I'm over here.

Eventually, in lowered tones – 'forgive me for being so blunt, Philip, but you wouldn't happen to be gay, would you?'

The sheer panic that struck his face spoke volumes. Despite hissed protests to the contrary, no matter what he said, I knew. I just did. So I let it go at that. We actually had a pretty good evening, once the cat was out of the bag, so to speak, but, as we bid each other good night outside the eaterie, his parting shot was – you won't say anything, will you?

'Not a dickybird,' I said kissing him on the cheek.

So it seems, we *did* have something in common.

Men.

*

Number three? Meet Doug. A fellow Scot, Doug was the kinda guy that you could imagine striding from peak to glen, all tweed, woolly socks and kilt. Broad of shoulder and square of jaw. Of course it was the contents of his sporran that was my main interest. That and would he be familiar with the sheepshank?

As it turned out, the only thing that Douglas was familiar with was the missionary position. Far be it for the man to be keeping his end up for bonny Scotland, the wee man (and I use the term advisedly) ran a mile when I produce my favourite toy.

'Err, no way. That's kinky!'

'Well, yeah, that IS the bloody point!'

*

So, three in three days. And then several more after that. None of them showed any real interest. At best, they thought it was just a bit of a giggle. A laugh. At worst, I scared the crap outa them. None of them took it seriously. Which was no good to me. I wanted serious. I longed for serious. I longed to be *taken* seriously. I mean, I tried everything, really I did. I teased, I cajoled, I goaded, I guided, pleaded, coaxed and yes even begged (begging is good!) but nothing seemed to work. More than ever I missed Henry. What I would have given for just one more night with him.... ?

But I could tell I was banging my head against the proverbial with these guys. It could take me forever to find a replacement. Someone with a bit of nous.

So I just gave up.

*

'Penny for them?' a male voice, someone was sitting next to me. Leave me alone. I don't want to talk. I was staring off into the middle distance again. Only this time the middle distance seemed to be the floor. 'You don't remember me do you?'

'Should I?' I didn't even bother looking up.

'Possibly not.' Then why are you talking to me, exactly? 'We errr....*met* about, I don't know, ages ago ... and err before that we saw each other ..err... well, right here. On the way into work.' I had absolutely no idea what this man was talking about. Please go away. 'We never even knew each other's name, even though we were ....erm, *close*....briefly.' Oh, for fucksake...

'Look what do you *want* exactly?' and I turned to face my harasser and I found that I was facing someone familiar and I'm thrown temporarily because I can't place him and then I do and I miss a beat and 'Oh. You.' He nodded. How embarrassing.

'There was erm...someone else and it didn't..... and we didn't really and...' oh, just get on with it, will you? '.......so I left and that was.......and I didn't even... much as I wanted to, you understand?'

'Not really. So far I haven't understood a single word you've said.'

Silence. Oh shit, I didn't really handle that very well, did I? He was trying to be nice. Just wasn't doing a very good job of it.

'So,' he said, having another crack at it, all joviality, '.... still with the same lucky guy then?'

'No. He wasn't so lucky. He died.' The silence is palpable.

'Oh shit! Oh shit, I'm *so* sorry. Why do I always put my foot in it like that?'

'I dunno,' I said, turning to face him again, 'maybe you're a bit stupid.' It's unkind, but that's me these days. Sorrow is long gone. It's only anger now. And bitterness.

'Yeah, you're probably right,' and he cracked a smile, lines creasing the corners of his baby blues. I remembered the fear in them when I flipped out. Only wanting Henry. No-one else would do. Poor bloke. Wanted a shag and got a mad woman. Maybe I should go easy on him. It wasn't his fault. 'Oh shit,' he's saying 'that's awful, *really* awful. When, I mean .... was it erm? ... errr, or did he...? Oh shut up James, you're making a complete twat of yourself!'

Well said.

Then - 'Look...' coz there's no shutting this one up, 'I'm *really* sorry. Honestly. Can I maybe, buy you a coffee or something. I don't know 'bout you, but I didn't get a chance to this morning ... always in a rush and stuff.... So coffee? No agenda ... just have a chat, you know?'

Yes, I did know. But coffee was out of the question. Not now, not ever.

*

A week later and I was sitting with James at a little bistro on our mutual way into work. Espresso was the order of the day, for both of us. Plus sugar, coz I needed all the energy I could get these days. I had balls to break in the office and I couldn't be seen to be flagging. I still wasn't really in a communicative mood but the wee shite had ground me down with his own brand of niceness. He'd made it clear from the outset that (as he had already put it) he had 'no agenda' and just liked to chat to people ... and to me in particular. Reckoned it was good to talk, sometimes, especially after such tragic circumstances .... and I probably would have, if only I could've got a bloody word in edgeways.

And it became a regular stop off for us. Early coffee break. We even arranged to get there earlier so that neither of us was late in for work.

Except Saturdays and Sundays, when I breakfasted and then worked alone.

*

Maybe it was the shagging disasters that had happened shortly after Henry's death that put me off asking James out. Maybe it was the fact that he had become my only male friend. I mean, I did fancy him. After all, I'd shagged him once before. Remember? But....... well, I think that I was actually frightened of losing him as a friend. Given my track record with blokes, there was a strong possibility that I would simply scare him stupid (again) and that we'd never speak afterwards. To my mind, that was a risk I wasn't prepared to take. I mean, this guy had taken the trouble to become a mate without the whole guy/girl thing going on. That hadn't happened since I'd been at uni, where there had been a few guys that I'd been friends with that I knew I'd never shag. Even the cute ones. *Especially* the cute ones.

And James most certainly wasn't going to ask *me* out. For that I only had myself to blame. Me and my big mouth!

*

So it was a very tentative James that broached the subject of a dinner party at the house of friends of his.

'Look, not as a date, kinda thing....but just as mates. It's just, well ..... I hate going to these things on my own....looking like a sad loser with no girlfriend or wife or .... whatever (whatever? Slave, maybe? Hmmm?) ...so I was wondering....erm, would you do me the honour.....of maybe....'

'"Do you the honour"...! Oh my god Jamesie, how posh do you sound?'

Raising his eyebrows a fraction 'Well?' is all he said.

I couldn't say no, could I? I mean, this guy had summoned up the courage to ask and there really was no hint of a 'date kinda thing' and I did enjoy his company and I could relax with him in a way that I couldn't with any other guy coz I was always on the lookout for what James called 'an agenda', i.e. can I get into your knickers? .....

leaving me to worry if they would stay around long enough to 'administer restraints and just punishments'.

So I said yeah (actually, I said 'it would indeed, sir, be an honour to accept your most kind invitation.') and I honestly thought that it would go no further than that.

Really I did.

*

James picked me up in a taxi that night. It was a long trip out to his friends' house. But it was worth it. They had this pile out in the country, well, out on the outskirts anyway. And when I say 'pile', what I mean was it was a proper detached house which had 'grounds' rather than just a garden.

Simon and Angela were something in finance, but didn't have that conceited and arrogant air that most seem to have in that 'profession'. On the contrary, these people proffered generosity like it was going out of fashion. Anything was on offer here. Their cottage in the country, their friends' ski lodge in the Alps, a yacht that was 'simply doing nothing' somewhere on the south coast.

I asked them if they had a large penthouse apartment in the city centre that they didn't have a use for ..... for, say, the next ten years or so. They ummed and ahhed for a few seconds before both nodding and saying 'Yarr, acksherly, yarr.' Then bursting into howls of laughter. I laughed til it hurt. 'Really? Seriously? Yarr?' I liked people like this. They were successful but wanted to share their good fortune (and, I'm sure, hard work) by spreading it around the people that they knew....without rubbing their friends' faces in it all.

It was while I was in the kitchen, doing the 'stereotypically women's thing' (Angie's phrase) of sorting the food, that I got the heart to heart treatment.

'James told us what happened to your boyfriend, Sophie. Not in any detail, you understand, but just what happened. And believe me, it wasn't gossip. I think he wanted to forewarn us, just in case it all got too much for you. Coming here. You know, if you were still a bit ..... delicate. I'm *so* sorry. It must have been a dreadful time for you.' The look in her eyes told me that this was no platitude.

'Yeah, well, I'm not sure '*boy*friend' was quite an accurate description. Try *married-man-twice-my-age* friend.' I smiled at her to let her know I was OK talking about this and that I was kinda joking too. There was a raised eyebrow in return.

'So I guess that gives you two guys something in common, then?'

'You mean me and James?' I was losing the plot here. James had an older woman....? Who died?

Angie just nodded. That look of sorrow hadn't left her eyes. That worried me. She was reluctant to take the conversation any further. But I wasn't.

With knitted brow.....'What, *exactly* do you mean by....... 'something in common'?'

Angie stopped dead. 'His mother....' and all I did was look blankly at her. 'You.... you don't..? Oh no!' A look of panic on her face and her hand went to her mouth... just a little late under the circumstances. 'He hasn't...? Oh shit!'

There was a struggle for me to keep my temper but I wasn't sure who exactly I was losing my temper with. Or why for that matter.

'He hasn't 'oh shit' what?'

We were standing face to face now. Angie silently weighing me up. Me standing with my arms folded. Tightly. Defensive.

One look towards the dining room, then voice lowered. 'There was a car crash. His father was badly hurt .... his mother...' and then she just trailed off and shook her head.

Now it was my turn to cover my mouth. 'Died?' Angie nodded, tight lipped. My head spun. 'But when?'

A shrug... 'maybe two, three months ago.'

Two, three *months*! But that was when Henry..... And James had said nothing. Not a word. While I went on and on feeling sorry for myself... He had..... And.....

'Oh shit, indeed.'

Then Angie grabs my hands in hers and makes me promise not to tell James that she told me about this. That it was up to him to tell me, but in his own time.

So it was with a different eye that I looked at James for the rest of that evening. All that suppressed emotion. Couldn't even bring himself to tell me. He shoulda said *something*. Was I that unapproachable? Was I that tied up in my own grief?

'You know, don't you?' he said in the taxi home.

'How do you know I know?' Were we playing games here?

'The look on your face when you came back from the kitchen. A mixture of sorrow and pity and anger, I'd say.'

'How do you know that it wasn't coz I'd just burnt the cabbage?'

'Coz it wasn't a burnt cabbage look.'

'Ah. You got me there! I never was any good at that old burnt cabbage look.'

Silence.

Then I turned to him and... 'so go on then. Why did I have to find out the hard way?'

More silence.

Then a deep exhalation. 'You had enough to....' Ah, back to the old half sentence routine. This I can do.

'So you thought it best to.....' See what I mean?

'Yeah. I thought it best.....was I wrong?'

So I turned to look him dead in the eyes. 'Yes James, you were wrong. But you thought you were doing the right thing... for me. So no, you weren't wrong. Got it?'

Raised eyebrows, creased forehead. 'I have absolutely *no idea* what you are talking about.'

I took his hand in mine and leaned against his shoulder. All I said was....

'Me neither.'

*

Later -

'How come you know such nice people, James?'

'I choose my friends carefully, Sophie. I always have.' He looked sideways at me, smiled, but said no more.

Go on, I was thinking, say 'Like you.' But he didn't. Implicit. Like Henry.

OK. So maybe this was a bit of flattery. But I honestly think he meant it and it felt sweet and kind and, yeah, it made me feel good about myself for the first time in an awful long while.

When we got back to my place I gave the taxi driver enough for the ride, much to James's consternation, he insisting he could pay it all when he got back to his place.

'But you're not *going* back to your place. Are you?' and I pretty much dragged him out of the cab.

*

That night I didn't want *just* a shag. And my handcuffs stayed well and truly shut in the bedside cabinet. Key and all. I wasn't scaring this guy off. Besides, there would be plenty of time for that......

Later.

I just wanted to take the pain away. Our pain. And I did my best to do exactly that.

*

Some men, no matter how assertive they are in everyday life, need to be led by the hand.

And so I led James .... by the hand*cuffs*. And then the riding crop. And then the ropes and chains. And then the ... well the list went on....and on .... and on.

With my expert guidance, he got to be very good. Very good indeed. Which is kinda ironic, if you think about it. It was never going to be the same as with Henry. I knew that, somewhere deep inside. But at least I had him all to myself, whenever I wanted him.

Which was an awful lot.

*

Emms interrupted me mid-flow. 'I suppose you're going to tell me that *this* is unlucky too?' I asked her, more than a little flustered, wiping my chin with the back of my hand.

Emms looked from me to James and then to which part of James I'd recently had in my gob – 'Oh no. Oh no, no, no, no, nooooo. Nothing unlucky about *that*, girl!' her eyes widening. She went on - 'Well, at least you got the 'something blue' sorted,' winked and shut the door, shouting from the other side. 'Altar in fifteen minutes... And no speaking with your mouth full!'

I wasn't about to.

*

I'd never seen James with a suit on before. I was hoping it was him anyway. I would be in for a bit of a shock if the man at the end of the aisle turned out to be someone completely different. All I could see right then were his golden curls. He was supposed to have had a haircut. Just this once!

There was Emms following up behind me and Guy hanging on to my arm. I wasn't sure who was the more nervous. Personally, I was surprised that he wasn't hiding under Emms's dress. I guessed that things had moved on since then.

Somewhere far behind me, I could hear a baby crying.........? Oh bum! Must be feeding time. Not now matey. Sophie's busy.

To think that it was only just over a year ago that I was following Emms up the very same aisle. Private chapel on a private estate. Well, look at me now.

And I know what you're thinking. Wasn't it all a bit soon? Was there a rebound thing going on here? Well, maybe. But there were many things that Henry taught me. Some deliberately stated, some, as I've said, implicit. Many not even appreciated at the time. The most pertinent thing was - not to waste my time. Decide what you want and go for it. So I did just that.

*

Same staircase, different bouquet. Although I can honestly say that I had absolutely no intention whatsoever of copying Emms in actually handing the bouquet to a specific person, I did have every intention of aiming the bouquet in someone's direction. So, as I stood halfway down, I surveyed those below me with one particular person in mind. And there she was. Looking absolutely stunning, as usual. And just too far away to risk a throw. So I sauntered on down, ignoring the gathered crowd, and crossed the room to where she was standing, close to the wood panelled wall.

'I know I've told you this already, but I have to say it again. You look amazing.' I couldn't think what Henry ever saw in me when I saw Sarah looking like this. Boy, did I feel flattered? Pressing the bouquet into her hand, I added 'Please find someone, Sarah. Please.'

'No hurry. He's a pretty hard act to follow, you know?'

'Yeah' is all I could manage, only to find the flowers pushed back into my grasp.

'Someone else needs the luck, Sophie. Go on. Do it.'

So I did. And do you know who caught it?

Carla!

As Henry Blythe, himself, would have said......

Good grief!

*

He wasn't angry, you must understand. He just couldn't see the funny side. He was embarrassed more than anything. Let's face it, you don't *normally* expect to see pink fluffy handcuffs hanging from the rear view mirror of the open top sports car that is about to whisk you away on honeymoon. When everyone is watching. And pointing. And giggling.

'I didn't say a word. Really. Not everyone knows about my penchant for gadgets.' Well, not *absolutely* everyone.

'I bet they're yours.' He accused.

'Uh uh. I've *packed* mine.' Poor James was horrified.

'And how, exactly, are you going to explain those to airport security?'

'Ah.' Think, think..... 'Well, I guess I have twelve hours to come up with a reason. Besides, we're on honeymoon, they'll understand.'

Won't they?

*

Some sixteen weary hours later, we were descending into the Caribbean island of Tortola, having chased the sun to sunset. The sun itself was hovering low over the peaks and beaches as we touched down in what seemed to me like a toy plane compared with the one in which we had crossed the Atlantic. I suppose I should have been pleased to arrive and I was certainly excited but, despite dozing on and off for the last eight hours, I was fit to drop by the time we got to customs.

The last thing I wanted to have to deal with, in that late afternoon heat and humidity, was some jobsworth who insisted on asking silly questions like any illegal drugs, pornography, firearms et cetera? I mean, honestly! Would we be bringing drugs *to* the Caribbean? And as for porn? I felt like telling him that that was why we were here...to make our own, but I didn't think he would see the funny side.

Of course, then he asked to see inside my suitcase. That's when my attitude changed. So did James's.

Yeah, I know we *talked* about sorting out my packing when we got to departures, but we were running late by then and I just didn't get time. So I knew what would greet Mr Customs Man when the lid was flipped on my case. My pink furry ones. James slapped one hand across his eyes. I just stood my ground. You're not phasing me, mate.

And this wasn't phasing the guy in the uniform either.

'Honeymoon?' was all he said.

I just nodded.

'Welcome to the British Virgin Islands,' then he flipped the lid closed, scrawled a chalk mark on our cases and waved us on. 'Enjoy your stay,' was his parting shot.

You betchya.

Our onward journey was by ferry from right next to the airport. By this time the sun was kissing the horizon but we had no time to watch as the boat was due to leave. Once aboard, however, we took in the setting sun and the mirror finished sea, now black with the approaching night. We didn't get to our destination until well after dark, by which time we were too shattered to do anything but fall asleep.... after a rum cocktail or two, of course.

Check in was a bit weird, though.

The receptionist remained polite and pretty much straight-faced throughout, welcoming us in his slow West Indian drawl.

'Ah yes, the booking that was made, *and paid for*, by Mrs De Giverny. She was most insistent that we put you in the same suite as the one that she had when she stayed here last year....on *her* honeymoon, I seem to recall. The bed *has* been replaced since then...well, we had to ..... but otherwise the suite is in pretty much the same condition as it was then. Ah. We have also redecorated. Again, we *had* to.'

I grimaced at James, trying to picture the scene of destruction that Emms had left in her wake. I could only imagine. We'd have to watch our step.

The next morning brought back fond memories of Capri. As I wandered bleary eyed from our wee villa at sunrise, I was met by the most awesome sight. It stopped me dead in my tracks.

We were high up on a hill slope surrounded by lush green forest. The vista ran eastwards towards the rising sun with a crescent of white sand beach in the distance and the sheer, turquoise and deep blue Caribbean Sea beyond. Distant islands lay scattered to the hazed horizon. I sat on a nearby rock wall. It didn't just remind me of Capri..... I thought of H and our tree in the country, which I felt a little guilty about, given why I was here, but it pleased me that it wasn't a unique experience after all. New memories were crowding in on the old ones.

I heard James moving behind me and then his hand on my shoulder. 'Impressive, huh?'

'Yeah, impressive.'

He sat beside me and we just drank in the view.

*

Breakfast was on the terrace and, even though I was with my new husband, I just couldn't take my eyes off the scene in front of us. Lovely as he was, I figured that I would have a lifetime to gaze upon his delightful face. I may never come back this way again.

'I wanna learn to scuba dive! I wanna shag on that beach down there! I wanna walk through the jungle ..... and shag in the jungle. I wanna go sailing, I wanna shag on a yacht, I wanna ..... erm, oh let's just do it all, eh?'

'Yeah mon. Noooo problem.'

'Ouch. You'll have to work on that accent, Jamesie! That was nearer Scottish.'

But we did. We did all of those things. Some of them an awful lot. Mainly the walking and the scuba diving. There wasn't much sex, of course ..... (yeah, right) and we didn't use the bed much either. Four-poster or no four-poster. I wasn't going *there* again.

*

About a week into our trip, things took a sudden turn.

James found me pacing the main villa room when he got out of the shower one afternoon, after a diving trip. There had been a note slipped under our door to the effect that that there was a hurricane warning in force.

'We're gonna have to leave Jamesie.' I got one of his askance looks that said 'seriously?' ... or, maybe, 'are you *completely* mad?'

The more I thought about it, the more panicked I became. A hurricane. Shit. But I clearly had to explain it to hubby. There was no reason he should know. Some things I'd kept secret from him, hadn't seen any particular reason to tell, especially given the consequences.

A summer storm was one thing. A hurricane was a completely different matter.

So in words of one syllable, (not for his benefit, for mine. I couldn't use more than one syllable at a time. Not right then.) I explained the circumstances of the storm in the country which had lead to my fear of the approaching cyclone. A fear that was rapidly becoming a full blown phobia.

'So you see, I can't stay here. Not if there's a chance that ....'

'It's not going to happen, hun. Really. Even if it does come this way, this place is bound to be hurricane proof. We just hunker down and sit it out. No big deal. Honest. The worst we'll have is a sleepless night. So no different from the last eight nights, is it?'

'Someone *died* last time. There's no way I can go through that again.' And I know, I know, I was beginning to sound paranoid, neurotic even, but I'd checked before we even booked anything. Hurricanes rarely happened this early in the year. Not here. It hadn't happened like this for well over a decade. And the chances were that it'd head somewhere else anyway, but I couldn't explain the fear that gripped me. Was this a post traumatic stress thing going on? I had no idea, but it was scaring me witless and I was serious about leaving this tropical nirvana.

I pleaded...no, I insisted.

James just said 'no'.

End of story.

*

So I did what I usually do in times of stress. I hit the bottle. Fortunately for me there were plenty of bottles to choose from. I had made friends with Mabel, the lady that cleaned the rooms during the day. On the odd occasion that we were in when she was there, we chatted. Sometimes while she worked, most often I told her to take the weight off. She deserved it. I could see it was a guilty pleasure. Mainly I loved to hear her Caribbean drawl, softer than the mock Jamaican one I'd entertained Henry's clients with on the phone back home. It gave me a chance to practice my mimicry.

But when I told her about the weather warning, she just said not to worry. We might get a bit of a blow, but it'd be 'no problem'. It didn't help. As the hours ticked by, the stress levels rose and rose. I asked if there was any hooch liquor to be had on the island. Bootleg booze. Something with a bit of a kick to it. Next day she turned up with two empty coke bottles. Evidently I hadn't made myself understood. But, when she waved them in front of my face, I could then see a clear liquid inside.

I was betting my eyes lit up. 'Strong?'

'Killer!' and she wheezed a laugh.

*

As I sat on the verandah, I could see that things were changing. Gone was that mirrored sea and the wall to wall blue sky. There were white crests in abundance and heavy clouds were scudding in from the north and east. I wouldn't fancy my chances on that sea now. And you could forget flying in one of those single-engined toy things that occasionally flew by. I might be going quietly mad, but I wasn't completely crazy. Not yet.

Just permanently drunk.

I found it was the best way. And Mabel's liquor really was killer. I took a neat shot on ice when it first arrived. I really, *really* wished I hadn't. Jeez! Teeth abraded of enamel, tongue and throat stripped of their skin, stomach lining scoured raw. A bit like a major oral session with H or Jamesie ...... only without the pleasure of the final mouthwash. Even when I diluted the tiniest of shots with a whole can of coke, it still retained its paint stripping qualities.

It was probably fair to say that I wasn't the best of company. I was painfully aware that I might be cocking up our honeymoon. But the way I looked at it was that a hurricane was cocking up our honeymoon ..... along with James's stubbornness not to let us leave.

*

A day later, I could see that he was beginning to regret his decision. Things were not looking promising. The skies were almost completely cloudy, the wind had picked up to a permanently strong and gusty breeze.

I was on edge from the moment I woke til the moment I fell asleep. We couldn't go into the sea, as it was now deemed too dangerous. The weather forecast just kept getting worse. I just kept getting drunk. Or rather kept *staying* drunk.

To my mind, we should have been writing out our last wills and testaments rather than just sitting there watching the weather worsen. Jamesie did his best to keep my pecker up, so to speak, but it just wasn't working. If I'd had my way we would have been out of there days ago and residing somewhere well out of harm's way, exploring calm white sand beaches with no regard for clothing or celibacy.

Instead, I was now on my seventh coke bottle of gut-rot firewater and had given up cleaning my teeth, figuring that I probably had little left worth cleaning anyway.

Day ten and I was sitting curled up on our bed, knees under my chin, arms wrapped tightly around my legs. I was off on one. I'd been here before and was no longer scared witless.

I was scared shitless.

There was a full blown tropical storm howling outside and James was packing all of our stuff, while trying to make soothing noises for my benefit. He was failing. Miserably.

We had to move into the main building which, he assured me, was hurricane proof. Certified. Certified? Yeah, that was me, right then and there. Fully certifiable. I had visions of being trapped, having stuff falling on me, not being able to move, wet through and dying a slow lingering death, dead bodies scattered around and on top of me. I mean, people did die in hurricanes. *Thousands* of them.

Outside, the air was surprisingly warm and humid, despite the wind. There was no sign of rain yet, but it couldn't be far off. Just over there probably. Where the sky and sea were so black that they'd merged.

In the main reception there were people milling around wondering what to do. I hadn't seen so many people in one place since we arrived. They looked lost without their usual tourist pursuits. About the only thing to do was hit the bar. Worked for me. But James was getting more than a little pissed off with my drinking habits. He said he could understand, but stressed that it wasn't the answer.

'Yeah, so what *is* the answer then?' I waited. 'Huh, gotchya!'

There was already a bit of a buzz at the bar with people trying to form a queue to begin with, until they realised that it was every man or woman for him or herself. I pushed in at the back and saw James watching me from a distance. Even from the back of the room and over the constant roar of the wind, I could hear him say 'Oh, fuck it!' He strutted to the bar, eased passed me, ordered a full bottle of the finest local rum, an ice bucket and two glasses. The benefits of being tall....and gorgeous!

'Right', he says, 'you wanna get pissed? We'll get pissed. And the first one to fall over, or asleep, loses.'

'No contest!' And I pour the first. 'And what do I get when I win?'

'Anything you want, baby,' and he winks.

Then the rain started .... and it was torrential.

Instantly.

*

Half a bottle later and I was lying there on the sofa, relaxing into James. I'd pretty much tuned out of the whole hurricane situation, thanks to the brilliant idea of James's of blocking my ears up with those wee foam things that people use to keep their ears water free when swimming. So I could hear very little. I *could* still hear muffled noises, but the howl outside was simply a constant drone now.

The booze was working its Caribbean charms and I was back on the beach that James had taken me to about five days earlier. I had no idea how he knew, but there was this tree..... Yeah, I know that was kinda spooky, but .... There was this tree, OK? ... like the ones you see on tropical beach scenes, postcards, posters ..... porn magazines, you know, a coconut palm leaning almost horizontally over a white coral sand beach with some gorgeous babe draped over it. Well there was this palm tree and there was this beach. And there was this babe. So I draped this way, then I draped that way, then off came my top, then off came my bottoms, then off came James's trunks, then out came the handcuffs and click click and Bob's yer wotsit. An hour or so of hot, tropical sex on the beach. And, no, the sand didn't get everywhere. We both made absolutely sure of that. Mainly by me being chained onto, or hanging from, the tree, thereby keeping the important bits well clear of the coral beach. And when I say 'hanging', this time it all went according to plan. Suspended with my arms high above my head so that James could have his wicked way with me, any which was he felt like it and without fear of interruption.

And not an ant or wasp or old woman in sight. Nice view, too.

Well, OK, on the jungle walk back to the villa we *were* eaten alive by mosquitoes, but hey, it was a small price to pay. Frankly, I felt myself lucky to be able to walk at all.

*

I was woken by a rocking sensation and it took a while to regain my bearings.

'Looks like I won,' said Jamesie.

'Eh? What? I wozn't 'sleep.'

'Hun, you've been out cold for over three hours.'

'Oh bum! So, sir,' turning to face him on the sofa, 'what is your command?' and I gave him the mandatory wink.

'Later hun. This you have to see....' and he lifted me up and dragged me towards the door. It was then that I realised that my earplugs were gone, I could hear James's voice, and that there was no wind. It was ominously quiet.

'Is it all over? Did I sleep through it?' Not a word from James coz he was busy at the door. Other people were milling round. The door swung open and a warm breeze drifted in. Then I was outside and there was a small circle of blue sky way up above, but it was what was ahead of us, all around us, that stunned me.

'Ohmyyygaaaard!'

'Awesome, huh?'

I was over to James in a flash. 'What the ffff.........? James? What's going on? What *is* that?' In all directions there was just this wall of boiling, swirling cloud in every shade from off white to near black, with hints of greens and purples mixed in, maybe miles high, I didn't know. There was no way to gauge just how huge this thing was. Lightning flashed inside it but the air stayed eerily calm. Birds sang. I could only describe it as like looking into the centre of a giant whirlpool.....from beneath. The whole thing was rotating!

And, dead centre, a rainbow arced from sea to sea.

All around was destruction. The main building had stood up to the onslaught but some of the villas had lost their roofs and most of the palms had been stripped of their leaves. There were branches and foliage all over the place.

'We're in the eye of the storm, hun.'

'Jeezus James. You mean it's not over yet?' .... he just shook his head. 'A few more hours yet, babe. Wouldn't have missed this for the world. We'll never see the likes of this again.'

I wasn't that chuffed seeing it the first time round. But it *was* strangely intoxicating. The way this wall of liquid cloud seemed to writhe in turmoil. Scary? Yes. But I'd done scared before and survived. Suddenly I reckoned I could take this on, rum or no rum. Come on then, I thought, do your worst.

And, OK, so the rum could come too.

*

A few of the brave ones stayed and watched for about half an hour as the cloud wall drew close. I'd had enough long before then. Just when you thought it was all over ....

The hotel staff was doing its best to keep the guests entertained, or at least keep their minds off the matter in hand. Food was served in the restaurant and the drinks continued to flow over the bar. There was a distinct party atmosphere but with a definite undercurrent of latent fear. It only took one solid bang on the exterior walls or metal rollerblinds for all faces to turn white and anxious looks to be exchanged all round, before dissolving into nervous laughter.

Reggae rhythmned out over the sound system but was outdone when the winds rose again, then hit hard. There was deadly silence from those gathered for about a minute before someone shouted – 'OK, whose round is it?' 'Yours!' replied everyone else and we all got down to some serious partying.

Then the world exploded

The lights went out.

And the sky fell in.

*

'James! Jamesie!! JAMESIE!!!' Oh shit, here we go again!

But this time my screams were echoed all around. Women screamed, called names, and deeper voices responded and called for calm.

Fortunately, when it went dark, I was reclining in hubby's arms with a full glass of rum on the rocks. Fortunately, *this* time, I was on top. And come hell or high water, I was bloody well staying there.

'S OK, babe. Just a power cut. There's plenty of candles around. It'll be light again soon.'

I didn't mind admitting that I was shaking by now. This was déjà vu to the nth degree. Was my whole life to be re-runs of what I'd done before? And no, this wasn't just a power cut. Something large had hit the roof. 'So what was that noise then, smart arse? You bin at the baked beans again?'

'Tree is my guess.' Oh, well done mastermind, must've taken some brainpower to work *that* one out. And then, sure enough, the odd candle got lit and soon it was a winter wonderland in the middle of July. James had decided to go walkabout ... and he was taking me with him. I didn't want him to go anywhere. Not after last time. But he was insistent.

So he grabbed a candle in a glass holder and he took me on a site seeing tour.... to the ladies loo. 'Oh Jamesie, you do take me to the nicest of places...' I kidded, as I canoodled up to him. But then he took me by the hair, pulled my head back and whispered 'winner takes all', before blowing out the candle.

I really don't know what came over my other half. I mean we were in the middle of a hurricane here. Everything was rattling like an old jalopy in a car wash and there was an almost constant scream penetrating from outside.....and all James wanted to do was penetrate me. So, OK, I had no problem with that. He really did choose his moment though. At least this wasn't a re-run of past events. This time I did get a good seeing to. Inside this room, door locked from the inside, pushed face forward against the wall, half-disrobed and well and truly *had,* my screams competing with the racket outside.

'Oh god, yes, oh baby, yes, yes, oh fuck me harder, yes just like ...oh babe. Yes, yes, yes !!!!' And its brutality matched the raging storm furore. Just how I liked it.

And as his final spasm subsided, James breathing hard in my ear, the lights came back on. Perfect timing.

Then there was a cough.

It wasn't James. It certainly wasn't me.

I froze. James froze.

He was still inside me. Somehow, given the reaction of a certain part of me, I didn't think he'd be going anywhere soon. Yes. I'd clenched.

Closing my eyes, I said out loud, slowly, 'Oh. For. Fucks. Sake!' I turned, as best I could.

A fragile old lady was sat on the toilet, her skirt up round her waist and her mega pants round her ankles.

A meek smile on her face, she said - 'I don't suppose that you could pass the toilet paper? ..... erm, when you've finished with it, of course.'

I shuffled towards the door with James, still attached to my backside, shuffling awkwardly behind me like some kind of comedy double act. I resisted the urge to come back on for an encore. Thank you and goodnight.

James managed to free himself once we'd checked that the coast was clear in the corridor outside. 'Excuse my French again, James, but for fuck's sake! I just cannot believe this. Am I gonna be plagued by old women *every* time I want a shag anywhere even vaguely public?'

'What? This has happened before?'

'Err, yeah. *Twice*!' I shouldn't have said that, of course. The poor boy thought he was being original. Which he was .... to a point. The last thing he wanted to hear was that it'd already happened .... especially that it had already happened with Henry.

He looked pensive for a moment. 'Manager's office, now, Ms MacDonald' and stalked off down the corridor. Recovering my shorts from around my knees, I hobbled after him.

I found James sitting at the manager's desk, drumming a pen on its wooden surface. 'You're going to tell me you've done *this* before, aren't you?' and he indicated that I should sit down. He was just a teeny bit angry.

'Oh no. Oh no, no, no, no, noooo.' But I *so* wanted to.

'Well, Miss MacDonald .... I'd like you to take something down.'

But I've only just pulled them up...was what I nearly said, but instead... 'Certainly, sir....' and I wriggled in my seat...... '*anything* you say. Now where shall I start?'

And so James fulfilled one of my favourite fantasies, in a wonderful hour of sluttish, sexual debauchery. Sure, it wasn't quite how I'd imagined this particular role play. What I'd *imagined* was me dressed in typical office gear, all, neat and tidy in a sensible skirt and blouse, barely concealing my undercover vamp, all black lace, stockings and killer heels .... with my partner in lust all suited and booted. What I got was maybe the Caribbean version. Skin tight top and shorts. For both of us. Still, who was I to complain? I got what I wanted. Got what I deserved, according to Jamesie. And I'm betting that the real manager would never guess how his ruler got broken. We celebrated afterwards with champagne .... and rum, of course, opting this time to stand at the bar. I wouldn't be sitting down for a wee while yet.

By late that evening, the storm had downsized to 'bloody awful' from 'OH, SHIT!' It was still raining and blowing a gale, but nothing serious. People were bedding down for the night and the sense of relief was tangible. James and me shared a large sofa. We were tempted to indulge in round three, but I really didn't want an audience of old ladies .... again. So we just messed around under the blanket and stifled grunts and sighs when we came.

*

Next morning, I was one of the first to wake and was the first to the door onto the restaurant's verandah. A strong breeze still blew and there were plenty of clouds in the sky, as well as patches of pale blue, but the rain had stopped and the air smelled fresh and clean. On the western slope of the hillside a whole swathe had been cut through the trees and the road down to the beach and beyond was littered with fallen trees. Distant shacks had been laid to waste, their white clapboard walls and tin roofs scattered the hillsides, like so much trash. I hoped that the occupants had got out safely. When I got to our villa there wasn't honestly an awful lot left to see. The roof had gone and so had most of the contents.

When James sauntered up behind me, I suggested he took a photo. 'I think Emms needs to see this. All she did was break the bed. We took the whole bloody roof off!'

*

Later that morning, after a hearty breakfast, including the requisite strong coffee and two ibuprofen, the clean up began. Everyone mucked in, sorting through which villas were still habitable, clearing the gardens of debris and then venturing out onto the entry road with a 4 x 4 and a winch to clear the trees.

Not being their busiest time of year (some people weren't as stupid as us), rooms were re-allocated with villas to spare. We got the 'honeymoon suite'. Yeah, that's what I thought!

We collected bedding from the laundry and were halfway through making the beds when it occurred to me that Mabel wasn't here. So wrapped up in our own trials, we'd all but forgotten about those people that actually lived here. So we resolved to track the lady down, just to make sure that she was OK.

She was local. Just the other side of the hill crest. The road wasn't too bad in that direction, as the forest thinned a little with the altitude. Mabel's house had been described to me as a pale blue and white shack with a white fence out front. If you'd blinked you would have missed it. The only thing remaining that matched the description was the walls of pale blue. The white fence and roof were gone. We found Mabel sifting through the wreckage of her home in the back yard. It was obvious to us both that it hadn't been much of a house in the first place. It wasn't fit for anything at all, now.

Mabel was simply overjoyed to see us. Throwing her arms in the air and then around us in turn. 'Now where did I put ma tea pot?' I know iz 'round 'ere somewhere. Ah,'ere we are,' and she picked up a teapot handle from amongst the wreckage. Just the handle, you understand? No teapot attached. 'So, d'you take sugar?' she said, shaking her head, then wheezing one of her laughs. I tried to smile, but just thought, jeez, it's all gone. Everything. No possessions. No home. Nothing.

'Where did you sleep last night, Mabel?' feeling tears welling up.

'Dere,' was all she said and nodded at some heavy timbers and wooden sheets arranged in a kind of tent design, leaning against a remaining wall. 'Dear god, Jamesie, we had nothing compared to this. What she must have gone through.'

'Don' worry 'bout me, darlin', when you got 'most nuttin', you don' miss it.'

Or when you got almost nothing, you miss what little you had?

We were both agreed that we had to help clear up. See if anything at all was salvageable. There was just so much chaos, it was difficult to know where to begin. By five, the sun was heading for the western horizon and it hit us both about the same time that we hadn't eaten since breakfast. Mabel said that she was going to head to a friend's house about two miles away and see if she could stay, if the house was still there, of course. We promised to be back in the morning to see if we could make her house habitable again.

Me and James looked at each other.

'I'm not going home just yet.'

'No, me neither.'

*

So we stayed an extra week on Virgin Gorda, (or Virgin Gorgeous, as I'd started calling it – despite the destruction), helping with the clear up and reconstruction . In the end, we had to admit that what it was costing us to stay (speshul redewced rayte for speshul redewced accommodayshon) would have been better spent on building materials and donations to rebuild and replenish Mabel's home ..... and pretty much anyone else in the neighbourhood. What we had become were merely very expensive labourers. So we gave cash and left them to it.

But we felt as though we'd done something, at least.

*

The final night we watched the sun go down, like one of those classic movie endings, all slush and sentiment, and next morning, as we rode the ferry back to the airport terminal, we sat at the back of the boat again, taking our last glimpse of the island that we had ended up spending nearly three weeks on. Somehow I doubted we'd ever be back, but you could never know, could you?

Still, hurricanes? Been there, done that!

I was looking forward now, to seeing my friends and family and one very special person in particular. It seemed like a lifetime since we'd left. Now we had a whole lifetime to live.

At least, I hoped we did.

*

'Mummmy, mummy, can you eat woollies?' .... this really is getting too much.

'No darling you *cannot* eat woollies,' and I really hate to think what the wee brat has in his hands this time.

'Good, cause they're horrid' and he opens his hands to reveal three creepy crawlies. 'Nothing like spetty!'

'Wood lice, Harry, not woollies.'

And he runs off to find some more vileness in the garden.

And I know what you might be thinking, and you'd be wrong.

Harry is not Henry's son.

Nope. Not by a long chalk. Harry's father is very different. He's tall and he's strong (so, OK, not *so* different) and he's kind and he's gentle and, although he can have a firm hand when he wants to, it's his physical and emotional strength that gives me comfort. Sure he can dither and ramble on, but that makes two of us ..... sometimes.

And talk of the devil.......his golden locks, long and curled, just like his son's, a halo with the sun behind him. He could be a saint ..... if I didn't know that he could be a complete devil when the fancy takes him ..... with or without the right encouragement.

It was James's idea to name our son Harry. Henry just seemed a wee bit too pompous, a little passé, for either of us. But he knew how important Henry was to me, so Harry seemed a good compromise. James didn't mind one bit. But that's James for you.

Henry, James and Harry. All very regal isn't it?

*

Even after all these years, there's barely a day goes by that I don't think of Henry and the games we used to play. And I have absolutely no doubt that time heals the wounds, just as people said it would, even though the scars still linger.

And he was right, wasn't he, about not wasting time? Before you know it, sometimes when you least expect it, the sands of time run out. That last grain falls between your fingers. Irretrievably.

He said - savour every last second, Sophie. Every single one.

And I try to do just that. Really I do.

Under the circumstances, wouldn't you?

*

And there are other questions too. Some that are impossible to answer.... like what will the future hold? Will we be happy? Will we lead a good life?

And those that maybe we don't want to confront, don't even want to consider.....

Like why was I so damned stupid? What was I thinking? Why on earth did I do that? And that dress with those shoes! Really?

But, of course, the big, BIG question, for me, is ……

……… given the chance, would I do it all again?   Now?

Take the rollercoaster ride that was Henry Blythe?

Well, no, probably not. Not now.

But time was, Henry……..

……… Time was.

Author information

If you enjoyed this novel, please leave a review at -

Amazon.com

http://www.amazon.com/dp/B00BVKW9CA

OR

Amazon.co.uk

http://www.amazon.co.uk/dp/B00BVKW9CA

and

Goodreads http://www.goodreads.com/book/show/17663195-time-was

The sequel to Time Was, 'Blythe's Spirit', was published on 4th July 2013 and is available at –

Amazon.com

http://www.amazon.com/dp/B00DSEDZAC

OR

Amazon.co.uk

http://www.amazon.co.uk/dp/B00DSEDZAC

Book three in the Henry Blythe series of novels is planned for publication in early 2014.

Working title – 'Bad Man Rising'.

Join Paul Adams on Facebook to keep up to date with news and new publications

https://www.facebook.com/pages/Time-Was-Paul-Adams/464991426913353

'Like' on this page and 'share' with your friends.

Also become a 'friend' or 'fan' on Goodreads at

http://www.goodreads.com/author/show/7047257.Paul_Adams

CPSIA information can be obtained at www.ICGtesting.com
Printed in the USA
LVOW08s1530230214

374826LV00005B/493/P